Sam Atlas's hopes are at an all-ti
ing the third wheel to her two be:
tic life is nonexistent—until Sam
elusive Tamara King, and it changes everything. Sam learns quickly of Tamara's unreliability, and their complicated relationship grows with them as they move towards their thirties.

CW01655142

In her search for closure, Sam's friends support her through comedic rebound dates, defend her many drunken mishaps, and stand by her side right up until the event she never expected she would see—Tamara King's wedding.

Sam learns how first loves often leave scars that are hard to heal, but finds that letting go can bring laughter, heartache, and unexpected love.

TAMARA KING

Emily Wright

A NineStar Press Publication
www.ninestarpress.com

Tamara King

This is a work of fiction. Names, characters, places, and incidents are either the product of the author's imagination or are used fictitiously. Any resemblance to actual persons living or dead, business establishments, events, or locales is entirely coincidental.

ISBN:

First Edition, October, 2021

Also available in eBook, ISBN:

CONTENT WARNING:
This book contains sexually explicit content, which may only be suitable for mature readers. Depictions of

For Barrie and Bea, always in my heart

Chapter One

2021

It was just a wedding.

At least that's what I was telling myself, sitting on the cliff's edge as the waves lapped at my calves. Happy place, happy place.

The water was always cold in England, leaving red bumps rippling across my skin like Braille. I longed for the water. For the cry of the gulls above, spiralling and diving over the people who meandered across the sand. The wind whipped at my face, carrying the thought that echoed in my head. It's just a wedding...

"Hello, Sam? Are you even listening to me?"

The dress hung perfectly on my wardrobe door. I wasn't sure how long I had been staring at it until my brother waved his hand in front of my face.

"Oh. Sorry. Yes, I'll remember." I rubbed my eyes. The dress lingered still, the image burned into the back of my eyelids. "Twelve o'clock."

"Eleven!" Jake rolled his eyes. "I know you pride yourself on being fashionably late, but a wedding is no time for that." His expression turned serious when I didn't reply. "Hey, are you okay?"

My mind wandered idly back into the room, away from the damp sand and waves that were previously pulling my body towards the seabed. The sea often soothed me. But Jake's deep voice was dragging me out of my happy place and back to the four walls of my bedroom. At this rate, I was prepared to suck my lungs full of air and drift away from the room on the current.

"Yeah. I'm fine," I said, closing my eyes and moving further and further away, my head tilted back to the sky as the waves tipped me over the horizon.

"Don't be nervous." He placed his big hand awkwardly on my shoulder. "You've nothing to worry about."

"I know. I know." I tried not to look at the dress, but it was staring back at me. The same way it had been for the past few hours.

Jake followed my gaze. "Is it the dress you're worried about?"

I didn't answer. I didn't know what to say.

"That is the least of your problems." He flicked my arm when I didn't reply.

I rubbed the spot absent-mindedly, still watching my dress hang loosely over the door. I briefly thought about dragging it into the hallway and letting Flic rip it to shreds with his claws.

"Come on, Sam. Lighten up. It's a wedding, not a bloody funeral."

He watched me for a moment and then shrugged and stood to leave. "I'll be here at quarter to. Try not to have too much fun while I'm gone."

I stayed still, perched on the edge of the bed until I heard him shut the door and drive away. He was right. It was just a wedding. A wedding I had been dreading for the last few months, but nonetheless, just a wedding. Besides, Ellie and Tom would be there, and I didn't want to let them down, embarrass myself, or lose face. I held a deep breath in, promising myself that after I exhaled, I would start getting ready.

A fierce knock at the door pulled me back to reality. I forced myself down the hallway, almost tripping over one of Flic's plastic toys. Despite tidying them up daily, they were always scattered around the house. I was surprised I hadn't broken anything with the number of times I had fallen over them. I understood why some people believed cats were conspiring to kill their owners. Another knock.

It was the postman, delivering my last-minute gift purchase from the late hours of the night before. I inspected the contents, the packaging now scattered on the floor. Looking at it, I wasn't sure it was a good idea. It seemed like the stupidest thing in the world.

I placed it next to the pre-existing present I had on the mantelpiece, wrapped prettily in silver paper and purple ribbon. My view flickered between them for a minute. Maybe it would be a nice surprise. Or maybe it would ruin the whole day. Surely a kind gesture couldn't be interpreted as a bad thing, could it? I took the gift into my hand again and turned it over and over in my palm. Then I noticed the time on the clock and ran back to my bedroom to start getting ready.

Chapter Two

2010

The good thing about Petey's was the cheap beer. It was also the bad thing.

Since Petey bought the bar two years ago, renaming it after himself, it was our favourite place to hang out. Though he was a fair deal older than us, he had a soft spot for our group and paid off our bar tab from time to time.

It was a decent-sized bar, with a handful of booths spread out along the sides. The seats were tired and old but comfortable; I don't think they had ever been replaced since the place first opened. The dark wooden tables were almost always sticky, with dozens of ring-mark stains scattered across the wood. The floors matched the tables, the wooden flooring a mosaic of all the spills and spatters from nights before. Hung on the green walls were old photos of various musicians on stage with guitars in the air, belting into microphones or stage-diving. There were even a couple of old guitars mounted but with no strings—Petey had learned his lesson there. A drunken first-year student had snapped them off and used them to fight half of the bar staff when they had refused to serve him.

Ellie stumbled over to our booth, clutching three beers to her chest.

I glanced at Tom and Matt, and we laughed. Ellie always had a little too much to drink whenever Blue Rooms were scheduled to play. Of course, being the girlfriend of the lead singer had its benefits: she had every piece of merch they had, taking every opportunity to talk them up. Ellie never shied away from weaving the band into conversations; she was like an unpaid walking sponsorship. Needless to say, this was a lot more professional and a great deal more convincing when she wasn't pissed.

"Sorry, Matt, yours—yours is still on the bar. I—I couldn't carry another," she spluttered, brushing her hands down her Blue Rooms T-shirt.

"Baby!" Tom protested. "Your top."

"The beers are sticky! It's fine." She plonked the glasses down onto the table, the beer sloshing over the sides. "I've got like five hundred more of these at home."

"Maybe if you didn't spill it everywhere, your hands wouldn't be sticky," Tom said, mopping up the spill with two old beer mats from the table.

"Right, I guess I'll get Matt's, then," I said, ushering Ellie along the worn-out red seats. I made my way through the group of people crowding the bar. It was starting to heave, as it always did at this time. Two women, who didn't look old enough to be there, were eyeing our table from afar. Must have been new groupies.

The haze of alcohol descended over me like a warm blanket. The steady buzz was a must to keep me in good shape for the evening—*if my date ever turns up.*

Standing on my tiptoes, I could see Matt's beer waiting awkwardly on the bar. I reached in between two tall guys and managed to clutch the glass.

"Hey! That's my free beer!"

I looked up to a tall man. His T-shirt had faded from white to a dreary yellow colour, and his brown hair was dragged back into an oily quiff. He shrugged under a leather jacket, leering down at me, unaware that his T-shirt label was sticking out of the front. The moron had it on backwards.

I leaned away from him, fearful of getting grease on my outfit. "Excuse me." I turned to push past him, but he grabbed me firmly by the waist.

"Finders keepers," he slurred into my ear, the stench of alcohol on his breath.

"This is my friend's beer."

"Tell you what, you can have it." His fingers curled around my back. "If...you give me a kiss."

I pushed him hard in his big chest, and he let go of my waist.

"What's going on here?"

I turned to see a young woman propped up on the inside of the bar. Her hands cupped her face delicately, her blonde hair tucked behind one ear. I didn't recognise her.

"James, when are you going to learn that being an over-exertive caveman is not impressive?"

His cheeks flushed.

"And harassment is not tolerated in this bar. Now piss off, or I'll get you thrown out." She flashed him a quick smile, and he shuffled off, his friend in tow. She flung a white cloth over her shoulder and popped down beneath the bar to produce two shot glasses. “Rum or tequila?”

“Pardon?”

“We should celebrate.”

“Celebrate what?” I asked.

“Getting one up on that greasy ape.” She leaned forward on the bar. “I’m not supposed to shit-talk about customers, but that one really gets on my nerves.” She straightened herself up. “So, rum or tequila?”

“Tequila.”

She disappeared again and returned a few seconds later with a bottle of Jose Cuervo, two slices of lime, and a pot of salt.

“What’s your name?” she asked, filling the glasses.

“Sam.”

“Emma.” She pushed a glass towards me. “Us girls have got to stick together. May I?”

She reached out to cup my hand and, when I nodded, tipped a little portion of salt just above my thumb. She arranged the salt on her hand, her green eyes reflecting in the bar light.

“Cheers!” She clinked my glass.

“Cheers!” We held each other’s gaze for a short moment and then quickly licked the salt, shot the tequila, and squished the lime into our mouths. Her face scrunched up from the fierceness of the alcohol, and she muttered some swear words under her breath. She recomposed herself and smiled back at me, holding eye contact until I looked away.

"You'd think I'd be used to the taste by now." She shook her head. "It's a love-hate relationship."

I nodded in agreement, unsure what to say. The burn of the tequila tainted my mouth, and any attempt to swallow the taste away was futile. A man approached the other side of the bar, eyeing us carefully. He twiddled his card between his fingers impatiently, resting his elbows on the bar.

"See you around," Emma said.

I uttered something of a goodbye, took the cold beer in my hand, and headed back towards the booth.

"Here she is! Hero of the hour!" Ellie shouted, patting me on the back as I scooted along the seat.

"Have you been drinking more since I've been gone?"

"I'm just loosening up for your big date."

"Why would you loosen up? It's not your date," I laughed. "Tom, where is this cousin of yours anyway?"

Tom checked his phone. "She said she'd be here half an hour ago."

Ellie sucked on her teeth. "Not looking good, Sam."

"Blind dates are never a good idea," Matt said. "Trust me." He glanced over his shoulder like he was expecting someone. "You know that girl I was seeing?"

"Lauren?" Tom said.

"No, she's long gone!" Ellie slurred.

"Why?" I asked, though I didn't feel like talking. "She was nice."

"Too clingy." Matt shrugged. "Wanted to take me to a christening."

A handful of women surrounded our table and asked if the boys were "The Blue Room". Tom and Matt smiled and politely corrected them—"It's Blue Rooms"—posed for a picture, and then sipped their beers like they weren't the talk of the town—even if their band name constantly got mispronounced.

Petey had asked them to play tomorrow night, so they discussed their setlists while Ellie giggled to herself.

★

"Sorry about my cousin," Tom said, fiddling with his sleeve. "She doesn't like to stick to a schedule."

I glanced at my phone. She was over two hours late, but to be honest, I wasn't expecting much.

"It's fine," I lied. "But it's been good to get out anyway."

"Where've you been lately?"

I looked down into my empty glass. "Just been busy with stuff."

"That means sleeping and eating food in bed," Ellie added.

"Shut up." I elbowed her playfully in the ribs. "I do more than that."

"Do you want another drink?" Matt asked, reaching for his wallet. "You can talk to that hot new bartender again."

"Emma? That's Petey's new wife," Tom said. "Him and Sarah got divorced, you know."

"What? He got married again?" Matt said. "That's so fast. Even for me."

It had been months since I had seen Sarah. I assumed she had just got another job somewhere, not that they'd split up. Weird. Petey hadn't seemed any different at all.

"Anyway, I think I'm gonna go soon." I turned to Ellie. "Do you wanna split a taxi?"

Her head was resting on the table, her black Afro curls flopped over her face. When she didn't reply, I gave her a little shove.

She raised her head slowly, eyeing me with suspicion. That girl could fall asleep anywhere.

"I'll take her home with me," Tom said, lifting her gently out of the seat.

We stepped outside, and the cold night air whipped against my face. The street was empty. A single beer can blew across the road.

"You. You—you're my best friend," Ellie slurred, reaching over to hug me.

"I know, you're mine too. You idiot." I hugged her close, the stench of beer invading my nostrils.

"My best friend," Ellie said again, assertively, swaying on her toes.

★

The next day I was late for class. With a little bit of pleading, I convinced Dad to let me borrow the car so I didn't have to take the train to the university. Dad detested driving. Though he always caught the bus to the hospital for work and left the car on the drive unused, he still hated the idea of anyone else using it. The old silver Peugeot, Stella, was living on borrowed time. The combination of the cold weather and very limited driving time made her very stubborn. Thankfully, today she grumbled to a start.

The morning fog had slumped down over the city. It was only a twenty-minute drive, so I was saving at least fifteen minutes by avoiding the train. I ran a couple of amber lights, anxiously checking the clock on the dashboard every few minutes. John, my old and ill-tempered lecturer, *hated* when people were late.

My stomach twinged with embarrassment as I remembered the no-show of Tom's cousin. I wondered if she had turned up, seen me sat with the others, and thought, *oh God. No*. And left without any of us knowing. It had been so easy for Ellie to convince me to come and meet her. Maybe I needed to be more stubborn. Like this old car.

Two girls stepped out into the road, and I slammed on the brakes, my bag flying to the floor with the stuffed zebra my Dad insisted sit on the dashboard. They lingered on the street, nicely demonstrating their lack of respect for the Highway Code with their middle fingers. The taller girl of the two adjusted her mustard beanie and added a few more gestures before scampering away, shouting things muffled by the radio. I shouted a few back and then screeched off, trying to find somewhere quick to park.

I burst into John's class fifteen minutes later, red-faced and out of breath. He tapped his watch and tutted, motioning for me to sit down. Glancing around the room, I noticed Ellie wasn't there—nursing a hangover in bed, no doubt.

I turned to go sit in my usual seat, the farthest seat on the left facing the window, but to my surprise, someone was already sitting there.

She looked up at me, and her mouth twisted into a smile. It took me a second to recognise her mustard beanie. It was one of the girls who had stepped out into the road. Embarrassed, I quickly sat at the nearest spare seat, knocking into the table as I did.

I kept my eyes down most of the class, tearing them away only to glance at John every so often. As soon as the lecture finished, I ran for the door, took the stairs six floors down, and pushed through the crowds to get outside.

I pulled out my phone. Two messages from Ellie and six from Grace, a persistent girl I had met twice and since would not leave me alone. Ellie was still in bed, as expected. Grace was hounding me with questions: Was I okay? Did I want to meet? Did I want to go with her to meet her grandparents for their Ruby wedding anniversary? A big fat no to all.

Someone tapped me on the shoulder.

It was the mustard beanie girl. The girl who had already this morning flattered me with an extended list of expletives.

"I thought it was you, but I couldn't tell for sure." She reached into her back pocket and pulled out some Rizla rolling papers and a pouch of cheap tobacco. "You running off kinda confirmed that for me."

"Yeah, about that—"

"Oh, don't worry about it. Apology accepted." She briefly stopped rolling her cigarette and glanced up at me.

"Actually, I wasn't going to apologise, since it was you that stepped in front of me." I watched as she quickly rolled and licked the paper before popping the cigarette into her mouth.

"I think you'll find we were both at fault."

"Erm, no—"

"Have you got a lighter?" she interrupted.

I raised my eyebrows, caught off guard by her question. "Sorry, I don't smoke."

"Of course not." She turned to ask a cluster of students nearby and returned a few seconds later, puffing smoke through the air.

"How is it my fault if you step in front of me?"

"You were going way too fast. Now I get why though. I'd speed, too, to get to that old guy's lectures." She smiled at me playfully.

This made the anger in my chest melt away, along with any other clever response I could have thought of. "Why were you even in his class?" I asked.

"I transferred."

She took a long drag of the cigarette. Something was nice about how she did it. The captivating way her lungs lifted and inhaled the rolled tobacco, exhaling a small whisper of grey in return. I hadn't noticed there was a particular art to the way someone smoked a cigarette. Too much smoke or too little. Mouth too wide or too small. There was a silence when she took another drag. I fidgeted with my hands in my pockets, feeling suddenly shy.

"Do you know a band called Blue Rooms?" she asked.

"Yeah, they're my friends' band."

She laughed loudly, making me anxious.

"What?"

"Tom's my cousin. I was supposed to meet you guys yesterday." She paused to puff on her cigarette. "Damn, they say it's a small world, but Treaton Vale is something else."

This was Tom's cousin? I wanted to take a proper look, but I was conscious of her gaze on me. Her features were petite. She had a small oval face with freckles placed carefully across her nose and cheeks. Her eyebrows moved independently from her face, knotting when she spoke with her cocky allure, lifting high when she smiled.

"So, you're my date," she announced, watching me carefully, a smile tugging at her lips.

"Well, you were supposed to be," I pointed out.

"There's always tonight. I take it you're going to see them play?"

I had actually forgotten. With Ellie not here mentioning them every five minutes, it must have slipped my mind.

"Maybe."

"Cool. I'll see you there, then." She flicked her stub on the floor and stamped it out. "Sorry, what's your name again?"

"Sam."

She held her hand out. "Tamara."

★

Petey's was always rammed whenever Blue Rooms were scheduled to play. People were grouped outside blocking the entrance. The sound of bellowing laughter rang out into the air as they sipped out of pint-sized plastic cups. I nodded at a few familiar faces as I pushed through the door. Ellie was meeting me in the back booth where we usually sat. It would take more than a bad hangover to keep her away from Tom when he played. She had been to every gig they had since they met; she even frequented their band practices. It's a wonder they didn't get sick of her.

I spotted her sitting, cradling an orange juice, and she waved me over.

"There better not be vodka in there."

"God, no. I nearly died last night. I need all the vitamin C I can get."

"You're so dramatic."

She took a big gulp of her orange juice, eyeing me. "Someone has certainly dressed for the occasion. Look at this!" She pulled lightly on one of my brown curls. "You're defo hoping to score. Eyeliner and mascara too!"

"I don't know what you're talking about."

In fact, it had taken me almost an hour to get ready, double my time taken the previous night. After meeting Tamara, I was much more eager to capture her attention. I had never been called beautiful much, aside from my dad when he waved us off to prom and Mum when I was younger. My hair was much curlier then, and she used to twirl it around her fingers when I was sleepy. As I grew older, my curls fell loose, and now I had to rely on the curling iron to bring them back to their former glory. Ellie, on the other hand, with her half-Caribbean heritage, had naturally tight black curls that framed her face perfectly.

"Do you think Tamara will show this time?" she asked.

"I guess we'll have to wait and find out."

The bar was starting to crowd. People spilt in through the doors, filling up all the empty spaces while some indie band played from the speakers overhead. Everyone bobbed their heads rhythmically to the music whilst they chatted amongst themselves. I caught myself looking for Tamara, scanning the room for the mustard beanie as Ellie complained about her hangover.

The speakers cut the music and started crackling with static, pulling everyone into sudden silence. A voice called out, introducing the support acts, and after a muted round of applause, they stepped up on to the stage. To call it a stage made it seem impressive, but it was more of a platform, not quite big enough to fit all the members of Blue Rooms on when they had their gear. Ash, the lead guitarist, usually had to play standing at the side of them, but he didn't mind being so close to the crowd.

Petey's itself was known for its music scene. Bands played on Thursday, Friday, and Saturday nights, but Blue Rooms were an exception. Since they first played for Petey last year, he got them in whenever he could, including times Tom, Matt, and Ash were just in for a drink.

A couple of support acts played, and with each one, the crowd grew more restless for Blue Rooms' appearance. I couldn't spot the mustard beanie anywhere.

"We've got some special guests in the house tonight!" a voice bellowed out. "Ladies and gentlemen, I'd like to welcome to the stage Blue Rooms!"

Tom, Matt, and Ash stepped up onto the stage just as Petey burst through a door at the side of the bar, his arms extended.

"Boys! Great to see you again, as always!" he beamed, bringing them in for an embrace. There were some unheard exchanges, and then Petey switched on the microphone in his hand.

"Playing us a sneak peek of their EP—which is going to be a *must-have* by the way—the incredible...Blue Rooms!" Petey bowed off the stage after clicking the microphone into its stand. Tom welcomed the crowd that had gathered near the front while Matt and Ash tuned the instruments.

Tom swaggered around the stage. "We're gonna play our new single, 'Missing You'." He combed one hand through his shaggy hair and flashed Ellie a big smile. They counted in together, and as soon as Ash played the opening notes, Ellie grabbed my arm, squeezing it tight.

"I love this song!" she screamed. Ellie and I had pushed down to the front where the majority of the crowd had collected, most of them familiar faces and who no doubt had already seen Blue Rooms play before.

Everyone bounced along to the music, a sea of arms waving in the air. The crowd left a gap towards the bar, and in the clearing, I spotted Tamara. She had on the same black jacket she was wearing earlier but no mustard hat. She was with the same girl from this morning, and they were both leaning on the bar, speaking to Emma. Blue Rooms played a handful of songs. The whole time Ellie swayed along, staring at Tom in adoration. I could see why she found him attractive. He was tall and handsome, with dark eyes and high cheekbones. He often wore his signature denim jacket, tonight being no exception. He'd embroidered it himself with band patches and had a habit of flicking it open while he sang. Underneath, he wore a white T-shirt tucked into his skin-tight jeans and some low-cut black Dr Martens.

An arm swooped in around my back, and Tamara appeared with two beers.

"I know I'm the worst date in the world. Standing you up and then showing up late—but...I brought you a beer." She held it out towards me, grinning. "I hope you like beer."

I smiled. "Beer is a good start."

Tamara glanced at her own and then to Ellie.

"Oh, God. And now I'm the rudest date in the world. Here, have my beer." She held it out to Ellie.

"Oh, no, really it's okay. I'm still hungover—"

"Please. I insist," Tamara said.

Ellie reluctantly agreed and took a small sip.

Blue Rooms played the rest of their set, and we danced and sang along to the music together. Tamara linked her arm around my back every so often, and I couldn't concentrate on the music, just where her fingers rested on my skin. After their set finished, everyone started making their way to the bar and the outside smoking area.

"Come outside with me?" Tamara shouted over the noise. Before I could answer, she continued, "Just for a chat? I can't hear myself think in here."

I nodded, and she took my hand and led us through the crowds of people. Outside, the smoking area consisted of four worn-out picnic benches, with a dozen people clambered over each one, laughing and blowing smoke in each other's faces. She pulled me into the far right corner, where the noise was just a background hum. The concrete was lit dimly by orange lights overhead, which coated everyone nearby in a golden glow. Two of the five lights had blown, leaving half of the area in shadow. Tamara flipped open her tobacco pouch and within seconds had rolled a cigarette and started smoking.

"So, where is it that you've come from again?" I asked, watching her mouth fold and caress the smoke perfectly. Her lips looked soft.

She smiled into her lap. "Manchester. We wanted to move here for ages, but my dad didn't want to."

"How come you're here then?"

"Mum finally dumped the pathetic excuse for a man, and *voilà*, here we are." She took a big puff of her cigarette.

"And here you are, jumping in front of cars and smoking all our tobacco."

She glanced at me, her gaze making me feel nervous. "You're funny."

"Thanks." I fumbled with my hair, wanting something to do with my hands. I briefly thought about smoking just so I had something to fidget with.

"Your hair is different," Tamara commented, a smile tugging at her lips. "It's cute."

"Thanks," I said again, my mind going blank. She drew hard on the roll-up, her gaze wandering over my outfit.

"I hardly recognised you earlier without that mustard beanie," I said.

She laughed as she exhaled, a short and shallow sound that I instantly wanted to hear again.

"Oh yeah." She brushed over her hair subconsciously with her free hand. "I left it in my car. Got about a hundred of them."

"They suit you."

She looked back at me, the warm lights overhead hinting at a golden streak in her dark irises. "Well at least someone likes 'em." She smiled. "My mum hates it. Says I look homeless."

"What about your dad?"

Tamara shrugged. "He's a bastard."

I immediately regretted asking. She glanced briefly over her shoulder and then ran one hand through her hair. Each ginger strand fell back into place slowly, framing her face perfectly in the golden glow. I decided not to press further. Tamara rolled another cigarette.

Once back inside, we joined the others at the booth. The band were all energised after their set, bouncing off each other to either get to the dance floor or the bar. Ellie, still sober, was asking Tamara endless questions. Tamara didn't falter and, instead, joked that she'd always wanted to be on *Oprah* and that this was good practice. Sometime later, Tamara excused herself to go to the bathroom. When she left, I watched her walk away. Ellie raised her eyebrows at me.

"Uh-oh," she teased. "You're so into her."

"Shut up." I hid my face in my drink.

"If you guys get married and me and Tom get married, then we'd be related!" She laughed. "Oh my God. We could have a joint wedding!"

"Jesus, no!"

My phone vibrated. Another message from Grace again.

Ellie glanced at my phone.

"I thought it didn't work between you two?" she asked. "Please tell me you're not cheating on my future cousin-in-law."

"No. Grace just won't stop texting me. And I'm not getting married to Tamara! We're not even together." I took a big swig of my drink. "Ellie, this is the first time she's actually shown up, and even then, she was late!"

We sat back into our booth, and after fifteen minutes, Tom, Matt, and Ash joined us. Ellie gave Tom a big kiss, and I hugged the guys.

I offered to get the next round. When I got back to the booth, Tamara still wasn't back. My face must have betrayed my thought as Tom asked where she was. I shrugged, feigning disinterest, and felt Ellie's eyes on me. Everyone's conversations faded into a blur. Each a string of words nonsensical, dancing above and around my head. What was Tamara's problem? Did she not like me? Was that why she left? *And Jesus, I'm going to end up alone.*

The night dragged after that. I was mad at myself for being excited about Tamara. Angry for feeling that fluttery spell in my stomach when she linked her arm around my waist. Furious for still looking for her coming through the door.

Chapter Three

2021

"Lottie, sweetie, don't chew on the bracelet." Jake peered at her through the rear-view mirror, his brow furrowed. Lottie sucked hard on a bead between her teeth. "Thought you were a little princess today? Princesses don't eat their jewellery."

She giggled at this, spitting out her saliva-soaked bead and throwing her head back in laughter. "I'm always a princess."

Jake smiled back at her, the proud parent-esque beam that came with any firstborn. It was the same way he had looked at her when she was born four years ago. Jake and Catherine had only been dating a couple of months when they found out she was pregnant. Jake was excited to be a dad, which surprised me, as he had appeared indifferent about their relationship before the news. Catherine lived an hour away, near Stockport, so they only saw each other on the weekend. After Lottie was born, they bought a house in between Stockport and Treaton Vale. A small, terraced house in Glossop that became Jake and Dad's DIY project for the years to come.

As he promised, Jake had picked me up at eleven. Something was unsettling about him. He watched me as I lingered on the doorstep, my mind failing to put a finger on what was different. Jake pointed a chunky finger to his chest, a large, clumsy arrow leading me to the obvious answer. It struck me—he wasn't wearing a hoodie.

How strange to see my brother answer the door dressed in a royal-blue suit with a pocket square and neatly shined black brogues. He posed on the doorstep, visibly impressed with his new wardrobe choice. I wondered if he had chosen it or if it was Catherine. When Lottie was born, he had worn the same green Nike hoodie for a month until she made him throw it away.

Jake had always had a simple style, even when we were kids. He wore the same four T-shirts and would scream and cry when our parents tried to dress him in new clothes. Aunt Marie hadn't taken it too well when he cut up a new striped shirt she had bought him one year for Christmas. Mum couldn't stop laughing, and they didn't speak for weeks. Somehow, I couldn't imagine him doing the same to a hundred-pound suit. Although it might make for some great entertainment.

Jake waited at the door, fiddling with his cuffs, uttering childproof curses like "fuddle" and "fudge" as he tugged at them. I bet he missed being able to swear properly. There's something very satisfying about reeling off a mouthful of expletives, feeling the anger or frustration cast out into the air and descend as nothingness. Something that "fuddle" and "fudge" could not replace. I bet he missed his hoodie too.

He looked much older now. When had time etched those crow's feet near his eyes? When had his hairline crept back those few centimetres? When did we stop fighting over Jelly Babies and paper planes? It was scary.

I assumed he felt the same about Lottie. How she had changed from a bald pink baby to the golden child with a gap-toothed grin and blonde curls past her shoulders. From crawling to walking and now dancing three times a week at ballet class.

“How are you feeling?” He was talking to me now, peering at me from the driver’s seat.

“I’m fine.”

He sighed. “Honestly, it’s not gonna be as bad as you think. There’s nothing to worry about. You’re such a worrier.”

“I’m not a worrier.”

Lottie giggled behind us.

“See, even Lottie agrees with me. Aunty Sam is a worry wuss, isn’t she?”

“Yeah!” Lottie laughed from the back seat. “Worry wuss.”

“Well. There are worse things you’ve called me.”

“Worry wuss. Worry wuss!” Lottie sang.

“That’s enough now, Princess.”

“Worry wuss,” she said under her breath.

“Catherine isn’t gonna be happy about that one,” I teased.

“Yeah, well. She’s not happy about a lot of things.”

The sternness to his tone threw me. He looked ahead at the road, twiddling his cufflink with his finger.

“You can talk to me about stuff, Jake. Or Dad even.”

"There's nothing to talk about really." He glanced back at Lottie, who had fallen quiet with the silence. "Daddy is a bit of a worry wuss too, isn't he?"

She giggled and rocked forward in her car seat.

"Who's the biggest worry wuss?" he asked her. "Daddy or Aunty Sam?"

"Aunty Sam! Aunty Sam!"

I turned to look out of the window, watching the trees sail by in a blur. That's what I was perceived as, then, a worry wuss. I must admit that I thought I might have more titles to my name by the time I was thirty-two. Perhaps Mother or Business Director. Instead, I was Cat Mother and Worry Wuss.

I knew I shouldn't complain. I had a lot of brilliant things in my life. It just so happened that days like these made me question every choice I'd ever made. I had a clean kitchen—that had to count for something. Mum always said that to us when we were kids. *If I can have at least one room clean, then that's a success.*

Jake pulled off the main road, following signposts for Tarnbourg Hall. The track was dusty and barely wide enough for one car. It was the most popular place to get married in Treaton Vale, and it was clear why, despite the ridiculous road size. It was the ancestral home of a French duke; all the heritage and history of the building made it unbearably romantic for some reason. Even though nobody present at the wedding would be able to name the duke in question who attracted all the attention. I certainly couldn't. The history and rumours were debatable. *Is it haunted? Do the ghosts of housekeeping steal your clothes in your sleep? Who knows?* But it was undeniable that the beautiful estate and the terrace and the twenty acres of stunning gardens made it a risk many people considered worth taking.

Jake parked the car, and Lottie and I walked hand in hand towards the entrance to the stately home. The archways were decorated with heaps of red ribbon and dozens of lilies parading the pathway to the open door. Lottie squeezed my hand. She always became anxious when she was somewhere new. Unbeknown to her, she had been here before as a foetus when her own parents had married. We waited for Jake beside a gigantic over-the-top welcome sign signalling guests where to go. Seemed the happy couple didn't have much faith in their guests to find the *only* door to the entrance. I assumed a great fear for the betrothed was forking out thousands of pounds on food for your guests, just to have them wandering around the car park, unable to get in.

"Are you supposed to take those?"

"You made me jump!" I said, swatting Jake with a piece of ribbon I had taken from the display.

"It's pretty," Lottie said, winding the ribbon around her fingers.

"It is, sweetie. But it's the wedding decorations. They're supposed to be for the *wedding*." He shot a warning look to me. A look I found amusing, as it was always strange to be scolded by my little brother.

"Can't I have it?" Lottie's voice was soft, bordering on a whine.

I tried to hide a smile as his eyes narrowed on me.

"I'm sure you can if you hide it," I suggested. It was such a thrill winding up a sibling. Something that never tired as you got older.

Lottie pouted and, as if to support her argument, held the ribbon up to her father, who reluctantly accepted it. Probably to stop a toddler meltdown and avoid attracting attention to ourselves.

“Okay. But make sure no one sees it. Here. Put it in your pocket.”

Jake took Lottie’s other hand, and we walked towards the entrance. A handful of people had gathered around a smartly dressed greeter handing out free drinks of champagne. As we waited our turn, Jake pinched my arm.

“What happened to being on your best behaviour?” He scowled.

“I don’t know what you’re talking about.”

He pinched me again, and I flinched. “There’s gonna be eyes on us here. Catherine is catering, and you said we’ll keep a low profile.”

“Maybe I changed my mind.”

“What?”

“I’m kidding! I’m kidding. Best behaviour it is.”

Chapter Four

2010

After the night at Petey's, I stayed in bed till noon. I told Dad I was hungover, but really, I was just disappointed. My desk was littered with torn-out, abandoned drawings from the week before. I could have focused on my course-work or at least started a sketch of something to distract myself. Instead, the night replayed over and over in my head. I rolled over on my squeaky mattress, admiring the walls and trying to envision myself in another place. My room had my favourite creations pinned on every surface. Watercolours of the seaside and the carnival in the Mayor's Gardens. I thought about the summer and the fun we had with the boys' band. Ellie and Tom, Ash and Yvette, Matt and whichever girl he was seeing that week...and then me.

I considered getting up and getting dressed but lacked the energy. I decided against it. The day could wait.

My phone had no new messages, just a build-up of unanswered texts from Grace. She needed to take the hint. I wondered if perhaps that's what Tamara had thought about me. Loud muffled music interrupted my cheerful thought process.

“Jake!” I shouted. “Turn it down!”

“It’s not me!” he yelled back from his room. Then the music cut out.

I went downstairs to make myself a cup of tea. Dad sat on the sofa, a steaming cup already between his hands.

“Morning, pumpkin,” he called from the living room. “I’ve topped up Stella’s oil and coolant. You’ve got to be so careful when you drive her.”

“I know, I will. Hey, where’s my cuppa? You could’ve made me one.”

“I thought you’d stay in bed till the afternoon with the time you got in. You met someone?”

I forced a laugh. “Good one, Dad.”

There was a loud thump at the door, followed by three smaller ones.

I ignored the door and walked into the kitchen to boil the kettle. A nest of teabags was building up on the side. Living with two messy men was hard.

Thirty seconds later, Dad called, “Sam, it’s for you.”

I glanced in the mirror. My curls had scrambled together into knots, and last night’s eyeliner was smudged down my face. Excellent.

Leaning in the doorway was Tamara. She had her hands stuffed into her denim pockets and a green beanie pulled over her head. My stomach clenched. But it was too late. She had already seen.

“Nice pyjamas.”

“Thanks,” I said, crossing my arms in front of the big *Lady and the Tramp* picture on the front. “What do you want?”

"I think I owe you an apology."

"Actually, how did you get here?" I asked. "How do you know where I live?"

"Tom told me. And I drove." She signalled over her shoulder to the old yellow car on the kerb. She paused, biting her lip. "I'm sorry. I'm just finding it difficult to take your glaring seriously when you look like Marilyn Manson."

I tried to hold back a smile. "Seriously, Tamara, what do you want?"

"I want to apologise properly. Please. I can explain. I just need you to come with me."

"Looking like this?"

"God. No."

I smiled, covering my face with my hands. It annoyed me that she had managed to make me laugh so easily.

"Please? I can explain." She jutted her bottom lip out and looked up at me with big brown eyes. When I diverted my gaze, she moved into view. "Please?"

"Fine. Give me ten minutes."

"Great, thank you. But I'm driving. I don't trust you with that big silver thing."

Tamara's car was dirtier than our kitchen. A carpet of old wrappers and papers lined the floor with empty fast-food boxes overflowing out of the side door. Upon seeing my expression, she apologised.

"Yeah, it's seen better days."

She produced a map out of the glove compartment, dropping some boiled sweets out onto the floor in the process.

“Where are we going?” I asked.

“It’s a secret.”

“No satnav?”

“No. I don’t believe in them.”

“What? Why?”

“Because they take the fun out of getting lost. That’s the best bit about driving.” She traced the roads with her finger, her tongue resting on her upper lip. “Okay! I need you to hold this.”

She tossed the crumpled map onto my lap and turned the key in the ignition. The car sputtered to a start, the loud rock music blaring out once again.

“Sorry!” She turned it down quickly. “You ready?”

Several wrong turns and a near miss with a cyclist later, Tamara pulled into a gravel car park littered with leaves. She drove into an empty space and shut off the engine. She bounded out of the car as soon as she applied the handbrake.

“Come on, then.”

She walked over to a gate labelled *Private land. No trespassing*.

“So, your way of apologising is, what, getting me arrested?” I asked.

“I might be a shit for showing up late—”

“—and standing me up,” I interjected.

She rolled her eyes. “Yes, okay, I’m sorry. I’m also a shit for that. But—” She held up a finger as if to stress her point. “I’m not a criminal.”

“I’m not sure whether I believe you.”

She led me up a barely visible path, striding ahead but glancing behind to call me on. I wasn't very athletic, but I tried to match her pace whilst hiding how out of breath I was. The grass grew longer the farther we walked, clinging to our legs like disobedient toddlers. The wet dew soaked through the bottom of my jeans, sending a chill up through my spine.

At the top, Tamara posed on top of a large rock, showcasing her biceps like two small oranges. She pulled me up to join her and spun me around to see the view. The sea was stretched out in front of us, teasing in the distance. I wasn't sure where we were. And we were higher up than I thought. Birds cooed overhead whilst the trees surrounding us shed quiet leaves, floating all the way down the hillside. I wished I had my sketchbook.

"It's really nice," I said at last.

"Nice? I share a piece of my soul with you, and you say it's nice?"

I laughed. "Sorry. I'm not the best at words."

She smiled at me. "Clearly."

"How'd you find this place?"

"Let's just say I've done my fair share of *exploring*."

"Exploring as in...trespassing?"

Her eyes flickered to mine, lit with excitement. "All the best places are hidden away. They want to be found."

We sat at the top of the rocks and talked while the leaves fell from the trees. While we spoke, Tamara tried to catch them between her fingers, but they caught the wind and floated away. Eventually, she got one and, unable to hide her excitement, turned to me and was adamant that

I made a wish. She gently placed the gold leaf into my palm and watched as I closed my eyes and blew it out into the air. Satisfied, she dug into her discoloured denim backpack and produced two foil-wrapped packages and two cartons of orange juice.

"I didn't know if you were veggie or not, so I just made cheese and tomato."

A laugh escaped my lips. She glanced at me, her brown eyes narrowed on mine.

"What?"

"Nothing. I just didn't expect you to be the home-made-sandwich type. Like a soccer mom."

Her face shifted into a playful grin. "Fuck off."

"The little cartons as well. I'm just shocked you're so organised." I unwrapped one package and took a big bite out of a sandwich. I couldn't look at Tamara without giggling and the sandwich threatening to come back up. Her lips pursed as she tried to hold back a laugh, and then she jutted me in the side with her elbow.

"Next time you can feed yourself."

The wind picked up after we finished our food, making the leaves dance around our legs. Tamara stepped forward on the edge of the rock and took a deep breath, looking out into the distance. I stood to join her.

"See that building down there?" She pointed a slender finger to an old stone house a few fields away. "Imagine having a place like that and it turning to a pile of rubble. It's mad."

"Have you been there?"

"Yeah. No one lives there. But it could be so good."

"It doesn't even have a roof."

"Yeah. Might get a bit cold in the winter." She laughed, nudging me with her foot. "I'll take you some time."

"Yeah?"

"Sure."

Birds chirped overhead in song. The breeze caressed my bare arms, and they rippled with goosebumps. "I just love this place," she continued. "Makes me feel like I'm not that mental."

I didn't say anything. I had been so consumed with her I hadn't had a chance to think. I watched her from the corner of my eye; her face seemed different. Serious, almost.

I jumped when her fingertips softly grazed my hand. She smiled, and I cursed myself for how easily flushed I was. Our hands stayed still for a moment, barely touching before she interlocked her fingers with mine. Her hands were cold and smooth, and I was worried that mine were clammy in comparison, but she didn't seem to notice.

"Thanks for coming." She said it so quietly it was almost a whisper.

"Thanks for bringing me."

She smiled again, and all the tension in her face disappeared.

★

We ducked and dived over the moors in Tamara's little yellow car, passing sheep and cows grazing in the fields. Every lonely house or closed fence made me question if

Tamara had been there and where we would go next. Tamara acted like she knew these roads inside out, and as she sang along with the music, I wished for that too. The music in the car was so loud that the speakers were vibrating, making the coins on the dashboard shake. The autumn breeze came through the rolled-down windows, blowing our hair around our faces. Tamara saw me trying—and failing—to stop my hair turning into a whirlwind and only laughed and turned the music up louder over the noise. I wanted to kiss her. I *so* wanted to kiss her. Instead, I sang along with the words I had caught from the chorus. After the song had finished, I restarted it. She glanced at me, surprised, and my cheeks reddened. I bet she loved that.

Tamara pulled onto the kerb in front of my house and switched off the engine. The loud music cut into silence. All the way back, she had sung along loudly with her CD, dancing and tapping her hands on the steering wheel like a drum kit. With the car now stationary, Tamara played awkwardly with her hands. She was looking straight ahead, a pensive look on her face.

"I'll see you on Monday, then."

"Yeah." She looked down at the floor of the car.

"Tamara?"

She turned to me, and my heartbeat quickened. In the fading sunlight, her eyes looked golden. Our faces grew closer until my lips hovered just an inch from hers.

Then she pulled back.

I had embarrassed myself again.

"I haven't earned it," she said quietly.

I opened the car door to leave, and she grabbed my hand. I tried to turn away so she didn't see the red flushing to my face.

"I haven't earned it yet," she said again, louder.

Without looking at her, I walked to my door and went inside. Earned what? A degree in how to lead girls on and humiliate them?

After a minute, the sound of loud music flooded the street, and her car screeched out of sight. It was only when I lay in bed that night that I realised she had never apologised to me in the first place.

Chapter Five

2021

My heel bounced against the chair leg with a repetitive clunk. The red chairs were lined up neatly in rows, decorated with sashes of white lace. They weren't as comfortable as they looked; the wooden structure of the base poked into my thighs, and I fidgeted to find a cushioned spot.

Under the drifting shade from the trees, it was a little too cool. Goosebumps pricked my arms and bare legs—newly shaven for the occasion—and Jake glanced at me as I shivered beside him.

"Do you wanna move over there?" he asked, pointing towards a sunlit spot near the front. By the wedding arch. The absolute last place I would want to be.

"No, it's fine. I left my wrap by the reception."

Before I could argue my case, he had vanished to go and fetch it for me. Usually a nice gesture, but in this case, I cursed my brother for making me wait there awkwardly without him. Lottie squeezed my hand. I squeezed it back, glad for the reasonable comfort from my four-year-old niece. I sipped at my champagne flute, conscious of drinking too much and making a fool of myself. Today was not a day for that.

Just as the thought of her whereabouts crossed my mind, Lottie called out, "Ellie!" across the terrace. A cluster of people turned their heads, one of them being the person in question. She spotted us, not hiding too well after all, and made her way over after pardoning herself from a conversation she was having with an elderly couple.

"Where've you been?" I hissed.

"What you talking about? I've been here." Ellie cooed over Lottie's dress and gave her a peck on the cheek.

"We said we would meet by the doors."

"I know, but you know what Tom's like. People see him, and we just get whisked away." She smiled, still his number-one fan after all these years.

"Well, you're here now." I pulled her in for a big embrace.

"My dress!" she fussed, laughing. "Seriously though. How're you doing?"

Terrified. Absolutely shitting my pants.

"I'm fine."

"That bad, huh?" She studied my face and then, perhaps sensing my unease, hugged me again, tighter.

"Your dress," I mumbled into her shoulder, her sweet perfume stinging my nose.

"It's fine. Now, let's get you another drink."

She took both of us by the hand and led us out of the shade and into the gathering of people. I looked down at the ground, which had been covered with petals and confetti, not wanting to catch anyone's eye.

Ellie nudged me. "You said you wanted to come."

"I know. I did. I just feel..." I was unable to articulate the mass of emotions I was harbouring.

"It's super weird. But you're here now. And you've gotta own it. What time does Slush Puppy get here?"

"She's hoping to make it for dinner. And stop calling her that."

Our eyes met, and we burst out laughing.

"Well, just get by until dinner, and then you'll be fine...with that hot piece on your arm."

"You can't say stuff like that now. You're a mum."

"I know. I know." She shook her head and then beamed, thinking of her son and prompting a check of his whereabouts. "Jasper's over there, Lottie. Go see him if you like."

Lottie looked at me for approval, and when I nodded, she scampered over to Jasper, who sat at a table with Tom's parents, fiddling with a pile of napkins. He sighed as his napkin tower collapsed, his floppy brown fringe falling over his eyes. We watched Lottie and Jasper clamber over each other in excitement, completely oblivious to the formal setting and constraints that apply to weddings: the *best behaviour* mantra. Tom's parents, Debbie and Phil, tutted over the children, straightening their clothes and telling them to be quiet.

"Come on. It's been a while since we had a good excuse to get drunk."

"It's nice to see motherhood hasn't changed you."

She pawed at me with her free hand and then picked up another flute and nodded over to an empty bench underneath a willow tree. The branches stooped over, providing a protective leafy curtain from the rest of the guests.

"You know me. Everything is a little better with a drink." She clinked my glass. "Now what shall we toast?"

"I dunno. To our friendship?"

Ellie scoffed. "I see your fat ass all the time. Pretty sure I'm stuck with you till the end of our days."

I nudged her, and she threw her head back in a sharp hoot of a laugh.

"To our *everlasting youth!"* Ellie cried out, saluting the branches of the willow tree and taking a big gulp.

The cool breeze danced through the vines, making them sway gently in the sun. Time edged on with each sip of alcohol, drawing the big event closer and closer. I hoped that just for once, time could take pity on me and stand still. So that best friends could gossip over the guests' questionable choice of attire, watching the kids play as Tom's parents fussed over them, and reminisce on the parts of life that brought us here, just for a little longer.

Chapter Six

2010

On Monday morning, Tamara didn't show up for class. I wasn't even sure if she was supposed to be there, but either way, I didn't see her. Afterwards, Ellie and I went to the Great Knight, a cheap but cosy pub not far from the university, for lunch.

"Maybe she's just old-fashioned about that kinda stuff," Ellie said, her mouth stuffed full with a burrito. "She might want to take things slow."

I considered it for a moment, pushing back into the stiff armchair. Maybe I had been too forward.

The sun moved from behind a cloud, blinding my eyes through the large wooden windows. I shuffled my chair around the table. Ellie moved my table mat and beer across to me, wiping at the condensation on the marked wood top.

I sighed, swirling my bread around my soup until it went soft and fell in.

"Hey, Sam!"

Someone tapped me on my shoulder. When I saw who it was, my stomach twisted into a ball.

“Oh. Hi, Grace.”

Grace pulled a chair out next to Ellie and sat down, not acknowledging her presence. “Where’ve you been?”

I hesitated, glancing at Ellie for guidance. She shrugged and went back to eating her burrito. Before I could answer, Grace slammed a poster down on the table. *Lovefest.*

“This month at Diamond, they’re playing the most romantic films. There are discounted tickets for students, so you can pay. They even have little heart balloons, look.” She pointed to a picture on the front of the leaflet. A couple stood holding a giant inflatable balloon between them, smiles plastered across their faces. I imagined Grace and me in their places and quickly rejected the thought. “They’re starting with *The Notebook* tonight. What do you think?”

Caught off guard, I struggled to come up with any excuses. I looked at Ellie desperately. Ellie took a deep breath in.

“Sam and I were supposed to hang out tonight. She’s been so *preoccupied* lately.”

“I noticed you haven’t replied to my messages. What have you been doing?” Grace asked eagerly.

“I’ve been struggling to keep up. There was Anita, right? Chloe, Rebecca, Jess... Am I missing anyone?” Ellie said, turning to me.

Grace’s face clouded; her eyes twitched between us. “I have the most perfect idea,” she said, her voice a little higher than before. Grace looked at Ellie for the first time since she sat down. "A double date."

Ellie's face fell. Before she could protest, I chimed in.

"Sure, why not?"

★

Just after seven, I pulled Stella into the car park behind Diamond, the small indie cinema. It was usually crowded with students as they offered discounted tickets and incredibly cheap pick 'n' mix. The owner, Robbie Kipper (just "Kipper" around Treaton Vale), was an aspiring director and was massively involved with the industry. There was nothing more he liked than a project to delve into. He was always showcasing low-budget films he had funded, and he held a premiere every year for final-year students to encourage them to show off their projects. Outside, huge billboards advertised Lovefest, and I wondered what Kipper was raising money for this time.

I had immediately regretted saying yes to Grace's invitation—well, demand. And not just because of the verbal abuse I had received from Ellie. The only thing that had stopped me from cancelling was the fact that Ellie and Tom were going to be there too, and Ellie and Grace spending time together was always going to be entertaining.

Kipper had rolled out a cut-out pink carpet to the entrance. Unfortunately, it was already stained black with cigarette butts, and the rose petals he'd sprinkled had turned to mush.

The three of them were there already. Grace had her back to me, her arms making wild movements as she spoke. Tom was nodding politely as Ellie stared off into the distance.

We bought our tickets and shuffled down towards our seats. Tom and Grace strode ahead. Ellie tugged on my arm.

“Dude. Honestly, she’s so fucking annoying. Please tell me this isn’t a thing.”

I laughed. “It’s your fault we’re here in the first place.”

“Mine?” she hissed. “You didn’t have to say yes to her.”

“I panicked. I’m sorry. But now you know the urgency of the situation, you’ll be able to help more.” I leaned in and whispered into her ear, “Otherwise, it’s more double dates for you.”

“This might seem crazy, right. But why don’t you just tell her you’re not interested? Moved on...found someone else.”

Right on cue, Grace shouted me over and ushered us into our seats. The cinema was almost full. Three quarters or so of the seats were taken by enthusiastic women clutching and cooing at not-so-enthusiastic men.

Whenever something romantic happened in the film, Grace pulled at my arm, shaking me as if I was a moron and had missed it. Each time, I nearly knocked the popcorn over. And I wished I had done. Normally, I would never conspire to spill delicious salty snacks, but it would have given me an excuse to go and get away for a bit to buy some more.

Partway through the film, I escaped to the bathroom without Grace following me. I sat on the seat with my head in my hands, considering if I could fit through the bathroom window.

After my bum was numb, I leaned my back against the cold blue tile, watching the door, telling myself that I would leave when the next person came in. I had my story ready. *Sorry, Grace! I got locked in the bathroom! I had to wait for the handyman to come and get me out.* A nice few minutes passed. The silence was sweeter after Grace had garbled in my ear all night.

"Are you...waiting for someone?"

I glanced up. I hadn't even noticed that someone had come in.

"I, erm, no...I'm just..." I motioned with my hands, unable to finish my sentence.

"It's Sam. Isn't it?"

I looked at her properly. It was Petey's new wife. What was her name? Becky? Definitely something with a B.

"Hey. Yeah. How're you..."

"Emma," she finished for me, laughing.

"That's it. Sorry."

"It's okay. I have a special talent for remembering names. Crap with dates, though. I forget every birthday, and I've missed so many parties." She smiled warmly. "Why are you hiding in the bathroom?"

I couldn't think of a single sensible reason, so I told her the truth. "I'm hiding from my date."

"Wow. That bad, huh?"

I nodded. "You don't know the half of it."

"This sounds like a story I want to hear the rest of. But right now, I really gotta pee."

"Oh yeah, sure."

She scuttled into a cubicle behind me and locked the door. I wanted to stay and talk to Emma but didn't fancy getting a reputation for hanging out in the bathroom and bothering women who needed to pee. I took a deep breath in and opened the door to leave.

"So, what's so bad about your date?" Her voice was more of an echo from behind the door.

"Besides her complete disregard for personal space and people's feelings? Let's see." I let the door close again softly and perched myself on the sink. "She thinks that the world is flat."

"No! She doesn't!"

"Oh yeah. She does. She's been to one of their marches and everything."

"That's mad." Emma came out of the stall, buttoning up her trousers. "More than that, even."

"Yep." I caught a glimpse of her pants and looked away. I didn't want a reputation as the girl who stalks women in the bathroom to peek at their underwear either.

"What're you doing on a date with her? She doesn't seem your type."

What was I doing on a date with her? 'Cause I was desperate? 'Cause I had been rejected by the first person I actually felt a connection with? And, at this point, I didn't think I had a type. Treaton Vale wasn't exactly bubbling over with attractive, smart women dying to ask me out.

"It's a long story."

She studied me for a moment and then wiped her hands dry on a piece of paper. “Again, sounds like a story that I want to hear the rest of. But I better get back to my husband before he leaves me for the usher out there.”

“Yeah, I guess I better go too.”

She held open the door, and we walked out together.

“Another time though,” she said as she parted ways to return to her seat.

I nodded, aware of the silence-in-the-cinema rules and the usher watching cautiously from the door, but she had already turned her back and was walking away.

★

When we left Diamond, it was dark outside. A cool breeze fluttered my dress, giving me goosebumps. I was dreading this part of the night; saying goodbye was always awkward. I wondered if I could outrun Grace to my car.

The four of us stood in silence. Tom was leaning back on the stone wall with his coat wrapped around Ellie, the top of her head resting on his shoulder. I hated that they were so cute.

Grace stared at me, her eyes so wide that they were bulging out of her head. I looked down at my feet, dreading whatever was going to come next. She lunged forward. I sidestepped, and Grace’s wet lips pressed to my cheek.

They stayed there for too long. When she stood back, her face was red. Her fists clenched.

“If you think you can friend-zone *me,* Samantha Atlas, you’ve another thing coming!” Her hand slapped me straight across the cheek, the same place she just kissed, and she stomped away, her heels clomping as she went. Ellie burst out into laughter.

"Oh my God. That was fucking brilliant."

★

I clutched the bag of frozen peas to my cheek. I wasn't sure if it was helping. My face was ice-cold, but my cheek was still sore. We were gathered around Tom's dining table drinking: cider for them, lemonade for me. Tom's house was the biggest in our friendship group. It was in the east part of the city, the posh part, with the Mayor's Gardens only five minutes away. The Mayor's Gardens were one of the most impressive things about Treaton Vale. They sculpted the acres with hundreds of flowers and trees, enveloping the landscape with boundless colour. In summer, the city held Gardeners, a free festival within the grounds. Thousands of people came to listen to the town's newest and most loved bands and try the different foods in the market. Two months ago, this was where I had met Grace.

★

It was the peak of summer. Yellow-and-blue bunting swung from the trees, and lights twinkled from the branches. I was in line for the mac 'n' cheese van. Ellie, Tom, and Ash were queuing for burgers whilst Matt chatted a girl up by the main stage. Wherever you looked, there were painted faces and costumes. The music floated in the warm breeze, and people swayed along, their faces coloured like frogs and butterflies. A group of girls walked by with fairy wings and wands, their eyelids sparkling with purple glitter.

"What about you, Tarzan?"

It had taken me a moment to realise the question was addressed to me.

"I'm not Tarzan." I pointed out my black nose and whiskers clumsily strewed across my face. "I'm a lion."

"What's with the loincloth thing?"

"It was too hot for my original costume. I had to improvise."

I cursed Ellie's spontaneous clothing choice. Afraid I would dehydrate in my full faux-fur lion costume, we raided Ellie's mum's old sewing box and had found some fluffy material dashed with spots, which resembled more of a cheetah than a lion. As I looked down at the pieces woven around me, I saw how Tarzan was more appropriate.

"Do you think I should choose the original mac 'n' cheese or go for something a bit more adventurous?" she asked.

"Adventurous."

"I really like original though," she whined.

"Why don't you get both?"

She laughed a little too loud. "Yes! Now that is an idea I can get behind. What do you want? I'll buy yours as a thank you, Tarzan girl."

Carrying our steaming trays of food, we walked over to an empty patch of grass and sat down. The sun was beating down on my neck; a damp layer of sweat started to pool underneath my makeshift costume. I wished I had brought more sun cream with me.

I waved the rest of the group over when they had their burgers. Ellie gave me a questionable look as she sauntered across, balancing two cans of Fanta underneath her arm. Tom took a big bite out of his burger, dropping sauce out of the bottom and narrowly missing his shirt.

“Guys, this is...” I started, forgetting the girl’s name.

She waited for me to finish the sentence and, when I didn’t, chimed in enthusiastically, “It’s Grace. Grace Bowerly.”

The group murmured a greeting, their concentration focused on consuming their food. We had waited in line for almost twenty minutes, and in the blistering heat, the time had felt much longer.

“Who are you here with?” Ellie asked.

Grace glanced in Ellie’s direction, surprised by her question.

“Just with my mum. I should go tell her where I am. She’ll be worried.” She turned to me, a stray piece of pasta on her bottom lip. “I’ll be right back.”

Ellie shuffled closer to me after Grace left, moving her two trays of pasta away from her with distaste. “She’s got those crazy eyes, that one.”

“What do you mean?”

“The *crazy eyes*,” Matt said. “The girl is a fruit loop. I’ve seen it a million times.”

“Really? She seemed nice to me.”

The group missed a beat eating their food to give me a dubious look.

“Trust me,” Ellie said. “You wanna steer clear of that one.”

★

Tom tried to stop Ellie from laughing at me, but he was struggling to contain his own. It was a challenge to put the lemonade bottle to my lips with the huge bag of frozen vegetables on my face.

"Well, all things considered," Tom began, "I think tonight went quite well."

Ellie nodded in agreement. "And holy cow, can that girl give a slap."

After I painfully finished my drink, I wanted to go home. We had a lecture the next day at twelve, but I wasn't sure if I was going to go. A giant red splodge on my face wasn't something I wanted to parade around at university. I could just imagine the look on old John's face.

I said my goodbyes, grabbed my keys, and opened Tom's door to leave. Someone sat on the doorstep. It was Tamara. She had her back to me and turned when she heard the door. She failed to hide the surprise on her face.

"Sam?"

"Tamara."

She glanced at the red mark on my cheek.

"Jesus. What happened?" She stood and reached out to me. I took a step back.

"Oh. It's fine. Just a misunderstanding."

"Can we talk for a minute?"

"Look, Tamara. I just want to go home."

"Can I give you a lift?"

I pointed to my car.

"Oh right. Yeah. Stupid question."

She watched me from the step, flicked her cigarette out, and sat back down. She didn't look away. In the rear-view mirror, I saw her watching the car as I drove down the street. I wondered how long she stayed outside after. Watching and smoking.

★

A few days later, Blue Rooms were playing in the city for the Oktoberfest weekend. There were lots of bands scheduled to play, and they had the headline spot for the Saturday. The sun had made a special appearance. Everyone was in much higher spirits, showing off arms and legs that hadn't seen the light of day since the summer. I was no exception, even going through the effort to moisturise my legs.

The smell of freshly baked buns and cakes filled the air. People gathered around stalls selling alcohol and hot foods, stuffing their faces with burgers and chips, ketchup smattered on their fingers. Live music played from the marquee. Ellie and I were on our third cider, and we stacked the plastic cups underneath one another, making a small tower. I was having a good time.

But I couldn't stop myself from looking for Tamara.

I was starting to annoy myself.

Tom, Matt, and Ash had spent the afternoon with us but now had disappeared to go prepare for their set. Ellie and I moved to the side of the square. Fountains guided the pathways from the high street. Small children played in the water, shrieking and taking their clothes off as they got sodden. Parents sat at the sides, happy so long as their children were occupied. We sat down on a wall facing the stage and waited in the sunshine.

I spotted Tamara lying on the small grass verge on the righthand side of the square. Her legs may have been even whiter than mine. It was the first time that I had seen her in anything other than her jeans. She wore little denim shorts and a blue tank top. Her beanie hat lay scrunched at her feet. She was with a dozen or so people, only a few of whom I recognised. One being the other girl I had almost run over. Almost all of them were smoking, each exuding a small trail of dark grey like an old chimney fire. Tamara stubbed out her cigarette and laid her head back on the grass. Ellie followed my gaze and rolled her eyes.

"I wish you two would stop playing whatever game this is."

"I just don't understand her."

"She's messing with you, Sam." Ellie finished the rest of her drink and squashed the cup in her hand. "Maybe you're better off." She aimed at a bin and missed.

"I don't know. I feel like this is different," I said.

Ellie gave me a sympathetic look. "Yeah. That's what they all say."

Shortly after, Blue Rooms started their set and we moved down to the front. I watched Tamara from the corner of my eye. When they announced the band over the microphone, she sat up. I hoped she would come over.

Ellie's mood lightened as soon as Tom stepped on stage. It was too hot for his denim jacket, but I could see it hung off a chair on the side stage, just in case. They got everyone dancing. Even some of the parents pulled their children into the square to dance, dripping water everywhere. Ellie grabbed my arms, throwing me to the left and then the right and spinning me in circles. Others started to join in. Tipsy men and women stumbled around, stepping on people's feet. But no one seemed to mind. Tamara had moved over to a stand selling alcohol out of small plastic cups. Feeling a sudden surge of confidence from my own helping, I strutted over.

"Hey."

"Hey." Tamara turned to face me.

"No beanie today?" I asked, wanting something to say.

She smirked, and I noticed a small dimple in her chin. "I got one, don't you worry. Just for you." She pulled the mustard beanie out of her pocket. "It's a little hot for it." She smiled at me, and my eyes drew to her lips.

"For me?"

"How else would you spot me? I can't be making that mistake again." She waved over the bartender. "I was hoping you'd be here. I'll buy you a drink. And one for your crazy friend over there." I followed her nod to see Ellie dancing frantically with an old couple near the front of the stage.

"Yeah. Sure. Thanks." I leaned forward on the bar and ordered two ciders.

Tamara pulled a ten-pound note out of her pocket. "How's your face?"

"Fine, thanks."

The bartender brought the ciders over, and I took one in each hand. Ellie had expanded her group, dancing with half a dozen people at the front of the stage.

"You wanna dance?" I asked Tamara.

She laughed, and it reminded me of wind chimes. I suddenly regretted asking. The breeze blew her hair over her eyes, and she rearranged it with a quick flip of her head.

"Sure. Why not?"

She followed me as I snaked through the crowds of people, making our way to Ellie. I handed Ellie the cider and then took a huge swig of my own. Tamara did the same. Then she took my drink and placed it on the floor with hers. I opened my mouth to protest, but she clasped my hand, spinning me into her body. Despite my slightly drunken state, she spun me effortlessly. One hand secured my waist, and we twirled around in circles. My vision started to blur from the motion. Both of her hands moved down to my waist, and with a pull, we were dancing with just a few pieces of clothing between us. She slowed down, rocking us from side to side so I could feel the warmth of her body. I glanced over Tamara's shoulder, conscious of the audience, but everyone was watching the band. She held me closer, wrapping her arms around my back. We stayed there, Tamara swinging and swaying us until Blue Rooms announced their last song and everyone pushed forward, forcing us apart. We joined Ellie at the front. Tamara linked her arm around the bottom of my back like the first time we saw Blue Rooms together. Her whole body was bouncing. She squeezed my hip, her smile stretched cheekily over her face. I couldn't help but smile too.

After the set, Tamara pulled me out of the square, away from the marquee and the busy body of people. Ellie went to find the others, giving Tamara her acceptance to drag me away with a nonchalant wave of her hand as if to say *do what you want with her*. I felt a little bad. But I had put up with being the third wheel with her and Tom for the last year. Surely, she would understand.

Tamara stopped at a bench a few minutes' walk from the square. It was strangely quiet. The marquee buzzed in the distance. She sat down and motioned for me to sit next to her. She watched the area silently.

"I know I'm shit. I'm sorry." She swallowed. "I don't know why I do it." Tamara was looking down at our hands. She rested them in her lap. "It's not an excuse...but sometimes I just find it so hard to say what I mean. What I feel. And for it to come out right." She paused. Her free hand softly traced mine. "There's stuff you don't know about me. There's stuff I don't know about you. Really, we don't know that much about one another." She looked at me for the first time since we sat down. "But I know that I want to." Her eyes flickered from mine to my lips and then back to our hands.

"I just don't understand..." I began.

"I know. And I'm sorry. I wish I could explain properly, but I'm not sure how."

My mind had been so active earlier, but now it betrayed me with its silence. Tamara was picking at the pocket on her shorts, her lips pressed together. She kept avoiding eye contact, looking everywhere but at me. I wondered if her face was as soft as it looked. I wanted to touch her. Run my fingers through her hair. To pull it. To kiss her.

Tamara took a deep breath in.

"I want to take you out on a proper date. Where I won't stand you up or be late or be an idiot." Tamara rubbed her forehead as if to erase the memory. "Please?"

I paused, although I already knew my answer.

“Okay,” I said. “But it better be good.”

Tamara laughed.

“I’m so fucking nervous, and here you are making fun of me.” She smiled. “Figures.”

My stomach tightened. “I make you nervous?”

She nodded, lacing her fingers in mine. She traced each one carefully.

“Just feel like I’m gonna mess it up.”

I didn’t say anything. I just squeezed her hand. Maybe because deep down, I thought Tamara was going to mess it up too.

Chapter Seven

2021

Weddings were never my forte. The idea still didn't appeal to me much. Dad said it was something I would want when I was older. Well, now, I was older. That was clear to me from the grey hairs I had to tweeze out of my eyebrows and the creases I couldn't pull out of my skin in the mirror. But weddings still seemed a foreign event. That's not to say I didn't enjoy them. What's not to like about booze and dancing and people being in love? With the exception of being single or waiting for your significant other to show up halfway through the wedding. What I would have given for a bloody cigarette.

"What's your secret?"

The question brought me back to the present. Thankfully, it wasn't directed at me, as I hadn't been listening.

"We tell each other everything," Ellie said. "And we have date night."

"Thank the lord for date night," Tom added.

The elderly lady liked this response. "Yes. Yes, it's so important that you two make time for each other." She grabbed Tom by the arm to make him listen. "Physically."

He gulped. "Uh-huh. I hear ya."

Ellie looked at me in horror. I was grateful I hadn't been listening to the other parts of the conversation.

"And you, dear. Any special men in your life?"

They turned to me. Ellie and Tom smirked, looking forward to the heat being on me for a moment. The lady peered at me eagerly. I tried not to look at the giant mole on her face. Or the two hairs protruding out of it.

"Actually, I'm gay."

She took a small step back to look at me more closely. "I would never have guessed."

"Really?" Ellie said.

"Shut up, you."

"Isn't your hair too long to be a lesbian?" She tilted her head to the side, inspecting me like a strange specimen she had found in her scone.

"Erm. I don't think there's really a checklist of qualifying criteria."

She nodded, absorbing the information. "Well, it does all seem very popular now. I think if I were twenty years younger, I would try it too."

We murmured some sort of agreement. Not one of us knew what to say.

"Anyway," she continued, unaware of the laughter we were trying to suppress. "It's time for my refill."

When she was out of sight, we let it out. People turned to try to catch on to whatever funny thing they had missed.

"Oh my God!" we chorused, laughing harder.

"Well, that's your backup wife sorted, Sam," Tom said, patting me on the back.

"I think she had more of an eye for you, *Mr Physical.*"

"What have I missed?" Jake sauntered over. "What's so funny?"

We all spoke over each other to fill him in on the conversation. He shook his head. "She was probably being sincere."

The three of us gave each other a knowing look. A look that meant we were going to make sure he had his own taste of Mrs Hairy Mole's delightful conversation later on.

"I think it's starting soon, so we should take our seats," Jake said, giving my arm a little squeeze. They all looked at me for a moment. A sympathetic gaze passed across their faces in unison.

"I'm fine!" Even I knew I sounded anything but fine.

The waiters moved through the clusters of people, dispersing them as people began to take their seats. Nerves gripped the inside of my stomach. Time would wait for me no longer. Or would it?

"Just give me a second," I said, pulling away from the group. "I need some air."

"But you're already outside," Jake said.

"Where are you going?" Ellie asked.

"I just need a minute. I'll be back."

Jake's eyebrows furrowed.

"I will. I promise."

"Remember what you said to me," Jake added. "Don't ruin this for Catherine."

“She’s the caterer, Jake. Not the fucking pope,” I snapped and stomped away from them.

It annoyed me that he felt the need to remind me every five minutes. I couldn’t give a flying shit about Catherine at that moment. Had it escaped his mind where we were? What about me? I couldn’t help but think about it every second; the sickness in my stomach wouldn’t let me forget it.

None of them understood. Ellie and Tom had been together since university. Jake was married with a kid of his own. They didn’t get that being at this wedding was like having a giant target on my back. I didn’t want to be *that* person who couldn’t handle tough situations, but maybe I was, and I had to be okay with that. Everyone had their fight-or-flight response hardwired into them, and if the past had taught me anything, it’s that I was definitely a flighter.

“She’s not coming back,” I heard Ellie say as I turned the corner.

But I would. I was almost sure of it.

Chapter Eight

2010

Tamara came to pick me up at six. I thought it was a little early, but she insisted. I nearly swallowed my tongue when I opened the door. A neat black dress hugged her body tightly, accentuating her curves. Her hair was tamer than usual. It had been curled and pinned, with just two acute strands lining either side of her face. I raised my eyebrows in surprise and made a conscious effort to not look at her breasts. She looked pleased with herself.

Her car was a little tidier than the last time. There were still clothes in heaps on the back seat, but most of the rubbish had been cleaned out. She thanked me for noticing.

In her usual attire—jeans, T-shirt and, of course, a beanie—Tamara looked hot. But seeing her like this had caught me off guard. I was a garden gnome in comparison.

She took me to a nice Italian restaurant outside the city, Gialeppo's, well known for having the best pizzas in Treaton Vale. After parking, Tamara rushed to the other side to open the car door for me. I told her there was no need. She ignored me, feigned a curtsy, and held out her hand. I took it willingly.

The restaurant was full of couples dressed in evening dresses and suits, pulling out chairs and thanking the other with a sultry bow of the head. A soft melody of string instruments played on the sound system, filtered by the quiet conversation of diners. We were the youngest ones there, and this made me more nervous. Tamara leaned back in her chair, unaware that we were like two fish out of water or too hungry to care, and studied the menu intensely, her lip rested between her teeth. We poked fun at the menu and the superfluous way they described the dishes. I ordered the butternut gnocchi, and Tamara had the spaghetti bolognaise—*whichever way they describe the cut of the tomatoes, it's still just a spag bol.* Then she ordered a bottle of pinot for the table and met my inquisitive look with a grin.

"You can't go wrong with a classic," she said, struggling to spoon the food into her mouth. The spaghetti unravelled itself from her fork, dropping sauce onto the tablecloth. She muttered some swear words, and we cracked up laughing. She tried to clean it discreetly but instead smeared huge stains of red across the previously spotless white. It didn't matter that everyone in the restaurant was looking at us in disapproval; it just made it harder to stop. I held my hand over my mouth and tried to stifle my laugh. It didn't work, and when our eyes made contact, we started howling again. A middle-aged couple across from us tutted loudly. Tamara knocked some cutlery off the table, and the sound echoed through the room.

"I don't think you're cut out for this big-date stuff," I teased.

After we finished our bottle of wine, Tamara insisted on paying the bill and left a handsome tip for ruining the nice cloth. We stumbled out into the crisp night air, clutching at each other, and bought another bottle of wine from the nearest off-licence. We ventured over the bridge and steadied our way down to the riverbank, walking hand in hand over the dirt path and taking it in turn to swig from the wine bottle. We followed the path around until it dipped into a small clearing. A few large rocks joined the river to the path.

"It's a bit dirty," I noted, disappointed.

"Fuck it." She kicked her heels off and sat on the edge of a rock. I did the same, and on the count of three, we plunged our feet into the water.

"Fuck!" we shrieked and then crumbled into laughter. We stayed like that for a while, drinking the rest of the wine and dangling our feet into the river as the night fell dark around us.

Tamara pulled out her pouch of tobacco.

"Let me try." I took it from her hands, and Tamara raised her eyebrows. She let out a giggle.

"This should be funny."

I pulled a skin out of the holder and held it between my fingers. Tamara passed me a filter.

"That goes at the end."

I nudged her in the ribs. "Yeah, I think I know that part."

The tobacco was harder to separate than it looked. It clumped together, forming hard bumps in the paper. Tamara's tongue pressed to her cheek. I tried to pull the tobacco apart, but the filter tumbled to the floor, down the rocks, and into the river. Tamara passed me a replacement, unable to hide the satisfaction on her face. I grabbed each end of the cigarette like I had watched Tamara do a hundred times and started to roll. It evened out nicely, but when I tried to lick the paper to seal it, it fell loose. I held the cigarette up to appreciate my creation, and we both burst out laughing.

"How on earth am I supposed to smoke that?" Tamara laughed and took the cigarette from my hand. She peered at it closely, like admiring a piece of artwork a toddler had made. She lifted it above her head, inspecting the filter, and it fell, tumbling down the bank and into the river to join its brother.

"Wow," Tamara said.

"I don't think that's bad for my first go."

Tamara looked at me, amused. She held the remains of my creation in her palm. Her lip curved upwards. Then, with lightning speed, she rolled another cigarette. She leaned back on one arm and placed it in her mouth, nonchalant.

"Show-off," I muttered.

A smile spread across her face. I watched her as she took a Clipper from her jacket pocket to light her cigarette. Her hands cupped it delicately, shielding it from the wind. On the second try, it lit. She took a drag and, with a fulfilled sigh, breathed out a puff of smoke. It danced through the air, contorting itself until it disappeared into the darkness. In between drags, she passed the cigarette from finger to finger. She saw me looking and offered it to me. I surprised myself by nodding, and she held the cigarette to my lips while I inhaled. Her eyes were on mine as

I breathed it in and out, the smoke filling my chest with a warm tingle. Her eyes stayed focused on mine, and a smile tugged at her lips.

"I thought you'd choke."

"Well, maybe you've got me all wrong."

"I better watch myself, then."

When the wine bottle was empty, we made our way back along the path to the main road. We walked with our shoes in our hands, our bare feet welcoming the cool dirt. Tamara hung her jacket around my shoulders, and though she claimed she wasn't cold, I noticed her skin prickle with goosebumps.

We were both too drunk to drive, so we ordered a taxi, abandoning Tamara's car at the restaurant. When the taxi pulled up, the driver made us put our shoes on before we got into his car.

In the back seat, Tamara gazed out of the window. Her hands rested on her thighs, her fingers tapping out a quiet rhythm. She guided the driver to her house. It was a few streets over from Matt's—I had been to watch a Blue Rooms practice there before. He had been dating a girl at the time who found out that he was dating her cousin as well. They had driven by, throwing eggs at his windows. His parents grounded him for a month and made him clean all of the mess off.

The driver stopped outside. A small silence hung in the air.

"Are you getting out?" the driver snapped.

"Give me a minute, man," Tamara barked back. "Do you wanna come in?" she asked.

I nodded, and Tamara got out of the car, pulling me behind her.

Her house was smaller than the others in the neighbourhood, but it was bigger than mine. We stood at her glossy black door while she fumbled in her pocket for her keys.

"Watch out for Puds," she murmured as she turned the key in the lock. Once inside, she kicked off her shoes and dumped her jacket on a dresser in the hallway. A big bound of black bumbled up to Tamara, its tail hitting the walls with loud repetitive thumps.

"Hey, boy." She fussed over the dog, and he rolled onto his side, making small whimpering noises. I placed my shoes neatly next to Tamara's heels and went to stroke him. He jumped up from his back and leaped at me, welcoming me with a big lick on my cheek.

"Puds! Sorry about that. He's really friendly." Tamara stumbled over to the kitchen and poured two more glasses of wine from an open bottle on the counter.

She headed out through a wooden back door, and I followed her outside to a little patio. There were two metal chairs and a small silver table with an overflowing ashtray. Puds went sniffing around the garden. Tamara automatically started to roll a cigarette. She offered me one. I declined.

My head was fuzzy. I took a large gulp from my glass, but the taste unsettled my stomach.

When she finished smoking, she headed back inside. Tamara was unusually quiet. I wondered if she wanted to be alone.

"Do you want me to go?"

"What? Why?" Tamara asked, surprised.

"I'm not sure if you want me here."

"I do. I do."

"You seem a bit...preoccupied."

Tamara shook her head. "Sorry." She reached out and touched my cheek. Her fingers were cold and smelt like cigarettes. "I've something to show you."

Tamara's room was littered with pieces of paper and empty beer cans. Her duvet lay scrunched on the floor in a ball. She quickly tried to tidy some bits, but she was uneasy on her feet.

"Sorry for all of the...the shit," she said, waving her arm in a vacant gesture.

"It's fine."

I perched on the edge of her bed and looked around. Her walls were plastered with posters of bands, most of them unfamiliar to me. Nearest her headboard was a picture of the frontwoman of a rock band. She had heavy black eyeliner and big blonde hair backcombed into a huge frizz. Her wooden nightstand was covered in loose tobacco and bits of torn-up Rizla packets. On her windowsill, a tower of glasses huddled together like they were trying to keep warm. Tamara kicked some clothes into a corner. I shuffled my bum back on the bed until it was pressed against the wall. My head felt full. Tamara pulled something out of a drawer and hid it behind her back. She wobbled over, a mischievous grin on her face.

"Close your eyes."

"Really?"

"Uh-huh."

I shut them and held out my palms. Tamara placed a large, thin package down. I opened my eyes to see a vinyl record. “Don’t Stretch the Moon”, Merlot and the Bakers.

“It’s the one that we were singing. In my car,” she said. “You seemed to like that one.”

“Thank you.” I ran my fingers over the red cover. “I love it.” The artwork was a giant black silhouette of the moon with a man in a top hat leaning on his side. I flipped it over and read the back. The artwork was the same, but the colours were inverted; the red moon rested prominently on the black background.

“It’s the acoustic version. It’s a bit more...meaningful,” Tamara said.

“Can we listen?”

Her eyes lit up. “Yeah, for sure.”

She lifted a few boxes off her dresser to reveal a black record player. She messed with a few of the switches, and then the record started to play. Gently, she danced her way back to the bed, softly humming along, and climbed back next to me. She kicked her legs out so ours were side by side, both smudged with bits of dirt, our feet almost black. Tamara sang softly. I closed my eyes and listened.

When the song finished, Tamara put it on again. She took my hand and felt over my knuckles and fingertips absent-mindedly as she sang along. After the song ended for the second time, she stood up, rustled through her drawers, and threw me a top. I didn’t catch it, and it landed on my face. The top smelt like mint, smoke, and lavender. It smelt like Tamara.

With her back to me, she shimmied out of her dress. It fell to the floor, revealing her small and perky bum. Her hair fell softly over her slender back, and my eyes followed down her waist.

I admired her quietly.

The sprinkle of freckles across her skin. The shape of her thighs.

She looked over her shoulder at me and unclipped her bra. It fell to the floor with a soft thud. She lingered, topless, then threw on a baggy T-shirt. She leaped onto the bed, banging against the headboard, and stretched out her legs. She nudged me with her toe, her smile bigger than I had ever seen it.

"Your turn."

Her eyes gazed at me, big and brown and inviting. I swallowed. My mouth was suddenly dry. I stood at the edge of the bed, facing her.

"I'm gonna need your help," I said shyly.

Tamara nodded and shuffled forward on her knees. I turned my back to her, and she slowly unzipped my dress, her fingers softly grazing down my skin. The hairs on my arms raised against her touch. Tamara moved back to the headboard, her eyes on mine. I let the dress fall to my feet, grateful that I had my favourite pair of black underwear on. I faced her and watched as her eyes flitted to my shoulders, breasts, stomach, thighs, and back to my eyes. My stomach tingled. Tamara's face was still.

I shrugged on the top she gave me, embracing the smell, and, without a word, moved next to her. The glimmering light from her bedside table cast shadows across the bed. Her lips rested, full and pink, and my hand longed to reach out and trace them. My pulse quickened at the thought, thumping loud and clear in my ears.

Tamara glanced at my lips. She reached out to tuck a stray hair behind my ear, then decided against it. Her hand hesitated in mid-air and rested on my neck.

Then we were kissing. Soft at first, then faster with a sense of urgency. Her mouth tasted of the sweet tang of wine and cigarettes. Her hands pulled me closer, and I grasped at her desperately. A quiet moan escaped her lips, and my insides throbbed.

She kissed me hard, her hands still entangled in my hair. Then she took a deep breath and pulled away abruptly.

"I haven't earned it yet," she said softly. Her eyes flickered to mine, and I wondered what they were looking for. She smiled gently. My stomach ached.

I kissed her again, craving the sweet taste.

"I haven't earned it," she mumbled into my mouth.

I kissed away the thought and trailed down to her jaw. Her milky skin was smooth against my lips. I nipped at her neck, encouraged by her soft groan. In one swift movement, she flipped me onto my back.

She pinned my arms above my head and pressed herself against me. Our kisses grew desperate, the hairs on my back rising to attention. With reluctance, she drew back to pull her top off over her head, her small, round breasts bouncing lightly.

"Your turn," she whispered into my ear, yanking my top off over my head and throwing it across the room. I lay exposed while she looked breathlessly over my body. Her eyes were darker than before, tinted with something unexplainable, holding something back that I wanted to understand.

She lowered her hand, letting it slip gently down my torso and into my underwear. Her breasts pressed against me, and my heart drummed loudly in my chest. She peeled my pants down my legs and moved her body down, planting kisses inside my thighs. She looked back at me, her eyes full of something unsaid, and then she parted my legs.

I fell back on the bed, grasping the sheets whilst the sound of ragged breathing echoed through the room. I gripped her hair and wound it around my fingers. She pressed harder against me, working tentatively until I folded up like an accordion releasing its favourite musical tune.

Tamara lay next to me, her breathing rasped, her hands behind her head.

"Your turn," I whispered.

★

I opened my eyes to Tamara face down, her arms sprawled across her pillow. I scrunched my eyes up tight and opened them again. She was still there, her hair stuck up on one side of her head. I traced my finger down her arm, her skin soft like cotton. Her chest rose and fell slowly as she slept. I lay and watched her for a while.

When she woke, Tamara made us breakfast. And each time she reached up to the cupboard, her top teased a flash of her underwear. I couldn't help but look. Flashbacks of the night before entered my mind, Tamara's face as I moved inside her, her mouth open slightly, begging for me to kiss her as our bodies moved together. My cheeks flushed red as I looked away, the memory fading behind my eyelids.

We sipped our tea and ate our breakfast with Puds peeking his nose out from under the table, desperate to catch anything that might drop. I stroked his large black head, and he sniffed my fingers, trying to lick the bread-crumbs. I moved them away at the last second. He looked disappointed.

"Puds," I said. "Why the name Puds?"

"He's so bloody greedy," Tamara said. "He can sense food from a mile off. We had to move all the food from the bottom cupboards because he knows how to open them. I've no idea how." She took a bite from her toast and then muttered with her mouth full, "Crazy dog."

"I always wanted a dog," I said.

"Why don't you get one?"

"Dad works all the time. He said it wouldn't be fair."

Tamara nodded. "Your dad would love him. He's a dog and a vacuum all in one."

Puds looked up at us both, his eyes wide, unaware that he was the topic of conversation. Tamara threw him a small piece of crust, and he leaped into the air and swallowed it instantly. He licked his lips and then curled up back under the table, pleased with himself.

Chapter Nine

2021

I paced around the side of the building, my heart pounding hard in my chest. My wrap got caught on a handle as I turned the corner, and it ripped, pulling a big hole down the seam. Great. Not only did I have to feel like an idiot at this wedding, but I had to look like one too. If any time was a good one to relapse on the tobacco habit, it was definitely then. Why had I ever quit in the first place?

Satisfied with the distance I had put between myself and the rest of the guests, I sat on a stone wall and looked out across the gardens. The wind drifted through the trees, caressing every leaf in turn. I took three deep breaths to try to steady my hands. The fresh air was tainted with the smell of cooking oil and freshly baked goods. I must have been near the kitchen. I wondered if they would serve cream cakes with the dinner or if it was freshly baked Yorkshire puddings. Whatever it was, it smelt good. And it was something for my mind to focus on for a few minutes.

Suddenly, I'm ten years old and Mum is serving us Sunday dinner. Mum makes the best homemade

Yorkshire puddings, crisp and light and perfectly golden. Jake is kicking me under the table, and Mum, noticing, gives me the most warped pudding out of the tin. This pudding is the *lucky* one, and whoever is served it doesn't have to wash up the dishes.

Dad had tried to recreate them after she died, but he was a terrible cook. The first few Sunday dinners were the worst. The mismatch of those days made the hole in our hearts deeper, the realisation that something so normal to us could never be normal again. All I longed for was one thing to stay the same, a Sunday dinner with the best Yorkshire puddings and Jake kicking me under the table. But it never did, and it never had since.

It's times like these when I wish Mum was still alive. I feel like she would know exactly what to tell me because isn't that their motherly gift? Dad tries his best, but when it comes to the matter of *love,* I imagine it would go as well as when I got my first period. If he wasn't sure about the difference between sanitary pads and tampons, I doubt he would know how to cope with this situation. Especially as he hasn't been with anybody since Mum passed away.

A door opened near me, banging into the stone wall behind it with a loud thud. Someone cussed under their breath. Probably a busboy or waiter on their break.

I turned back to the gardens, looking across the rolling hills in the distance. This is what I had wanted to avoid. Running away from the wedding like I had something to hide. I wasn't sure whether this counted as bad behaviour in Jake's eyes. I had said I wouldn't cause a scene, and I had promised not to drink too much, but I had never said I would be present for it. Surely that was better? A persistent clicking sound perked my attention. I turned to see somebody hunched over, attempting to light a cigarette in the wind. They cursed again, fiddling with a lighter that was obviously out of gas. I felt over the zipped pocket in my bag for the lighter I had placed there for emergencies. Perhaps it was time to break my cigarette silence after all. They turned around, trying to get a better angle for the job, and our eyes met. We watched each other for a minute, our brains working silently to piece the parts of the moment together. Me and her. Standing metres apart. Both craving nicotine and space. I moved closer, producing the lighter I had stashed in my bag.

"Do you need a light?"

She stepped closer to me, surprise and confusion painted over her face. Then a big smile, one that had both ignited and haunted me over the years, stretched out from ear to ear.

"I didn't think you would come," Tamara said.

Chapter Ten

2010

"It's fucking freezing."

Tamara stood in the sea, a blanket wrapped around her shoulders. The waves lapped gently around her calves.

"You can't go to the beach and not go in the sea," I said, kicking the water at her.

"Sam!"

"Is Tamara King scared of a little ocean water?" I teased.

She glared at me from under the towel, which she had now wrapped around her head like a nun.

"I'm *not* scared. It's just freezing, and I can't swim, so what's the point?"

"The point is to enjoy the little things. Like the sea in six-degree heat."

She laughed. "This is stupid." She kicked water at me and shrieked when some of the splashes covered her back. "We're going to catch something."

"Yeah, hopefully a crab or a lobster."

She splashed me again, her smile stretched across her face. "More like a cold or pneumonia."

"Be more like Puds. Look at him."

Puds galloped across the waves, trying to catch them in his mouth. His tail was wagging so fast I was surprised he didn't take off and start flying around the beach.

"Puds is an idiot. As are you."

I splashed her again, and she ran back towards the sand, screaming all the way.

I chased her, calling Puds behind me for backup. Tamara stumbled in the sand and tripped. I dove on top of her and pinned her down.

She struggled beneath me. "For someone so small, you're freakishly strong."

I kissed her. She stopped fighting and kissed me back.

"You're the idiot," I said.

Puds clambered over us, covering us in fishy sea water and wet sand.

"Puds!" we both screamed, jumping to our feet.

He stared up at us, his tongue hanging out of his mouth, his tail wagging. Then he shook himself dry, his whole body propelling water out of every surface.

Tamara ran again, and I picked up the towels and followed her with Puds in pursuit. At the top of the hill, she keeled over, out of breath. Puds sat next to her, looking up in adoration.

As the sun dipped overhead, Tamara popped open her boot with a creak. Puds jumped in, walking around with sodden paws.

"Oh my God, Puds. Get out."

He jumped down and licked her feet.

"You're such a weirdo," she said, throwing me a towel. "Take care of your dog."

"He's your dog. *And he's lovely. Aren't you?*" Puds wagged his tail in agreement. I rubbed his feet dry the best I could, then his body, and finally, his big head.

"That'll do," Tamara said.

"It won't make a difference to your car anyway."

"Bit harsh. But you're probably right." She gave me a quick kiss. "Let's go."

The clouds drew darker overhead as we drove back along the windy roads. I flicked through the CD to track three. "Don't Stretch the Moon".

"If you keep playing it like this, you're gonna end up hating it," Tamara said.

I shrugged and turned up the volume, singing along. She rolled her eyes. Then she sang along too.

"So, I'll pick you up tomorrow for the party?" Tamara asked once she'd pulled onto the kerb outside my house.

"I think I'm getting ready at Ellie's."

"Oh, okay. I'll meet you there then," she said, and she leaned over to the passenger seat to kiss me.

I stepped out of the car and waved to Puds in the back seat, but he was asleep. "See you later." I watched as Tamara pulled away, waving, and then I went inside.

"You had fun?" Dad asked before I had even taken my shoes off.

"Yeah, it's been great."

"Good."

I followed Dad's voice into the living room. He was doing the ironing whilst watching TV. Jake sat on the sofa on his phone, looking up when I came in. His hair was styled different, pushed backwards instead of spiked up. It made him look older.

"Tamara seems a lovely girl," Dad said as he ran the iron over one of his uniforms.

Tamara seems a lovely girl, Jake mouthed behind him. I shook my head at him. He smiled and went back to his phone.

I went into the kitchen and opened the fridge. "Have you eaten yet?" I called to them.

"No, love."

"Okay, I'll make something."

While I waited for the pasta to boil, I diced some onion and garlic and cut some broccoli into small florets. I simmered the vegetables in a pan for a few minutes, slowly adding in vegetable broth. Once the pasta was cooked, I drained it and mixed it together, adding cream cheese.

"It smells delicious, Sam," Dad said.

I brought in three steaming plates and placed them down. Jake rolled his eyes.

"Of course, it's some veggie shite."

"Why don't you learn to cook, then?"

"It's too much effort. I'd rather just eat three bags of crisps," he grumbled.

"Drop the attitude, Jake," Dad said.

Despite Jake's complaints, he ate it all and finished before anyone else.

"It wasn't bad," he admitted. "I wouldn't call you a culinary whizz or anything. But it sure beats Dad's veggie lasagne."

We burst out laughing.

"Hey!" Dad protested. "It wasn't that bad."

"Dad, I can still smell the burnt in the kitchen. It's clung to the kitchen tiles."

He dismissed the comment with a wave of his hand. Jake and I giggled. "I'd like to see you do better, Jake. Jam on toast is not cooking."

★

I arrived at Ellie's house at seven the next day. I exchanged a few pleasantries with Ellie's mum and dad and then headed up the two flights of stairs to the attic room, where I found Ellie sitting cross-legged on the floor

"Which do you think is better? This green? Or this one?" She held up two pots of nail varnish, her back to me.

The lighter green was electric against her dark skin. "Erm. The second one."

"Damn it." Ellie frantically scrubbed at her toes, trying to erase the previous colour.

I sat beside her and browsed through her bag full of nail varnish. She had so many that she'd accidentally bought some of the same colours twice. I found a soft indigo colour and started applying it carefully. The colour smudged across my skin, staining it a strange purple.

"What the hell is that?" Ellie laughed. "You should be ashamed."

"I can never get it to stay on the nail. It's so hard."

Ellie rolled her eyes. "You're such a bloody lesbian."

"Hey! That's offensive!"

She took the pot from my hand and placed it next to her foot. She sat with her legs propped up, balancing her heels on the floor, careful to avoid her toes touching the white carpet. She scrubbed off the messy creation and started again, the colour flawlessly covering my nails. She saw me admiring her work with a smidge of jealousy.

"It's art," she said.

After two hours, three outfit changes, and another last-minute change of nail colour, Ellie announced she was ready. I lay on her bed, stomach down, giving her a running commentary on her movements.

"Finally. We've got a winner, folks."

"Please shut up."

★

Ellie's mum dropped us off at the party, cooing about how beautiful we looked and how grown up we were.

"Mum, I am twenty-one, you know," Ellie said.

"I know, I know. But it's like you're both still at nursery for me. Arguing over the watering can. Fighting in the tree house."

We all laughed. I had nearly broken my arm that summer when Ellie had pushed me out. She had always been stubborn.

"Tell Tom and the others hello from me!" she called as we got out of the car.

Tom's house glowed on the street. Every light in the house was on, and in the dark night, it looked fluorescent, like the house had been overrun by aliens. Inside, people were just starting to arrive. I noticed that Tom had tidied away his parents' favourite artwork and hidden photo frames and vases so that there was nothing easily breakable in reach. The furniture had been pushed to the sides of the room, and the rug had been rolled up and stashed in a cupboard, leaving a big space for people to congregate, drink, and dance. In the kitchen, lined in rows, were half a dozen different spirits—the large bottles—and so many different mixers I couldn't count. Packets of plastic cups were in every room, bowls of snacks on most tables. Tom and Matt were there already, as expected, both wearing neat button-up shirts and tight black jeans.

"Where's Ash?" I asked.

"Take a wild guess," Matt replied.

Ash had been dating Yvette for six months now. She was older, twenty-five, and very middle class. She competed in pageants often—I saw from her Facebook—and dressed up in long and elegant dresses like she had stepped out of a 1930s film. Her lips curled when she pronounced her name, and her long blonde hair was often fancily pinned up like she was a bridesmaid at a wedding. She didn't seem like Ash's type at all, but he was besotted. I had only met her twice, and each time she didn't address me when she spoke. Ash took her to Petey's once to see them play, and she had refused to go again. Probably got someone else's beer on her dress.

"What's happened?" Ellie asked.

"He hasn't said. Just that he's running late," Matt said. "The dragon is most likely trying to change his mind about coming. And about being in the band, probably."

"Well, maybe she shouldn't come, then. No one wants her here," Tom said, anger building in his voice.

"She probably won't," Ellie soothed, her hand softly brushing Tom's hair down at the back.

I pulled out my phone and texted Tamara. I had messaged her at Ellie's, but she hadn't replied. She still hadn't. A peculiar feeling spiked in my gut. I couldn't put my finger on it.

Ellie and I poured ourselves drinks and went into the living room. The room was starting to fill with more people, and we recognised a few from our course and went to say hello. The music grew louder. People gathered in the middle of the room, dancing.

I checked my phone.

Nothing.

I went outside to try to cool down, reached into my purse, and pulled out a small pack of tobacco and some Rizla. I tried to roll the way that Tamara had shown me many times before.

"Since when did you smoke?" Ellie asked, surprised.

I hadn't realised she had followed me outside.

"I don't really. Just the odd one."

"Is this Tamara-induced?"

"What? No. Why?"

"Well, where is she?"

"She's just getting ready."

Ellie must have sensed the waviness in my voice. “Surely she can’t take longer than me.”

My phone vibrated.

Sorry, I’m on my way now.

“She’s on her way.”

Ellie kept her eyes on me. “Right,” she said doubtfully. She went back inside as if to prove a point.

I walked down the steps of Tom’s garden and sat on a swinging seat underneath a big oak tree. The big cushioned seat looked inviting. I crossed my legs and swung myself slowly. The cold teased at my skin, the alcohol protecting me with a dazed numbness. I pressed my cup to my cheek to try to sober up. My face was hot against the plastic.

I had been smoking so much more these past few months. It still wasn’t a lot. Maybe two or three cigarettes a day. But it was enough for me to buy my own bag of tobacco.

It was November, and Christmas loomed. The few months I had spent with Tamara had made me lose track of time. I understood now why Ellie never stopped talking about Tom. It’s the thing people write and dream about, it’s splattered across our TVs and every aspect of our everyday lives, and I had it. A strange feeling curdled in my stomach, like a knife twisting in my side. I tried to push it away. My heart and head were at war, and neither would listen. Or maybe I was hungry.

I finished my cigarette and had an overwhelming urge to stub it out on the plump, stripy cushion. That stupid cushion. I wanted to press small circular holes through its perfect fabric. I sighed and tossed the stub onto the ground, letting it fizzle out in the open air.

From the bottom of the garden, the music was comforting. People spilled out of the large double doors onto the decking, stumbling and searching for cigarettes in pockets and bags. Under the dark shadows of the tree, I felt invisible. It was a nice feeling. I was at the party. But I was also not.

Someone started making their way down the path. I wondered if they could see me. Tamara's silhouette gave her away.

Her long and shapely legs, her small and gentle shoulders.

As she came closer, her profile came into view. Her lips were pressed together the way she did when she was anxious.

"What are you doing over here?"

"Nothing. Swinging."

She sat next to me. "Are you all right?" she asked.

"Do you like Christmas?"

"What?"

"Do you like Christmas?"

"Why?"

"I feel like I still don't know you, Tamara." I squashed my empty cup in my hand. She watched me quietly, her eyes burning a hole in my face. It was a long time before she spoke.

"I used to love Christmas. When I was a kid," she said. "We used to come here every Christmas for dinner. Me and Tom would play in his room with our new toys, and

Mum and Dad would talk and drink champagne with Auntie Debbie and Uncle Phil." She paused and swallowed. "It wasn't until I was older that I realised how fake it was."

I turned to her, but she was looking straight ahead.

"All the shouting and swearing. Mum's crying. I could hear her at night while Dad was out. One Christmas, he got so drunk that he fell and crushed my new bike. I hadn't even had a chance to ride it yet." She took a deep breath in. "Sometimes, I would sit on the stairs while they argued to try and figure out how I could fix it. But you can't teach an old drunk new tricks."

"Where is he now?"

"Some prison in Doncaster."

"What happened?"

"He came back one night, pissed out of his skull. I was nineteen, and I'd had enough of him. I locked him out, and he was banging on the door, screaming for all the neighbours to hear. Mum gets real paranoid about all that stuff, and she was begging me to let him in. I did. And he was kicking off about how there's no respect for him and he works all day just to get locked out of his own house. My mum tried to put herself between us, and he punched her. Straight across the face. I can still hear the sound." She sighed and watched as more people stumbled out onto the decking. "Me and him started fighting then. He was strong, but he was drunk, so I had a little leeway. I got a good few punches in..." Tamara fiddled awkwardly with her hands. "He hit me, and then Mum screamed, and *she* attacked Dad. She'd *never* done that before. Then I was in so much pain I didn't see it happen. I just...heard it. The clattering when she fell—was pushed. My dad pushed my mother down the stairs." Tamara shook her head. "It was horrible—the noise. I think even Dad was shocked. Not that it matters." She looked away at the party. "The police were quick to come. But the trial took forever. Luckily, though I suppose that's a weird way to think of it, Mum had lots of bruises from him before, so there was plenty of evidence against him. Hope he rots in there."

We didn't speak for a few minutes while the words settled in the air. I sat beside her, both of us gently swinging in the cold night breeze.

"Come on. Let's go in." Tamara tugged on my hand.

Inside, the party was raucous. The house was humid, like when you step out of the airport into the blistering heat. People shrieked and shouted against loud, thumping music. Boys kissed girls against walls. Ellie was dancing with Tom and Matt in the middle of the floor. A brown stain decorated her dress. She'd probably spilt her drink from dancing too vigorously. Or maybe it was a bit of fly-away spew. Either way, she seemed past caring.

Tamara got us two drinks from the kitchen, and we filtered our way through the crowd of sweaty people. I spotted Ash in a corner with Yvette. His blond hair was trimmed much shorter than the last time I saw him. He was looking down into his cup as he drank, Yvette on his knee. She looked like she was casting a spell on the room.

We wriggled in next to the others and joined in dancing, linking our arms around each other's shoulders when our favourite songs came on and throwing ourselves across the room. Every time Tamara glanced at me, my heart swallowed itself. I watched her from the corner of my eye, searching for a bit of the vulnerability I had seen minutes before. Tamara threw her head back, belting out the chorus of the song up to the ceiling. Whenever she sang the *woahs* and the *aahs,* her mouth hung wide open like she was trying to catch something. Whatever sadness that plagued her outside had gone, or she was extremely good at hiding it.

We drank and sang until my head was dizzy and the room span. The only clear face was Tamara, beaming at me from across the group. Some of her other friends had shown up—the girl I almost ran over (who I now knew was called Tyler) and a handful of others I recognised from around the town. Tyler didn't dance. And she didn't speak to anyone outside of the group she came with, except for Tamara. A girl called Rhe was like her shadow. She followed her around the room, leaning into her shoulder and kissing her face. When Tyler left the room, Rhe did too.

"Let's see those moves again," Tamara enthused, pulling me out of the group circle. "But try not to stand on my feet this time."

I tried to keep my head up, but I didn't know where to look. Being so close to Tamara made me forget about keeping to the rhythm. I moved awkwardly, and she laughed and pulled me closer, trying to help me control my steps.

Suddenly, a sharp pain radiated through my back. Then I was on the floor, winded and confused by the array of shoes that surrounded me. I turned over and looked up to see Grace standing there. Her hands were shaking. Her face was red.

"What do you think you're *doing*?" Grace screamed.

I blinked, trying to focus on the scene in front of me. Pain surged up my back.

Someone pulled me to my feet. I heard more shouting.

People had stopped dancing and encircled the area. I pushed past their stagnant bodies and saw Grace on the ground, her nose bloody. Tamara towered over her.

“What is your problem?” Tamara growled.

“You’ve broken my nose, you utter lunatic!” she spat.

“Good. And I’ll break more than that if you touch her again.”

Grace pinched her nose and stood slowly, glaring at Tamara. “*You*. Are dancing with *my* girlfriend.”

The music cut out. A sea of voices murmured behind us.

“What? Grace. I am *not* your girlfriend. Why on earth would you think that?” I asked. A small group had gathered around us, excited for the drama.

“We went on a date, did we not?” Grace’s voice was muffled by her hand.

“And how did that date end, Grace? With you slapping me across the face.”

“*She* slapped you?” Tamara asked.

She shoved Grace again, and she fell back onto the floor. Grace looked up at her with fear in her eyes.

“Tamara, don’t!”

She turned to me, bewildered. Her fist clenched. “What?”

“Let’s just talk about this.”

“She just attacked you *again*,” Tamara spat. “She needs to learn her lesson.”

"Not with violence. You should know that."

As soon as the words left my mouth, I wanted them back. Tamara twinged. Her arm fell by her side. "Right. You sort it out, then." She pushed through the crowd that had gathered and was gone. Tom came the same way she left.

"What's going on?" He stopped when he saw Grace, bloody and lying across the carpet. "What the hell? What happened?"

"Tamara," Ellie said, resting her hand on her hips. Her chest puffed out, and her eyes were glazed over from alcohol.

"I don't think that's fair," I said.

"Well, who else punched me in the face?" Grace whined. "I seem to recall it being your new redhead love-bird, who has since left you to fight for yourself."

"Give it a rest, why don't you?"

Grace held one hand out to Tom. He took it reluctantly and pulled her up.

"These are the kinds of people you associate with," Yvette hissed from the back. I turned, and Ash glanced at me apologetically.

"Hey, Yvette, if you don't like us, then why don't you just leave?" Matt said.

Her eyes flickered over to his. She studied him for a moment and then left, dragging Ash behind her. Matt wandered away from the girl he was chatting to.

"Are you okay?" he asked me.

"Is *she* okay? What about me?" Grace shrieked.

“I’ll get some ice,” Tom muttered. “Show’s over, folks. Put the music back on!”

“Come on, Grace.” I rested my hand gently on her arm. She recoiled.

“Get off me,” she squawked. I acquiesced.

The party resumed. I sat with Grace in Tom’s bedroom upstairs. She pressed a bag of frozen peas to her nose.

“You know,” I said. “I had a bag just like that when you slapped me.”

She glared at me.

I sighed. I wanted to smooth things over. I wasn’t a fan of all the drama.

“Look, Grace. I’m sorry if you think I led you on. I guess I should have been clearer.”

She huffed. “I thought that you liked me,” she said into the peas.

My stomach rippled with guilt. I didn’t mean to give her that impression. “I’m sorry.”

She nodded. “Me too. For shoving you...and I messed up your hair...and everything. It looks like a nest now.”

I touched my hair. She was right. “At least you didn’t pull any out.”

“I wish I had.”

I gave her a look.

“I’m joking!” She rearranged the bag on her face. “I just wanted you to look at me like that,” she said quietly. “The way you were looking at her.”

I didn’t know what to say. We sat in silence for a minute while I searched for the words. I only found two.

"I'm sorry."

"Stop apologising. I know you can't force it." She placed her hand lightly on my thigh and then moved it away.

"This looks cosy."

I looked up. Tamara was standing in the doorway. She had her arms folded across her chest, her eyebrows knotted.

"Sam, please keep this hideous *dog* on a lead."

Tamara lunged forward. I stepped in between them.

"Please, stop! Both of you," I pleaded. Tamara rested back on the door, watching Grace carefully. I noticed Tamara's knuckles were red and swollen. We stood awkwardly for a moment.

"Okay, I'm going to go. Not that this hasn't been *lovely*...but I need to go bathe my face in aloe vera. It should help with the swelling," Grace said. "Call me if you get bored with her." She gestured to Tamara, who was sucking on her teeth. Probably to stop herself from saying something.

"Grace, you don't know when to stop!" I barked. "Just go."

She smiled half-heartedly, then pulled the door shut behind her.

A silence settled over the room.

"Wow. She's a real charmer."

"Yeah, she's something."

"One crazy ex down. How many more to go?"

"She isn't even my ex."

Tamara's voice softened. "How's your back?"

I stretched. It was a little sore. It didn't hurt though. "It's fine."

"Good."

"Jealousy brings out a whole other side to you, huh?"

She smirked. "Well, she called you her girlfriend, can't be having that."

Tamara locked the door behind her with a click.

"What are you..." I saw the mischievous look in her eyes that I had become familiar with.

She pushed me down on the bed and kissed me, her breath tainted with alcohol and the usual whisk of cigarettes.

"'Cause I want you to be my girlfriend," she said softly, grazing my ear with her lips. "If you would have me."

I kissed her neck, making my way to her mouth, hoping the dancing of our tongues would speak for itself. I concentrated my excitement on her body and the way it was moving against me. "What about your hand?" I asked when our lips parted for air.

"I'm sure we'll get by just fine," she said.

She kissed me again, and we started undressing each other at a rapid rate, clothes landing all over Tom's bedroom floor. The sound of the party carried on booming downstairs, fading to background noise.

Chapter Eleven

2021

"It's really good to see you," Tamara said, exhaling smoke into the air in a long sigh.

"It's really good to see you too. Weird. But good."

She smiled. The same smile that would've crippled me ten years ago.

"How've you been?"

"I'm good, yeah. Weddings are..." She took another drag while she contemplated the end of her sentence. "Stressful."

"I can only imagine." I rolled a cigarette between my fingers and lit it. Tamara watched me closely.

"You got better at that."

"I've had enough practice." The tobacco filled my lungs like an old friend's embrace. "I don't smoke anymore though."

"What are you doing, then?"

"Let's just say...weddings are stressful."

She nodded in agreement, brushing over her shoulder where she had dropped some ash. I had daydreamed about her on this day, wondering if she would wear a suit or a dress or something completely random—a kilt, perhaps, or maybe even a morphsuit. Nothing was ever certain with Tamara. That was her selling factor—and it was also her catch.

In the pictures my head conjured up, she had worn a long white dress with lace across her chest and embroidery across her veil. She had a long train that our bridesmaids gathered gracefully as she walked down the aisle to meet me.

My intuition was wrong. Instead of a dress, she wore a fitted grey-and-white chequered suit with a red pocket square and tie to match. I had never liked red much, and part of seeing this colour on her today made sense in my head. *She was never right for you. Look at her wearing red.*

Tamara shifted underneath my gaze. "What?"

"Nothing. Just, you...in a suit."

She smiled half-heartedly. "I always thought about it too."

"About what?"

"Me and you. What could've been. All that wishy-washy bullshit that people think about when they're getting married." She stubbed her cigarette out on the stone wall and hid it in a plant pot. A few seconds after, I did the same.

We watched each other in silence, taking in each detail that had changed between us over the years. Her hair was shorter. Nails were still bitten. Her right ear had a new piercing. Our eyes met, and we smiled, forgetting the strange situation and environment that had brought us here together.

"There you are," an unfamiliar voice sounded, pulling us out of our little bubble. "They're looking for you."

We turned to a tall, well-built man in a red suit, possibly a groomsman. He posed with his large arms across his chest like he had discovered two kids bunking off school in the middle of the day. "I almost thought you'd taken off." He scowled. "Was about to kick your ass."

Tamara laughed. "Nope...still here. Relax, man." She swatted him on his big bicep, and he unfolded his arms, relaxing them by his sides.

"Good. Come on. Let's go." He glanced at me, forced a smile, and turned on his heels, inviting Tamara to follow him. She was looking at me. Her mouth parted as she began to say something.

"Go on. Don't stand her up like you did me," I said.

She shook her head. "You'll never let me live that one down, will you?"

"Nope."

She followed the large man through the door, pausing in the archway to glance back at me once more before she went.

Chapter Twelve

2010

I clicked my pen and set it down. My paper was still blank, aside from the little black doodle of Puds in the corner. I picked up my pen again and held it between my fingers expectantly like the words were going to suddenly channel through me and onto the page. My coffee was too hot; my tongue throbbed gently where it had burnt minutes before.

I sighed and leaned back in the chair. An old man on the table next to me looked up from his paper.

John's assignment was due next week, and I hadn't even started. Jake was playing video games at home, and the loud gunfire was like someone hammering nails into my head. If I had managed to get into his room, I would've pinned him down, arms above his head, and flicked his ears until he cried. I doubt I would have been strong enough now to hold him down anyway, but I would've given it a go.

The bell jingled, and Matt ducked in through the door. He wore a crisp blue shirt that complemented his dark skin. His tousled black hair was shorter and neater than before. A short blonde girl followed him. She looked familiar, but I couldn't place where from. They browsed the baked goods stored in the counter, and Matt said something that made the blonde girl laugh. When they had their drinks, they made their way upstairs.

A while later, Matt came down to use the bathroom. On his way back, he spotted me and came over, a cheeky smile on his face.

"Hey, Sam. How're you doing?" He sat opposite me and glanced at the blank paper on the table. "Oh. Am I interrupting?"

"No. I can't think of anything to write anyway."

He nodded, mulling over my statement with a sincere interest. "I don't suppose you've heard from Ash, have you?"

"No. Not since the party. Why?"

"Yeah. Me neither. He didn't show up for practice on Wednesday. I'm worried Yvette has him in a basement somewhere."

"He not answering the phone?"

"Nope. Straight to voicemail. I know it's got something to do with her."

"I hope he's okay. Especially with that mugging on Monday." My dad had made sure to tell Jake and me about it multiple times since it had happened, begging us to *be safe* and *look out for each other* in the overbearing way that parents do.

"Yeah, me too. Did you hear that Andy Clems got jumped in the Mayor's Gardens?" he said. "If you can get jumped there, nowhere is safe."

"Shit. Is he okay?"

"I think so. Anyway. I better go. I have a date upstairs." He waggled his thick eyebrows.

"I noticed."

"Yeah, and you're gonna make me behind schedule. I have another date at four."

I smacked his arm. "You're terrible, Matt."

"I know. I know. But I'll need something to think about when I'm grey and in a care home. See ya later." He scraped out his chair and ran back up the stairs two at a time.

Defeated, I packed away my things. I slung my bag over my shoulder, nodded to Todd, the barista, and opened the door. My phone vibrated.

> *I'm busy at the moment. Can we meet later, after 8?*

For someone with so little to do, Tamara was always busy.

My shoulder caught someone, and there was a thud as a folder fell to the floor, some of its contents spilling out on the pavement.

"Oh, crap. I'm sorry. I wasn't watching where I was going." I bent down to help pick the papers up. It was handwritten sheet music.

"It's fine. Don't worry about it, Sam."

Emma tucked her blonde hair behind her ear, revealing her delicate pixie features. The skin around her eyes was darker than usual and a little puffy. I don't think she was expecting to see anyone.

"Sorry, Emma. How are you?" I passed her the papers back, and she pushed them into the folder.

"Yeah, good. Just getting some air. It's one of my few days off," she said. "How are you?"

"Not bad. Tried to do some work, but I'm lacking inspiration."

She seemed surprised. "Sorry to hear that. It sucks when creative juices just aren't flowing."

I nodded in agreement.

"Are you free? Do you want to go hunt some?"

I had some time before Tamara was free. And it sounded much better than listening to Jake shout at his TV screen. "Um. Sure."

We walked along to the Mayor's Gardens. Emma's blue silk scarf was wrapped carefully around her neck, and she gripped her coat tightly against the wind. A light rain pattered across the path. I hadn't planned on being outside for a long period of time, so I hadn't brought a coat.

"Even in the rain, the gardens are so pretty," Emma said.

I told her about the recent mugging.

"I find that hard to believe. It's too nice for anything like that to happen here."

"Maybe no one expected it, and that's why it happened."

She looked at me. "Yeah, I guess you have a point."

"What's in the folder?" I asked.

She held it close to her chest, protecting it from the rain.

"Some of my music. But I haven't done anything new in a while. Been too busy. Or I guess—" She looked at me. "Uninspired."

"I didn't know you wrote music."

"Yeah, I play guitar and sing too. Less often, though, now." The rain soaked through my hair, and it dripped down my shirt as we walked. I started shivering. Emma turned to me, her little mouth shaped into an *O*.

"Oh, God. You're soaking. Why didn't you say anything?" She started to unwind her scarf and wrap it around me.

"I'm fine. It's my fault for not bringing a coat. It is December."

"Oh, God," she muttered to herself. "I am quite self-indulgent sometimes."

"It's fine, Emma. It's quite liberating."

Her mouth hung open in surprise. "How is getting cold and wet liberating?"

"It feels nice sometimes. Being at one with nature and all that."

Her eyes were sad. She fidgeted with the scarf in her hands.

"My place isn't far. Please come and dry off. I make a great hot chocolate, even if I do say so myself."

The rain soaked through my jumper, turning it a dark grey. "Okay. But I want to hear some of your music."

She smiled, but it didn't touch her eyes. "I'm not promising anything." She linked my arm in hers, and we walked through the rain.

★

Emma brought us to a small flat five minutes away from the Mayor's Gardens. It didn't look much on the outside. The plaster was once a brilliant white but had faded from the constant English rain. Two potted plants that manned the gate had dried up and died, and the paint on the top of the gate had peeled, leaving it an uncomfortable grey.

Inside was modern and airy. Big windows cast pillows of light onto the marble kitchen counters. It was all open-plan: the living room was sectioned off from the kitchen by the change of flooring from tile to wood. The kitchen consisted of a few expensive counters with a small sink, a large double fridge, and an oven.

Emma wiped her feet on a bristled mat as soon as she stepped inside. She hung her coat and scarf on a hook beside the door and then turned to me.

"Okay. I'm gonna go get you some dry clothes. Just wait here." She walked over to the fireplace, lit it, and then left to go into the bedroom. I warmed myself against the fire until she returned with a T-shirt, a jumper, and some slack jeans.

"They're really old ones of mine. I hope you don't mind," she said. "You can change over there. I've left a towel in the bedroom."

I returned with my wet clothes scrunched in my arms. Emma was stirring some hot chocolate in two big Christmas mugs.

"I know it's not Christmas yet, but these are the only ones I keep here. I'll wash those." She took my sodden clothes and disappeared into the bathroom. A moment later, she ran back into the room, looking for something and tutting herself. “Sorry, I’m a bit of a mess.”

She brought over the two hot chocolates and sat beside me on the sofa, breathing a sigh of relief as she took a sip.

“Sorry, I haven’t been here for a while, and I forget where I’ve put things.”

“Do you...live here?” I asked uncertainly.

Emma blew in her cup to cool it and then took another sip before answering.

“Well. I used to. Before Petey and I got married. I still come back here from time to time. I didn’t want to sell it. And Petey said we didn’t need to. So, it’s my home away from home.”

“I really like it,” I said. “It feels peaceful. Like we’re not in Treaton Vale.”

She smiled. “That’s what I always thought. In here I could always pretend to be somewhere else.”

I held the cup close to me to savour its warmth. “Where would you wanna go?”

“New York, Vegas, Thailand, Australia, anywhere... More than that, even.” She placed her cup down on the glass coffee table. “I wanna see it all.”

“Why don’t you, then?”

“It’s just not realistic.”

“You can still travel.”

“I doubt Petey would like that.”

“Why?”

"He's a man of routine. The club is his life. I can't imagine him being impressed at me gallivanting across the world."

"Why don't you go together?"

She looked at me as if I'd suggested she go travelling with the Teenage Mutant Ninja Turtles. "No. No. He loves England too much. Our honeymoon was a stretch in itself. He can't separate himself from work. By the pool, he was on his phone sending emails or ringing bands and arranging meetings."

"Do you...do you want a cigarette?" I asked.

She glanced up from her lap, scrutinising me. "I haven't had one in years." Her eyes flickered away. "I didn't know you smoked."

I fiddled with my hands, feeling embarrassed. "Well, I don't really. Just the odd one."

She nodded. "You spend a lot of time with Tamara." It was more of a statement than a question.

"Yeah."

Emma lingered as if she was thinking of the right words to say. "Be careful there."

A peculiar feeling seized my gut again. I thought about Tamara. Standing in the sea, a towel wrapped around her head. Screaming as Puds chased her. Singing loudly in the car. Her eyes. God. Those brown eyes... I thought of her lying on her bed. Her eyes closed, concentrating. Her shoulders, her collarbone, her stomach. Each dimple and scar and freckle that decorated them. The way she pushed herself into me when we kissed. Her body as it tossed beneath me, soft gasps escaping her lips... A flush of heat rippled between my legs as I blinked away the memory.

Sensing she had said something to upset me, Emma placed a hand on my arm.

"Sorry. I don't mean to be intrusive."

I nodded, feeling embarrassed about where my mind had wandered. Emma's hand stayed on my arm. She moved it away to reach for the towel hanging on one of the barstools and rubbed her hair gently to help it dry. I wandered over to her bookshelf and browsed the books and DVDs.

"Which is your favourite?" I asked, brushing my finger along the top of *Pretty Woman*. A layer of dust coated my finger, and I wiped it on my jeans.

"Book or film?"

"Both."

With no hesitation, she replied, "My favourite book is *The Great Gatsby*."

"I haven't read it."

She didn't seem surprised. "You can borrow it if you like."

I nodded, knowing that I wouldn't read it. "Is it also your favourite film?"

"No," she sighed. "It's not quite the same."

"What is your favourite, then?"

She shook her head.

"What is it?"

She bit her lip. "Promise you won't laugh."

"Okay. I promise."

"*The Fox and the Hound.*"

"I love that film!"

"Really?" Emma eyed me suspiciously.

"Yeah. When I was a kid, my mum used to watch it with me every time I was ill."

She smiled slightly, with just a twitch of her lip. "I try to watch it every year, or I feel like I've betrayed a part of myself. And young Emma will come to haunt me in my sleep for being such a useless, boring adult."

Emma took a sip from her cup before joining me by the DVDs. I could smell the sweetness of her perfume mixed with the dampness of the rain. She traced her finger along the shelf, settled on the title, and pulled it out. "Shall we?"

★

As the credits rolled, Emma's eyes welled up. She wrapped herself in a red blanket like a child.

"Are you okay?"

"Yeah, I'm fine." She brushed tears away with her fingertips. "The ending always gets me."

Tears spilt down her face until her eyes turned red. Then she lifted out of her seat and went to the bathroom.

I sat and wondered about the last time I had cried. Properly cried. Red eyes, blotchy face, struggling-for-breath crying. I couldn't remember. All I could think of was Mum. Jake and I had stayed in the same bed for months after because neither one of us wanted to be alone. I must have cried since then. It was weird that I didn't know.

I traced my finger over the plastic DVD cover. I hadn't wanted to mention to Emma that I hadn't watched *The Fox and the Hound* since Mum died. I didn't want her to feel uncomfortable like most people did whenever I mentioned my mum.

Emma returned a few minutes later. She carried a small box of tissues under her arm. Her eyes had faint lines of black where her mascara had smudged.

"I'm sorry. I'm in such a way today."

"Are you okay?"

"Yeah. Yes, I'm fine," she said quietly. "I'm just a stupid woman sometimes."

"You're not, Emma. Don't say that."

She sniffed. "Thanks, Sam."

I smiled and then looked away, fumbling with the strands of my damp hair.

"Can I hear you play?" I asked.

I didn't see her reaction but heard her footsteps on the wooden floor as she left the room. The DVD had reset back to the title screen and was replaying snippets of the film. I switched it off.

The ring of guitar strings made me jump. Emma stood outside her bedroom door, her guitar slung over her shoulder. She laughed at my expression.

"This is Harrison." She walked over and passed the guitar carefully to me.

"Oh. Hello, Harrison."

She smiled. "He likes you."

I rolled my eyes.

"Hey." She nudged me. "He has a sixth sense with people. I trust it."

I brushed my fingers over the polished wood and gently plucked a string. The note hung crudely in the air.

"I always wanted to play guitar," I said, following the strings down the fretboard.

"I could teach you if you like." Emma collected the empty mugs and placed them in the sink.

"Really?"

"Yeah. When I'm not working." She sighed. "Which, as of late, seems to be all the time."

"Well, if you don't mind, yeah, that would be great."

"Okay." She turned to me, and her little button nose twitched as her laugh spread through the room. "Lesson one. You need to hold the guitar the other way. That's the wrong way around."

★

Emma hugged me when I left. It was comforting to know I had achieved some sort of productivity, even if it was not anything to do with my assignment. On the way home, I decided to stop by Tamara's house. The rain had passed and left a damp but fresh smell in the evening air. The sky was already dark, and the walk was quiet and peaceful.

Tamara's mum answered the door.

"Hey, Sam. They're just upstairs."

They're? I placed my shoes neatly by the side of the door like I always did and noticed a scruffy pair of trainers there. Puds nuzzled his wet nose into my ear. I tried to contain my laughter as he tickled my neck, and then I made my way up the stairs. I could hear muffled voices that became more distinct as I grew closer. My heart crept up into my throat.

"The thing is I'm sick of it."

"Well, what am I supposed to do?"

"It's simple."

"It's not as easy as you think."

The floorboards creaked as Puds ambushed me at the top of the stairs.

"Puds," I hissed. "Go downstairs."

The door opened. Tyler stood in the doorway. Her mouth drooped. Her bald head looked recently shaved. She clambered down the stairs and was out of the door in seconds. It was like she didn't even see me.

Tamara didn't say anything. Her lips were pursed, and her eyebrows knotted together in the way they did when she was pissed off. She went back into her room, and I followed. She stood with her back to me.

"I told you I was busy earlier."

"Yeah, but you said you'd be done by now."

"Yeah, well." She turned around. "You should've texted me."

"What's up with Tyler?"

"Nothing," she snapped.

"Why has she stormed off, then?"

Tamara's voice got louder. "What's with all the questions?"

Mine did too. "What's with the shitty attitude?"

She took a step back like I had shoved her. “Why don’t you fuck off and mind your own business for once?”

I stood there, speechless. Tamara crossed her arms in front of her chest. Without saying anything, I turned on my heels and left, not wanting to put my shoes on in the hallway. I stood on Tamara’s damp driveway while I pushed my toes into them, cursing her for making my socks wet. Cursing her for being such a temperamental bitch at times.

★

I couldn’t sleep that night despite going to bed as soon as I got in from Tamara’s. Luckily, Dad and Jake were out early in the morning, so I crashed out on the sofa, watching daytime TV and feeling sorry for myself. My knees were pulled close to my chest with my arms looped around them tightly. Dad had said it was exactly how my mum used to sit. I liked it when he told me that.

There was a knock at the door. I considered ignoring it, pulling the curtains closed, and ducking behind the sofa. Instead, I peered through the living room window, spotting Tamara on the driveway. It was raining lightly, and she had a black hoodie pulled over her head. She did an unenthusiastic half wave.

I forced myself to the door and opened it. She entered sheepishly and muttered a “hey” into the carpet, kicking her shoes off so they landed jumbled by the door.

She strolled into the living room, and I trailed behind her. A familiar pain gripped my stomach.

The daytime TV cooking host was cooing over a freshly baked apple pie that Elsie from Filey had made.

Tamara turned away from the TV, unamused by the host's fake *oohs* and *aahs* over the food. She moved by the window and looked out onto the street.

"Have you come here to apologise or to just admire my dad's shrubbery?"

She stayed quiet.

"'Cause you could've just done that from outside. And then I could've watched *Baking Babes* in peace."

Tamara glanced at the TV and rolled her eyes. Her continued silence and pointless visit and even her fucking face at this point, the still stoniness to her expression, made me even angrier.

She finally broke her silence. "Why didn't you text me back?"

"I thought I'd just come on my way home rather than text you 'cause you take so long to bloody reply."

"From where?"

"I was hanging out with Emma."

"Oh." Her eyes flickered with surprise. Then her brows knotted. She kept looking out onto the street.

"Don't be like that."

"Like what?"

"Like this. When you go all weird about something you don't have to get weird about."

She didn't say anything.

"Well. I'm going to have some tea," I barked. "You want one?"

She nodded slowly.

I didn't even want a drink but wanted to do something to calm me down. I took two clean cups from the cupboard, listening to the commentary on the TV as the kettle hummed. I returned a few minutes later, two steaming cups in my hands. I briefly thought about Emma's Christmas mugs.

Tamara stood in the same position. I handed her the cup.

"Thanks," she muttered.

"What is your problem?"

She rolled her eyes. The anger built up inside me again.

"You have such a pissing perfect life," she said.

"What are you talking about?"

"It doesn't matter."

"Tamara, you're so impossible sometimes!"

My tea was burning my hands, so I set the cup on the mantelpiece. As I turned back around, Tamara kissed me. She pushed me up against the wall, her mouth pinning me there. Our limbs melted into each other at the familiarity and the warmth of the touch.

I snapped out of it and shoved her back onto the sofa. She looked up at me in surprise.

"Do you think that just solves everything?" I shouted. "You just do what you want and act all distant, then just kiss and make it better? No."

She gazed back at me, her eyes filled with emotions I still didn't understand.

"Talk, Tamara."

She looked dumbfounded. Completely lost for words. She stuttered and then stopped.

"Tyler," she said at last.

"What about her?"

"You know we went to school together in Manchester." She fiddled with her hands. "We grew up together."

"Yeah?"

Tamara tapped the seat next to her. "Please?" I moved over and sat down, leaving a space between us. "She moved here before me," she continued. "She already knew everyone. And apart from Tom, I didn't know anybody."

"Okay."

"Well. We'd always get into trouble. Mum thinks she's a bad influence on me."

She laughed.

I didn't.

"We didn't fit in with the other kids. I don't want it to sound like a sob story or an excuse. But it's true. And me and Mum were skint at the time 'cause of all the stuff with the courts. We didn't have a lot to do. Tyler's older brother used to get us weed on the weekends. Then Tyler had the idea to start selling it at school. It was fine at first, and the money was good, but she got caught dealing and got expelled."

I knew Tamara smoked cannabis sometimes. I'd tried it with her, but I didn't like the way it made my body feel heavy. I had to go to bed early, and Tamara thought it was hilarious.

She looked at me to judge my expression, then continued. "Ty went to a young offender institution for twelve months, and I went to college and tried to forget about it." She was speaking faster, and I had to concentrate harder to not miss her words. "Met some friends, had my first girlfriend, got my heart broken. Got back into old habits and dropped out of college. Mum was furious, but at the time, I didn't care." She sighed and looked down at the floor. "It took me a long time to get over it. But that's something no one can take from me. I came out of the dark place." Her voice wavered. "Sometimes, it's still fucking dark, but you've just gotta hope you're not in a place where the light can't reach you."

Something about the way she looked, so vulnerable and delicate, made me want to hug her. Squeeze her so tight nothing could ever break her again. But I knew the story wasn't over, so I waited in silence until she continued.

"When we moved here, it was great to see Ty at first. There's something about her that makes you think you're kind of invincible. Which is stupid because, obviously, she isn't. She's the one who got expelled and went to the young offenders'. She's doing it again." She sighed. "And it's worse this time. It's serious. It's not just a couple of baggies at school. It's proper stuff, you know." She looked down at her hands. "She made me feel really guilty. She still does."

"You're dealing again?"

Her head snapped up.

"Do you have to be so blunt about it? It's not that simple. She's...she says I owe her, and I know deep down I do. She's got nothing."

"You don't owe her anything, Tamara. Sounds like you were stupid kids and she got unlucky. Doesn't mean you have to beat yourself up about it."

"You just don't get it, Sam."

"No. You don't get it. Shit happens, and you have to get on with it. If you don't, it'll consume you, and then you might as well be dead."

She turned her attention out of the window again. "Are you scared to die?" she asked.

I thought about it for a moment, letting the silence settle between us. "I don't know," I said at last.

She sighed, letting her head fall into her hands.

"You've got a lot going for you. Don't risk it all for something stupid."

"I'm not as smart as you."

"You are smart. I know you can do anything you want to," I said. "Don't be an idiot."

Our eyes met, and she smiled. For a second, I forgot what we were arguing about. She watched me for a minute, her eyes wandering over my face.

"I love you," she said.

"What?"

"I love you, you idiot." She sat up and pulled me into her, holding me so tight I could barely breathe. My mind enveloped her words, imprinting them on every surface of my skin, channelling them through my blood and out into my veins.

"I love you too," I said into her shoulder, my voice muffled.

She kissed me, pushing me down onto the carpet. In no time, we were both naked, lost in each other on the living room floor with *Baking Babes* playing in the background. Julie from Liverpool had got ten stars for her pie, but I didn't care. My head was spinning. *Tamara loves me.*

After, we turned our attention to the TV and cuddled up on the sofa, praying that none of the neighbours saw anything through the window. Tamara wrapped her arm around my shoulder, and I rested my legs across her lap. Her hoodie was slightly damp from the rain outside, but the smell was comforting. I relaxed into her arm, thinking that whatever had happened and whatever would in the future, right then, we were exactly where we were supposed to be. Curled up on the sofa on a rainy afternoon, Tamara hurling comments at the TV as our teas went cold on the mantelpiece.

Chapter Thirteen

2021

I tried not to look as Tamara's bride walked down the aisle. I only knew her name—April—and the fact that she was a lecturer at the University of Manchester. She was pretty, which made it a lot harder now to imagine her with giant boils on her face and a big bushy beard. She had two younger bridesmaids who led her down to the altar, both trimmed up prettily with red ribbons in their hair and small bouquets of red roses. They plucked petals from their arrangements as they glided down the aisle, beaming at the guests on either side. I tried not to look at Tamara either. The large man stood beside her with two other groomsmen, all watching the bride in enchantment. The guitarist picked the strings beautifully as they drew closer, leaving the notes ringing peacefully in the air when they were side by side. They uttered a quick, hushed greeting as they joined hands in front of the minister, and he began the recital of the vows.

It was strange because it didn't feel strange anymore. Seeing Tamara so happy, posing for photos with her new bride and their wedding certificate. The sick grip on my stomach had lifted and was replaced with the grumble of hunger. I hadn't eaten this morning from the nerves, or the night before, and now I was paying the price.

"What time is dinner?" I asked Ellie.

"Like three or something? I don't know. Ask Jake."

I searched for his face in the crowd of people. Everyone had moved forward to watch the pictures being taken, and it was hard to see anything in the sea of colour.

"Have you seen him anywhere?"

"Maybe he's with the kids."

"I'm gonna go look for him."

"Okay. Cool. And see if you can find out what's for dessert too," Ellie said. I rolled my eyes at her.

"What? It's the most important part."

I found Lottie playing Frisbee under the trees with more children. Tom's parents watched closely from the background. Lottie hadn't seen him; they hadn't either. I headed for the kitchen, suspecting he had gone looking for Catherine. She was one of the caterers for the wedding and would probably be done by now. I walked the same route I had taken earlier when I saw Tamara, following the fresh smells up to two big doors that rounded the corner. I pushed one of the doors open. Waiters and chefs charged about with red faces and steaming plates of food.

"Excuse me, guests aren't allowed in this area until four o'clock."

I apologised to the adolescent waiter, peering over his shoulder before I was ushered out. At least I had found out what time the dinner was. But where was Jake?

I called him, but his phone went straight to voicemail. I checked the men's toilets. No response. I checked the ladies' too, just to be thorough—nothing. I decided to head back to the main wedding party, thinking that he might be with Lottie now. As I passed the doors leading to the dining hall, I spotted Catherine inside setting porcelain plates out in neat circles. Her dark hair was pinned back into a tight bun, her overcoat drowning her in white like a little mouse wrapped in a tablecloth. Another person in a white overcoat strode over and set down a pile of napkins perfectly folded into roses. Their voices were too quiet to hear from the other side of the hall. One of them must have made a joke because they started laughing. The man leaned over and slapped Catherine's bum.

My breath caught in my lungs. I watched, expecting her to shout at him with a fiery rage I had seen unleashed many times before. Like when Lottie had ruined the newly painted kitchen with her watercolour paints. Or when Jake had a little too much to drink. But she didn't. Instead of scolding the man with her impressive (but scary) boisterous tongue—especially from someone so small—she hit him playfully on the arm. A harmless little nudge on his inner bicep. He moved closer to whisper something in her ear, and she giggled.

I knew Jake was too good for her. Fire filled my stomach, and I bounded across to them to give her a piece of my mind. Before they saw, Jake called out behind me.

Of course, now the mysterious disappearance of Jacob Atlas would be solved. All at completely the wrong time. I turned and spotted him waiting by the outside door where Tamara and I had shared a pre-wedding cigarette together. He waved me over. I approached him awkwardly, careful to block the view from inside the hall.

"Where've you been?" I hissed. "I've been looking for you everywhere."

"I left my present in the car. You'd left yours too." He handed me the package I had purposefully left on the floor of the car, pleased with himself. "What's it like in there?" he asked, peering into the dining hall. "Any food yet?"

"No! Not yet. I think they wanted us for some pictures." I tugged on his arm, pulling him out towards the terrace. "Dinner isn't until four."

"God. I'm starving. Catherine said they're serving the chocolate coulis. I can't wait."

I linked his arm in mine as we walked back to the wedding. Overhead, the clouds had parted, allowing a stream of sunshine to splatter the terrace in gold.

Chocolate coulis. Four o'clock. At least I had that bit of the wedding sorted. But suddenly, watching Jake run towards Lottie to gather her in for a hug, I didn't feel hungry anymore.

Chapter Fourteen

2011

Christmas came and went, along with the late dawns and early dusks. It had only snowed twice, one week covering all the roads with thick, soft inches of white and the other just a flurry. During that week, Stella was bound to the driveway (Dad's orders), and I had to walk everywhere. Tamara had tried to drive her car to mine and got stuck on one of the steep side roads. After bribing Jake with a fiver, he and I walked down to help push her out. After four failed attempts, we abandoned the car and headed back to mine to warm up.

Winter was Tamara's favourite time of year. We had spoken about visiting York for a weekend and exploring the Christmas markets, but we never ended up going. Instead, we spent most nights inside watching crap but entertaining TV and drinking apple cider, waiting for the warmer weather.

Tamara spent a lot of time at my house. Her mum had got a new fancy lawyer boyfriend or a Tory Boy, as Tamara kept saying, and she didn't want to be there while they fooled around.

She and Jake got along really well, which was surprising, as he'd been distant lately with Dad and me (I figured it was just part of the territory that comes with being fifteen), but he'd taught Tamara how to play shooting games on his console and didn't even shout when she screamed at the screen like he did with me.

Dad had been working more shifts at the hospital. A lot of the staff had come down with the flu, and they were struggling for numbers. The bus service was always running late in the winter too. This meant that I was cooking dinner for them both after class—which I didn't mind—but Jake protested, either by retreating to his room and locking the door or going out somewhere and not telling me. Having the house to myself was great, no one to fight over the channels with and no one to judge me when I ate a full litre of triple-chocolate cheesecake ice cream to myself.

Apart from the nights the snow hadn't allowed, every Tuesday, I had been going over to Emma's flat to learn guitar. It was difficult at first. My fingers were sore, and I didn't have the strength to push the string down hard enough on the fret. By Easter break, I was starting to make faster progress. I knew a lot of chords—the strumming was the hardest part. My hand wanted to go with a different rhythm and kept falling out of the sequence. Emma was patient, though, and without her, I think I would have given up again.

I think she enjoyed spending those nights away from the bar. She spoke so passionately about music and art that we'd get lost in the conversation for hours. She was right about one thing; she did make the best hot chocolate, and it got me through those winter night guitar sessions.

★

"G, C, D, F," I said to myself, trying to burn the order into my brain. With each chord change, I counted the beats and moved to the next one, my fingers sliding easier now over the fretboard. Emma was busy tidying the kitchen, nodding her head along to each beat and lifting her hand with every chord change as encouragement. She stacked the pizza boxes that we had finished earlier and moved them next to the bin. Then she wet a dishcloth she took from under the sink and wiped the counter down. The sweet scent of lemon invaded my nostrils. I fumbled a chord, and Emma glanced up, catching me eyeing her as she cleaned.

"Don't get distracted. I'm not doing anything interesting."

"When can I move on to something else?" I asked.

"When you can do it without thinking."

I put Harrison down gently on the stand Emma had brought in from her bedroom and had a sip of orange juice. I sat on the barstool opposite her while she fiddled with some scented candles, trying to get them to light.

"You are getting better," she soothed, sensing my frustration.

"I'd hope so. I couldn't have got much worse."

"It just takes time. All good things take time."

I grumbled something in response, and she laughed.

"With that attitude, it's no wonder you never got further than holding the guitar—and the wrong way around, I might add."

"We didn't all have a guitar tutor for a dad, did we? You never had to pay for a single lesson."

"Well. Neither do you," she said. "But I might make you start."

We laughed. I liked making her laugh. She looked so much lighter. Like she wasn't carrying around this invisible weight on her shoulders all the time.

She got the candles to light.

"What flavour is this one?" I asked.

"Cranberry and elderflower. It's one of the good ones from the market."

"Ooh, well, la-di-da."

She rolled her eyes. "Nothing wrong with liking things to smell nice."

Emma's phone sprang to life, making us both jump.

"It's Petey," she said. "I better take it."

She picked it up and walked into the bedroom before she answered. I listened quietly from the kitchen but couldn't hear much. After a few minutes, Emma came back in the room, her phone by her side.

"Sorry. We'll have to cut this one short. Petey needs me back at the bar."

"Okay. No worries." I gathered my things and put on my coat, zipping it all the way to the top. We walked outside together, hugged goodbye, and then walked our separate ways. It was still light out. The sunset was getting later day by day, and people were taking advantage of it. Though the air was chilly, people sat outside the pubs under the heaters, sipping various beverages and laughing.

Kids played on the park nearby, screaming as they chased each other around the monkey bars.

I cut through the Mayor's Gardens, as it was the more scenic route, and throughout winter, I had been taking the long way around the village to avoid it at night. An elderly couple sat on one of the old wooden benches, holding hands. A grey-faced dog with long whiskers sat at their feet. The old man stroked the dog's head appreciatively.

My phone buzzed. Dad was attempting Mum's veggie lasagne recipe. If I walked quickly enough, I could get home before he burned it.

A cluster of teenagers rode past me on their bikes. The one at the front pulled his bike up onto one wheel as he rode past the elderly couple. They cut across the grass, which had a sign that specifically said not to do so, and stopped beside the green shelter next to a gathering of people.

I saw her first.

That fuzzy bald head.

Then I saw Tamara.

My stomach clenched. Tamara had promised me she wasn't going to get involved with Tyler and her drugs anymore.

It was like someone had punched me in the gut.

They were kissing.

My eyes wouldn't believe it. I moved a little closer. But I recognised her jacket. And the unmistakable fall of her hair.

Push her off. Push her off, I willed.

This wasn't happening.

Notice me.

Notice me.

My heart felt like it was going to explode. I gripped my chest instinctively.

"Are you all right, love?" The elderly woman approached me and put a concerned hand on my shoulder. Without speaking, I nodded, but I was pretty sure I was going to throw up.

Notice me.

How can you not see me standing here?

"You don't look so good," the old lady fussed.

Tamara pulled away from the kiss and let her hair fall over her face. Tyler's gaze wandered the park, and then she spotted me, frozen and staring. Her lip curled up in a sneer. Tamara followed her glare and looked right at me.

I was running before I had even thought about it. My legs were propelling and moving me as far away from them as I could go. I heard Tamara shout behind me, but I just kept moving. I ran out of the Mayor's Gardens and back down past the pubs, where people were laughing and enjoying their night. And suddenly, I hated them. I *hated* them for smiling and having fun when I'd just seen the woman I loved kissing someone else. Tamara was still calling behind me.

And I hated her. I hated her more than I had ever hated anyone.

"Just wait. I can explain!"

Yeah, just like all the other times you've explained so well.

My legs kept moving, trying to put as much distance between us as humanly possible.

I heaved over, trying to catch my breath. I couldn't stop the picture of the two of them in my head. I felt sick every time I saw Tamara's hands on Tyler's waist. Her mouth on hers. I tried to blink it away, but there they were again. Behind my eyelids. Taunting me.

"Sam, wait!" Her voice was closer now. I didn't know where I was running to, but I couldn't stay here, and walking couldn't get me away from them fast enough. I picked up the pace again, but she caught up to me.

"Sam!" Her face was red and out of breath. "Please! It's nothing. It means nothing!"

"What the fuck were you doing?" I paused to take a breath. "You know what? Don't bother answering 'cause I'm sick of it."

"I didn't want to do it!"

"Then why did you?" I shouted. "You're in charge of your own actions, Tamara!"

Her eyes filled with tears. "I—I don't know." They spilled down her cheeks. She brushed them away, embarrassed.

"I'm not gonna be your doormat. I'm not just gonna roll over every time you do something and brush it under the carpet!" My voice was hoarse, not confident and determined like I wanted it to be.

"I wanted to stop! I told her I didn't want to do it anymore."

"Yeah, it sure looked that way." My chest was swollen. "How long has this been happening?"

She closed her eyes. More tears spilled out. Her silence gave me the answer.

"Leave me alone, Tamara. Seriously, just fuck off and go be with her now. All your secrets are out—just fuck off!"

I turned and ran. I felt a little childish screaming and running away, but I didn't know what else to do.

Tamara stood crying in the street, but I didn't care. I told myself I didn't care.

★

An hour later, I stood outside Ellie's house. The lights were on downstairs, but the attic room was dark. I sent her a text asking if she was home, and she replied almost instantly.

At Tom's, you ok?

I knew she would come if she knew what had happened. But I suddenly felt so stupid.

I told her I was fine and kept walking.

I stopped outside Emma's paint-chipped gate. I knew she wouldn't be in. And I didn't know what I would say even if she answered. But I rang the doorbell anyway and listened to the inevitable silence that followed.

I sat on the step and let my head fall between my knees. The picture sprung into my mind again of them kissing, kissing, and kissing. My heart thumped loudly inside my chest as anger and sadness and self-pity and heartbreak flowed through my veins. I hated Tamara King.

And I hated myself even more for loving her.

★

I stayed at Ellie's house for a week and told Dad that we had a project we had to work on for uni. He probably knew I was lying, but he didn't pry. Ellie had bit back the *I-told-you-so's,* which I appreciated because I knew how much she enjoyed gloating. We spent most nights with Ellie asking if I was okay and her moving the box of tissues closer to me, expecting me to cry. But I wouldn't. And I still hadn't cried.

We stayed up late watching rubbish and predictable horror films. Somehow, they made me feel better. And when Ellie would fall asleep, I would reread Tamara's messages.

I hated Tamara texting me, but as soon as she stopped, I missed it. I kept checking my phone, but alas, she had gone quiet. It made the whole thing more real. More concrete. Like ending.

It scared me that I couldn't remember her face or hear the exact tone of her loud and charming laugh. It made me feel sick. The distance between us was so obvious, and my stomach would not let me forget it. It throbbed whenever I thought about her, squeezing and suffocating me.

Two weeks after "the incident" (I couldn't think of another way to refer to it but couldn't stand to call it anything else), I went looking for her. I searched obvious places first—her house, Petey's, Mayor's Gardens—but she wasn't there. Even at the riverbank where we'd had our first proper date. I don't know what I would've done if I saw her. If I would've said anything. But I just needed to see her.

I remembered the place where Tamara drove us to when she first held my hand, and we listened to Merlot and the Bakers, and I had felt electric and vulnerable and hopeful all at the same time.

I set off driving in the general direction, but I didn't know where to go. I tried my hardest to remember, but Tamara had the map, and I couldn't think properly. I drove and drove and got nowhere. Every road looked the same. I couldn't even find the stone rubble house. Tamara never took me to see it, and now we never would.

I pulled up at the side of the road, frustrated. I felt stupid again. Anger bubbled inside me. Even without her here, she had still managed to make me chase her again.

I set off home, turned the music up loud, and stared out onto the road. Without realising, I had my foot down flat on the accelerator, and the car was picking up fast down the small country roads. I kept pushing, watching the speed climb up and up on the dial.

"Fuck this!" I yelled to no one. "Fuck Tamara King!"

Stella's wheels felt wobbly, so I slowed down, my heart sinking with the speed. I felt sick with guilt and stupidity. Then a loud bang hit the front of the car.

Oh my God, I thought. *I've killed someone. And it's Tamara's fault.*

The car screeched to a halt, probably doing damage to the tyres as the smell of burnt rubber invaded the fresh air.

My heart thumped hard in my chest, expecting the worst—a small child with a skipping rope in their hand, all life and hope crushed by an old silver car.

It wasn't a child.

Or even a person.

It was a hare. Quite a big one.

I stared at it for a while. Pink, mushed guts and unidentifiable body organs splattered across the road. It didn't look real.

Once back in the car, I sat and looked out at the road and the poor hare that had met its gruesome end.

And I cried.

And cried.

And cried.

Chapter Fifteen

2021

"Where's your date?"

"She's running late. She'll be here for the evening do."

"*Running late,* I getcha." Tom's dad, Phil, winked at me. "Say no more."

"What do you mean?"

"You're saving face. Couldn't get a date, so you made one up, right?" He scratched his white sideburns. His hair had receded fast over the last few years, making his fore-head large and shiny.

"No, she's real. I promise."

He sighed. "Just when I think I'm getting the hang of the ways of the youth, it all changes—"

"Phil, leave her alone." Debbie marched over, holding her pink fascinator to her head so it didn't blow away in the wind. "Is he bothering you, honey?"

"No. No. It's fine."

Debbie pulled him back towards Lottie and Jasper, who were colouring together on a nearby table. "Let's leave the kids to have some fun."

"Wait. Sam! Do you have Snapchat?" Phil held up his phone, but Debbie swiped it off him. "Never mind," he called. "I'll get it later."

The wedding had reached a quiet equilibrium. Guests wandered around the grounds, moseying themselves into conversations and enjoying the last of the free champagne. Tamara and April were off having their couple photographs, something I was glad I didn't have to endure, especially as now I was dateless for another few hours.

While the dining hall was being set up—and I was debating the Catherine crisis—the musician plucked at her guitar and sang softly into the hum of conversation. Jake sat with Lottie, helping her colour her picture, completely unaware of the catastrophe I had diverted him from. His bushy brows were knotted together in concentration as Lottie passed him each coloured crayon in turn. How could Catherine do this to them? And at a wedding that they were both attending? Lottie was too young to understand the complexity of these things—even I was barely capable at the ripe age of thirty-two. How could a four-year-old comprehend the idea of their parents splitting up and one destroying the other in the process? They had been together almost five years. That was a whole era for Jake: becoming a husband and a father. Becoming a responsible adult. Becoming the things his older sister still wasn't yet: married and with a family of his own. Dad always said it would be me first. *You'll see, this time next year you'll be settled with the girl of your dreams,* he'd say. *I knew within ten minutes of meeting your mum that she was the one for me.*

Dad and Mum met in their last year of school at a celebratory barbeque his mother had insisted on hosting. It was 1973, and Robert and Eileen Atlas had volunteered to host the gathering to congratulate the new mayor. Eileen worked as a receptionist on the council and loved any excuse to delight others with her culinary skills. Robert detested any fuss. He was a simple man, just like Dad, and neither of them cared for large events overcrowded with people. Eileen was stubborn, definitely the decision-maker in the house, and usually what she said was adhered to. Grandpa Joe, the newly appointed mayor, was the focus of the barbeque. Mum told us many times that this was a dream of his, and the three years that he spent in that role were the happiest she ever saw him. Sadly, both of them had passed away before I was born, so I never got the opportunity to ask. Joe and Annie Sinclair had bought a house at the bottom of Dad's street the previous year, and they had two daughters, Joanne and Marie. My mother had been born first, and expecting a boy, they christened her Joanne instead of the predetermined Joe Jr. Mum didn't like her name—she thought it was a cop-out—and Dad teased her endlessly, calling her Joseph and asking about her technicolour dreamcoat.

Dad was sixteen, and the last thing he wanted to do was attend the barbeque, which would be frequented by all the middle class, who wholly radiated the stench of desperation in everything that they did. Grandma Eileen scolded this out of him sharpish. She, too, desired to climb the social ladder, and she roped him into preparing the food with her on that Sunday morning. The weather was appalling, even for a British autumn, and the darkened skies haunted the event with the promise of rain. Eileen refused to cancel, and the showers held off until after the food was served, with fifty guests cramming themselves into their small house for shelter. Dad noticed a girl standing on the porch, looking out at the sodden paper plates and spread that he and Eileen had slaved over all morning. He liked her navy dress and the way she slumped against the doorframe. Indifferent but upright, strong arms and legs that exhibited a lingering trace of her summer tan. She barely turned when hc approached her with a plate of cheesecake, only declining in a polite but unwavering manner. She looked at him properly when he returned a moment later with a bottle of beer, and *that* time she didn't refuse. The two of them snuck away to the bottom of the garden, where, underneath the shelter of the trees, they shared the rest of the bottle in laughter and hushed conversation to avoid attracting attention from the rest of the guests.

You have her eyes, he would tell me, time after time. Both a happiness and a hardship that reminded us both of her absence. *So blue, like the best and unseen parts of the ocean.* I was glad that she had passed those genes to me, and I hoped that I, too, could carry them down the ancestry lineage so that my children and grandchildren would have at least the tiniest insight and reminder of the amazing woman she was.

Chapter Sixteen

2014

It was autumn when I missed Treaton Vale the most. The dusty red of the leaves would cover the Mayor's Gardens in a thick blanket, spilling out onto the streets and colouring them with warmth. Squirrels and dogs leaped across the piles of foliage, diving in and out like children into a ball pit. People sat out in their T-shirts with goosebumps on their bare arms, taking full advantage of the last of the daylight, knowing soon enough it would be taken back by the darkness that rolled around every year.

I missed the quiet too. In London, you were never alone. There was always a buzz of traffic and always people: loud and hurried, drunk or high, quiet and lingering, but always there. Stuffed into corners, reading books close to their chests, or tourists taking photos of everything in sight, pickpockets eyeing them up for an easy target. The city was so sticky too. Walking through the underground was a maze of sidestepping old chewing gum, abandoned half-eaten food, and, unfortunately for me—on more than one occasion in the two years that I had been there—dog poo. But there were many great things about being in the city. Always something new that I seemed to have missed. It was forever changing. And the people were too. Jerry on the Jubilee Line who played the marimba and gave away apple stickers to children who put money in his case. The juggler at Covent Garden who chased a pickpocket and returned the money without any altercations. The young man who watched his equipment without anybody asking him to. With such a big city, it was easy to focus on the bad things. The litter, the smell, the extortionate prices, and the busy and rude businesspeople. It was harder to appreciate the smaller things because, in Treaton Vale, they were a given. They were consistent like the leaves that would shed in the Mayor's Gardens. And I was waiting for the change.

★

"I cannot believe you haven't packed yet!" Ellie sat on my bed with her arms folded across her chest. "Seriously." She scowled. "We leave tomorrow."

"I know, I know. Don't bloody remind me." I dumped my bags on the plush corduroy chair I took from Dad's—one of the only things I managed to fit in the car, as it took up all the space, and I had refused to hire a moving van.

Ellie heaved a sigh that erupted into a long and dramatic raspberry. "Sam. Please. Pack. Now."

"I can't. I'm meeting Rachel for drinks."

"Rachel? Why!" She put her head in her hands. "Don't you ever learn your lesson?"

I was working in the HR department for Sisters, a company that dealt with the discrepancies of its larger and co-founding companies. At my interview last winter, my graphic design portfolio had captured Mr Armstrong's attention. He was a barrel-shaped man with a brown tuft of hair that clung to the top of his balding head. He was nice enough and usually wore a smile in the morning with an ill-fitting suit and a mismatched tie. He had promised to help push me into a more relevant department, which was seeming less and less likely as time wore on.

Rachel was in her mid-thirties and was the marketing manager for Finer Falls, a business we worked with in designing the website and promoting the new lines. After begging Mr Armstrong to let me attend some board meetings with clients, he agreed for me to sit in and take notes.

Rachel Davis was known throughout the company. Her name was muttered around the office and in the stairwells; people loved to gossip about her. In preparation for what might come, I had taken a seat near the back, eager to not draw unwanted attention to myself. As soon as she had entered the room, it fell silent. She had a sinister but captivating look that could halt all chitchat with a glance. I was grateful for my seat at the back, for every time she looked my way, I would cast my eyes down into my notebook and frantically scribble notes. Her stare would make even the strongest pelvic floor weak.

"She wants to see you," Alex, one of the new junior directors, had said as people packed away their pens and pads.

"What?" Panic struck through me. "Why?"

He shrugged. "She wants to see your notes."

As the room emptied, Rachel had perched herself on the edge of her desk, smiling and nodding nonchalantly as people said their thanks and their goodbyes. When I approached, she flicked a card towards me and headed out of the door, not once glancing behind her.

★

"I thought it might be...nice." I unpinned my hair and brushed it through my fingers, trying to distract from Ellie's disapproval.

"Nice?" Ellie laughed. "There's nothing about that woman that is *nice*." She picked my case up and threw it onto the bed.

"You've never even met her."

"I don't need to meet her. I just know." She raised an eyebrow at me, an offer to challenge her statement. I sighed. I knew she was right. Most of the time. "Still. Pack before you go?"

"I don't get why I have to come anyway."

Ellie's eyes darted up to meet mine, causing my chest to tighten. "I'll pretend you didn't say that," she said, pulling open my drawers and sifting through my clothes.

"But really. I hardly talk to them anymore—"

"That's not the point." She held up a crumpled blue dress and rolled her eyes, casting it into the ever-growing "no" pile. "We're a weird little family, and it's a milestone that we have to be there for."

"Fine," I agreed, defeated.

"Now...where are all your nice clothes?"

★

I met Rachel at the De Lavu, one of the finer restaurants overlooking the Thames. She would not dine anywhere that didn't have black-tie service at the door, and she was always fashionably ten minutes late so she wouldn't ever be sat alone.

"Darling." She slinked towards me and kissed me once on each cheek. "So good to see you."

"And you," I said, my tone limp with feigned interest.

A waiter pulled out Rachel's chair, and she sat slowly, brushing down her skintight black gown. She flashed him a dazzling smile before turning her attention to me. "Don't tell me you're upset with me? You know how I'm busy."

"I'm not upset with you—"

"Good," she interrupted. "Because I would hate for something childish to ruin our evening." She chose the wine from the linen-draped trolley, and the waiter poured two small glasses. He left the bottle in the ice bucket and excused himself from the table.

"So—" She paused, pursing her crimson-painted lips. "How have you been? What's the latest on the twelfth floor?"

I was a little put off by her questions. One, because it was unusual for us to begin a night talking about myself, and two, because she most certainly knew what had been happening on my floor, as she typically knew most of the office business before anyone else.

"Just normal, really. Nothing worth reporting."

"Armstrong still seeing that impish blonde?"

"Kristina? Yeah, I think so."

"He doesn't change, that man. The only thing he changes is which girl for the month and, hopefully, his bedsheets. Mary knows, you know. She has for years." She sipped at her wine. "But she won't divorce him. She loves the money too much, of course. Most of them do."

I murmured in agreement. As if I would know anything about driving flash cars and living on an estate with four times more bedrooms than people. I lived in an average-sized flat in Ealing with Ellie, and we had barely enough room for ourselves, never mind any lavish furniture. Rachel knew this, naturally, although she had never been herself. *Why go to yours when we could just go to mine?* she would say. *You don't stay in the rubble when you could go to the Ritz.*

I didn't mind it. I wouldn't want her seeing and asking me about all my things. She could store up any information in her head like a giant filing cabinet. Picking and choosing when to use it for later.

"Enough about work anyhow," she continued. "Aren't you going to Brighton this weekend?"

Of course she knew. "Yeah. I still haven't packed. Ellie is doing it for me now."

"And how is she? Excited to see Tom, I bet."

Strange. She never asked about Ellie before. "Um. Definitely. She's been talking about it for weeks. The band's been away for a couple of months sorting everything out."

"I expect you'll be happy to see them all." She fluffed her black pixie cut with a ruffle of her fingers, a habit she used in moments of silence to readjust. She would do this after she finished a meeting. And also after sex. She laughed when she saw me watching her. I had pointed this out to her a few times and called it "the rumble."

"I'm rumbling, I know." She grinned at me, and a dewy warmth fell over my skin like the first time we had met.

★

After attending Rachel's first meeting, I followed the instructions on her card telling me to meet her at The Grand Gavront at six. The Grand Gavront was just down the road from the office, a highly established hotel known for its heavy prices and elite clientele.

There was no sign of her in the bar, so I asked for her at the reception.

"Ms Davis will most likely meet you in the bar. I would recommend two glasses of the Chateau Latour over by the back on the left." He gave a smile, the right corner of his mouth pulling upward suggestively. "That's her favourite seat, ma'am." I glanced at his name badge. Troy. *Troy. I can only imagine the stories that you have to tell about her.* I wanted to ask him so I could prepare myself for what might be on the way. I also didn't want to come across as pathetic, but I had probably done that already.

I took the two glasses of the most expensive wine I had ever purchased in my life and sat where Troy had advised, the seats at the back, tastefully decorated with plants and candles, swan napkins, and three sets of cutlery. I thought this strange, as it was only a Thursday night, but maybe this was an everyday occurrence for people with money.

Five minutes later, I spotted her gliding up to the bar. She wore a tight leather pencil skirt (I later learned she *loved* all manner of leather, especially lingerie) and an ivory blouse, delicately revealing her cleavage. After exchanging words with the barman, she glanced over her shoulder at me, making my palms sweat. I stood instinctively to greet her, bumping my knee against the table and spilling part of my wine.

"Samantha Atlas," she declared, kissing me once on the cheek. I winced at the use of my full name, which she noticed. "Or do you prefer Miss Atlas?"

I started to redden. "Sam. I usually use Sam."

"Ah." She looked into my eyes. "I prefer that actually." She sat, and I did the same, trying my hardest not to look down her top.

"Did you bring these over?" She motioned to the glasses.

"Yeah."

She laughed. A little giggle that belonged to a fairy. Not what I expected her laugh to sound like. "You needn't in the future. The bar staff do that. That way you don't have to worry about any spills." She smiled. "Eli has very safe hands."

I nodded. It was about as much as I could do.

"So." She smiled, obviously loving the power she held over me. "I have been ever so curious about those notes that you were writing. I've not seen someone so eager to transcribe what I say in a long time."

The redness again. How embarrassing.

I fumbled in my bag and passed her my notebook. I had since googled important marketing and media statements and etched them in at random entries to make me seem smart. She skimmed through the pages, testing me on some of these, which I brushed over quite successfully. We spoke about Sisters and Finer Falls. Well, Rachel did, mostly. Talking and drinking as Eli replaced our empty glasses. I took big gulps of mine to keep up with her, hoping that I wouldn't be charged for the new round.

"What's this?" She pointed to a drawing on the back page. Something I had been doing when I had spare time at work, usually after dinner when we were quiet.

"Just a doodle."

She inspected it closely. "It's very good. Reminds me of the young blonde in your office."

Actually, it was of her. She was called Naomi, and we had spoken in the lift a few times. She was smart and witty, but I didn't know her sexual preference and so had never asked her out.

"I have to say I'm a little disappointed," she said, finally closing the book and laying it on the table. She waited before continuing, making sure she held my eyeline for a few seconds. "That you had all these notes and not one about my breasts."

My eyes darted down at the mention of them. The blouse hugged them tightly, the slit down the middle aptly placed to display them in all their glory. "Not one," she said, pushing them together subtly as she reached for her glass.

"I'm not sure any words could do them justice."

She laughed, making my arm hairs stand on end. I brushed over them self-consciously.

"Tell me, Sam. Have you heard what people say about me?"

I hesitated before answering. "No, not really."

"Don't lie." The sudden sharpness in her voice pricked my skin. "I know what they say." I met her eyes, hazel and burning back into mine. My heart crept up into my throat. A moment's silence fell between us.

"Don't you want to find out if it's true?"

I did. I really did.

I jumped as her heel brushed against my thigh. A warmth spread through me, racing between my legs. I held my breath as I grazed her hand softly with my fingers, feeling my gut clench with excitement. Her heel moved farther up my leg.

Perhaps sensing the tension, Eli approached with another bottle. "Would you like more wine?"

"I think we will retire for the night," Rachel said, pressing harder against my crotch. "Would you send it up to my room, please?"

"Of course, Ms Davis." He removed our empty glasses, gave me a knowing look, and moved to the next table.

After a moment, Rachel stood, holding out her hand for me to do the same. As she led me away, she glanced back at me over her shoulder.

"Don't forget your notebook. You might need to take some notes."

★

Rachel had the same allure as she did upon that first meeting. Age had been kind to her, though I severely doubted it was from nature's blessing. We ate in scattered conversation, filling in any silence with the cutlery scraping plates. I hadn't heard from her in a few months, as was the norm. She would vanish suddenly, appearing again gracefully sometime later, wanting to know what she had missed.

It was hard for me to accept at first. The abrupt cut-off from Rachel poured salt in old but not forgotten Tamara-shaped wounds. I wondered if that was what most relationships were like, two people trying to find their balance. One person enamoured and the other indifferent, trying to bring themselves to the same mediocrity of happiness. As soon as life sparked a change, they would be gone, and the balance would be shifted, catapulting one into adventure and the other into darkness.

Surprisingly, I enjoyed the to-and-fro of Rachel's relationship. She always returned when I needed something. Be it excitement or sex or her veracity. Sometimes all three.

When we finished our food, the waiter came to collect our plates and fill our glasses. Rachel was overly friendly to him. Touching his wrist whilst saying her thanks and casting her famous Rachel gaze upon him. I could see her donning her bow and arrow, ready for the hunt. She turned her attention back to me.

"So, is there anyone in your life I should know about?" she asked.

There was a new woman in the office who was cute. But I didn't want Rachel to get there first. "No. Not really. I've been busy with work and things."

She raised her eyebrow. "You expect me to believe that?"

I laughed. "Well, what about you? Or had I better get my notebook to list them all down?"

She burst into laughter, something she did very rarely. It always made me feel special to create those fairy notes.

"That *notebook!"* She giggled. "We do have fun, don't we?" She pressed her fingers underneath her eyes to stop her makeup from smearing.

"That we do."

"Although," she began, "there is a reason I asked to see you tonight."

"Another booty call?"

With a shake of her head, the smile on her face disappeared. Her lips rested plump and red. I watched them as she spoke.

"I'm getting married."

★

After a three-hour drive, Ellie and I arrived in Brighton at Tom's parents' beach house. Stella had just about made the journey; she had taken a few more scrapes since moving to London, and I wasn't sure how she would manage a longer trip. Her CD player was going faulty, and when it overheated periodically, you had to give her a strong smack on the dashboard to stop it skipping. This was Ellie's favourite job.

"It takes Tom half the time to get here," she said, fiddling with the latch on the boot to try to get it to open.

"Well, next time you can get the train. Or learn to drive."

"Fat chance of that. What is wrong with this?"

I pushed down hard on the latch until it clicked and sprang up. Ellie shook her head. "This car is a death trap."

We lugged the bags inside the door, and Ellie showed me around. It was just as I had expected from Tom's parents—a lavish but tastefully decorated interior, with lots of old pine furniture that you could smell as you walked through the house. Probably gifted to them from a famous sailor they were friends with. If anything, the house was small for them. Just two bedrooms, with huge plush beds and small balconies facing the sea. A beautiful decking surrounded the entire house with stone steps leading down the garden and out of sight.

"The beach is down that way." Ellie gestured with a flick of her hand before turning quickly to the kitchen. "But this is the good stuff." She pushed one of the cupboard doors, and with a click, it slowly opened and rotated, revealing forty or so bottles of wine. "Right?" She turned to me, and her plans for the weekend suddenly became clearer. "I mean, there's about a grand's worth of booze here, right? It's been ages since we got proper fruity."

"Fruity?"

"Yeah. If you use more sophisticated words, then it's more excusable to get wasted."

"And *fruity* is what you went for?" I laughed.

"It's better than *pissed*, though, isn't it?" she said, picking up one of the bottles and examining it. "Or hammered or...bamboozled? This one's 17 percent!"

"Well. Let's get fruity, then."

We sat with two huge glasses of wine on the decking overlooking the sea. You couldn't see much of the beach, but you could smell the salty air and hear the seagulls cawing above, eyeing out potential targets to steal from.

"Are you sure they won't mind us drinking this?"

Ellie shook her head after taking a big gulp. "Nah. They've got wine like we've got debt. Just stacks and stacks of the stuff. You should see their house back home."

"Yeah, I remember Tom's parties."

"When you puked all over that Persian rug."

"It was all green. But I'm not sure why." I laughed, the wine stinging my throat. "And when you peed yourself outside."

"Hey! Tom still doesn't know about that." Ellie spluttered her wine down her top. "I said it was the neighbour's dog."

"We had some great ones, didn't we?"

"We still will." She nudged me with her toe. "Tonight will be no exception."

Tonight. I kept forgetting about tonight. It had been months since I had spoken to the gang. Even longer since I last saw them. It had become so hard to keep in touch since we moved. And I felt awkward being around Tom in case *the* dreaded name was mentioned. I pushed those thoughts out of my head and took another swig of wine. Ellie watched me, her mouth pursed.

"Refill?" She emptied the rest of the bottle into my glass and winked. "It's gonna be a good one. I can feel it."

★

"Married? You. Married?"

Rachel smiled. A sympathetic smile that I had been on the receiving end of many a time but now had a subtle and sickly sting.

"God. There's no need to look at me like that." When I didn't answer, she sighed and put her hand on mine. "Sam," she began, tracing my fingers softly, "if it helps, it surprised me too."

I scoffed, and she paused her futile attempts at comforting me.

"How are *you* of all people getting married?"

"I don't care for your tone." She had a sip of her wine. "I knew you would be upset, but—"

"Upset? I'm not upset."

She watched me while she took another sip as if trying to infiltrate my brain and scoop out the emotions I was feeling. We didn't speak for a few minutes, just each taking turns at drinking.

"It doesn't make sense. After everything you say about marriage."

"I know." She smiled to herself. "Like I said. It surprised me too."

"How did this even happen?"

"Well, he was a director. And we would have our monthly get-togethers and such. A few mini-breaks and weekends away...and then he told me. He was leaving his wife."

"Oh, how very romantic."

"You're too young to understand."

I hated when she said that. And she knew it. Making out that I was a stupid teenager who couldn't understand simple concepts.

"I'm twenty-five, not twelve."

"And I bet you feel like you know so much about the world, don't you?"

"What is your point?"

"My point is that you don't. You can go through so much of your life thinking something is the truth, only to wake up one day and see it flipped on its head. Something sat right in front of you the whole time. And now it makes sense."

"Marriage? Now marriage makes sense to you?"

"Marriage. Love. The whole package."

I rolled my eyes. "Right." I topped up our glasses with more wine. "Marriage. Marriage makes sense to you now, when your new fiancé destroyed his *marriage* to be with you?"

"Look, Sam. You don't have to understand. And I'm not asking you to. I just wanted you to know."

"That's fair enough." I watched her watching me closely. The feeling of being under the microscope didn't sit well with me. Why was I so bothered about this news? It wasn't like I had ever envisioned myself being with Rachel. Most of the time, I didn't give her a second thought. I enjoyed spending time with her—and we had fun. But it wasn't electric. It wasn't fire.

I looked at her more closely, noticing the big diamond ring on her finger. How had I not seen that before?

She held it up for me to inspect. "Isn't it nice? It's Cartier."

I nodded, pretending I had heard of it before.

We glossed over the subject as our food was delivered to the table. I could sense her watching me as I poked at my food. It was a strange, harrowing feeling, like embarrassment, curdling in my stomach, ruining the delicious smell of the moussaka in front of me. A deflated energy, an unexplainable emptiness, occupied the spaces between my vital organs. My fight-or-flight response, urging me to run.

"Well. Thank you for dinner. And for sharing your... news." I thanked the waiter as he removed our plates before continuing, "But I better be going now."

"You don't have to rush off, you know."

"Don't you have another fifteen or so booty calls on your breakup schedule? I wouldn't want to keep you."

She rolled her eyes. "Fifteen? I know I've had my fun, but even *I* couldn't keep up with fifteen at once." She was trying to make me laugh. I offered her a smile. "I don't know why you think so bad of me."

"I don't think bad of you, Rachel. It's just...weird."

She gave her hair a "rumble" and asked for the bill. Instead of the usual seductress moves she would make at this point of the date, she took my hand in hers and kissed it. A long and meaningful kiss that left a lipstick imprint below my thumb.

"Now, go. I release you." She placed my hand back on the table. I didn't want her to let go. My hand felt cold without her holding it. She smiled, her famous Rachel dazzle, teeth white and perfect. I smiled back at her, pulled out my chair, and shrugged on my coat, ready to leave.

"Sam."

I turned back to face her.

"You were more than just a booty call to me." Her eyes were dark, lighting up with the flicker of the candle-light.

I paused, a grin tugging at my mouth. "I wish I could say the same."

She laughed. I was going to miss that fairy giggle.

"Goodbye, Rachel. And congratulations. He's a lucky man."

Chapter Seventeen

2021

Dinner was served. And a full vegetarian menu, to my delight. I assumed April was vegetarian also—Tamara had dipped and dabbed into the lifestyle but always caved at the sight of anything fried chicken. I had told her that I didn't mind many a time after nights at the bar or dining out in town, but I did. It annoyed me that she was so flimsy. She wouldn't commit to the idea but would be the first to tell somebody that she was vegetarian. Her decision-making always baffled me.

From the corner of my eye, I watched her tucking into her risotto cake and wild mushroom salad, whispering something into April's ear, the two of them laughing. It was strange. She looked like Tamara and had the same Tamara-like mannerisms: her overactive eyebrows, rising like arches across her forehead, thick and brown and full of life; the incessant way she played with her hands, even during her speech, which was short and sweet; that golden glow to her brown eyes, the hidden innocence lying within them along with the secrets that made Tamara who she was. She looked like Tamara; that was indisputable, but she wasn't the same Tamara to me.

Tom sat at the top table, along with his parents, Tamara's mum and boyfriend (a new Tory Boy, I assumed), and April's parents. Ellie and I were at a round dinner table with Jake, Lottie, and Jasper, Tamara's cousin and their boyfriend, and two of April's friends. I was grateful we hadn't been seated with Mrs Hairy Mole. She was on the other side of the hall and, from the look on their faces, was terrorising her fellow table guests. We ate in sporadic conversation, from names and careers to funny wedding anecdotes and jokes that were followed with polite laughter.

I brushed over the subject of the empty seat next to me, reiterating what I had told everybody who asked me: my plus one was running late, yes, she was still coming, yes, she was real, and no, I hadn't hired her. (Phil came back to question me some more once Debbie was distracted.) The table mulled this over with a feigned interest and expressed desire to meet her once she arrived. In reality, their foremost concern was probably the waiting time for the dessert, as Jake had been hyping up the chocolate coulis whilst waiting for our main to arrive. Jasper and Lottie and the other children at the wedding had their own little menu printed out on a colouring sheet that distracted them adequately.

Catherine ducked in and out of the hall, collecting finished plates and returning with the famous chocolate coulis. As much as I disliked her, it sure smelt damn good.

"Sam. Can you help me here?" Jake exhaled a hoot of laughter. "God, what a mess." He dabbed at Lottie's chocolate-smeared cheeks with a napkin.

"It's on her arm too. How have you even managed that?" I asked her as she scooped in another mouthful.

Lottie giggled with delight. “Cos Imma princess.”

“Ah, yes, the famous chocolate-covered princess from England.” Jake dabbed at the sticky goo around her mouth. “Your Highness, if you wouldn’t mind next time wearing a bib.”

My personally allocated and perfectly folded rose napkin stared back at me. I wanted to crumple it in my hand and shove it down Catherine’s throat. Instead, I unravelled the cotton with a spin and diverted my attention to scrubbing Lottie’s dress, which was dappled with chocolate finger stains. My phone buzzed in my bag, the vibration tickling my ankle. I pulled it out and read the message.

> *Just wrapping things up here. Hope everything is okay?*

I texted back quickly before slotting the phone back into its pocket and zipping it shut.

> *Great. Hope all went well? I can’t wait to see you.*

The plates were collected, and the wine was drunk, laughter and conversation filtering my thoughts from my messages. April’s dad clinked his glass with a fork, the chime hushing the room into silence, and announced that the evening would continue in another room at the opposite side of the building. Everybody stood to gather their things and followed in a surprisingly organised line, snaking through the corridors of Tarnbourg Hall towards the evening celebrations. I clutched my bag close to my torso, hoping for a vibration to say that she was here. My heart fluttered at the thought of her walking through the door. Perhaps this wedding would be a good one after all.

Chapter Eighteen

2014

Ellie and I were drunk before we even got to the party. Tom had arranged for a car to pick us up at seven. It wasn't far away, only about a fifteen-minute walk, but by the time the doorbell rang and the driver was standing on the porch, it's fair to say we were both relieved that we didn't have to stumble our way over there. Blue Rooms had finally signed a major record deal and had been backed to record two studio albums and a European tour. This was a huge night, not just for the boys but for all of us from Treaton Vale. It was the affirmation that with hard work and determination, success could rise out of a small city. Treaton Vale was the kind of place that when shared with others who were meeting for the first time, they'd squint their faces. *Treaton what? I've never heard of it.* Now, it would be Treaton Vale: the birthplace of Blue Rooms.

Petey would have a big night up there for them too, no doubt. He had done a lot for the band and truly believed that this day would come. The boys would always tell us about Petey's crashing their band practices and scolding them for drinking too much on nights out. Matt had referred to him as his dad a few times, which Petey found hilarious. Emma was going to be there too. We had kept in touch since I moved to London, catching up over social media every couple of weeks and the odd phone call if I was waiting alone for a taxi. The fact she was going to be there made me less nervous.

I was apprehensive to see the boys. It had been so long that my brain had started playing tricks on me, warping my memories into tainted goo and undermining our friendships. Part of me had been so worried about things changing between us all. Unfortunately, lost in that worry, it all did change regardless, and there was nothing I could've done about it. We didn't drink at the bar every night or hang out at the Mayor's Gardens anymore, but it was okay. Life moved on in different ways; it didn't mean that it was lost. I had to remember that.

We showed our tickets to the muscle at the door. He inspected them closely before waving us in. A young man, dressed sharp in a tux, greeted us, handing over a glass of bubbly.

"Now this I could get used to." Ellie clinked her glass with mine.

"So, what's the etiquette here? What are we supposed to do?" I looked around at the immaculately dressed people surrounding us. "It all seems so *sophisticated.*"

"Hmm." Ellie pondered this. "Not something that we do well."

In terms of parties, we were at stage one: the quiet before the storm. Everyone was looking their best, settling into the environment and adjusting themselves to the company. Ellie and I were more of a stage-three kind of people: loosened up from the alcohol, inhibitions lowered, ready to dance and not care about said company's opinion.

Two huge banners hung from the walls, congratulating the band in big block letters. Balloons were pinned to the ceiling in netted string, two hundred blue and white sacks of air ready to be dropped onto the currently empty dance floor. The bartenders, fresh-faced and suited up, waited at their stations, preparing themselves for the crowds that would descend on them in the next hour. The spaces were quickly filling up. Young, attractive women hung on the arms of potbellied men. The DJ played a compilation of indie tunes, saving the most popular songs for when the party was in full swing. A group of men a similar age to Blue Rooms were gathering a small crowd about them. Ellie informed me that they were the supporting band for the tour. There were a lot of familiar faces from home, acquaintances who had frequented many Blue Rooms sets at Petey's and had always supported them. In each cluster of people, there was a friendly smile and an acknowledgement of the common past we shared.

I spotted Kipper nursing a large glass of white. Half a dozen people enclosed him, captivated by his conversation. He was probably rounding up some investors for his new projects. The man had a way with words, and the people here had a way with money.

"He's working with the guys to soundtrack a project he's working on," Ellie said too loudly into my ear. "Gonna pay a lot for it too."

Kipper gestured wildly with his arms. He must have been coming up to a big selling point in his proposal. He took a swig from his glass after he finished orchestrating his work, his eyes wandering over the guests to spot his next opening. A whooping cheer drew our heads to the far side of the room, where big sliding glass doors opened out onto a large garden. My heart felt full as they each ducked through the door, and all nervousness instantly vanished. Matt, in skintight black jeans and a crisp white shirt that complimented his dark skin beautifully. Tom, a second behind him in a double-denim combination, light blue and expertly fitted, sculpting his muscles tightly.

"I picked that for him!" Ellie squealed into my ear. "He looks so good!"

Ash was wearing a blazer, dark blue with a burgundy shirt underneath. Standing next to the others, he looked a little out of place. I wondered if Yvette had picked his outfit for him.

"Are they still together?" I whispered to Ellie.

Before she could answer me, Yvette slunk her way over to Ash and draped herself around him. How had she, even in this setting, managed to look overdressed? Tom spotted us in the crowd and called us over, and everyone parted to allow us through.

"Congratulations, guys! You so deserve this!" I hugged them each in turn, bombarded by their individual taste of aftershave, and gave a nod of acknowledgement to Yvette, who gave a half smile in reply.

"I can't believe this. It's all so mad," Matt said.

"I know. It's like a dream. Pinch me! Pinch me!" Tom feigned injury. "Ouch! Matt!" The two had a little pinch-off, forgetting that all the guests were watching.

"Behave, you two. Honestly, how many times do we have to tell you that?" teased a familiar and soothing voice.

"Emma!" The boys turned and hugged her tight, picking her up off the floor. She screamed as they lifted her high, her small pink calves kicking against the air. Then the boys screamed as Petey squeezed them both together, releasing Emma.

"Getting this new deal means I can finally sue you for all the wrongdoings over the years. Finally!" he boomed.

"Like what?"

"Where to start? How about all the free drinks? The broken stage? All the damages from Halloween?"

"That wasn't our fault. We didn't start that fight," Ash chimed in.

"Oh, really?" Petey turned to Matt. "Wasn't it one of your many lovers' rivals? Huh?"

Matt laughed. "He punched me first. I went straight through my snare."

"And then he went crashing over the cymbals," Tom laughed.

"And who paid for it?" Petey asked.

"You?"

"Yes. Me. You idiots." Petey opened his huge arms. "Come here!" He gathered them in a big embrace, like three little birds nesting in the wings of their mother. "I wouldn't have it any other way." He released them from his grip with a sigh. "And look at you all. Dressed so smart. Barely recognisable."

"You don't look bad either. I've never seen you in a suit before," Tom said. "Who knew that they had them in the Middle Ages?"

Petey gave him a light clip round the ear. "Give over. It's not about me tonight. It's all about you!" He whistled loudly to gather everyone's attention and then toasted his half-empty flute to the ceiling. A chorus of cheers echoed through the room, followed by each of the boys being pulled in a different direction to be questioned and praised. Tom pulled Ellie into the crowd with him. He was shy around strangers, and Ellie loved to talk and fill silences. They were the epitome of the couple who left that sickly sweet feeling in your stomach, from the way they watched each other to how one knew what the other was saying before they did themselves. The comfort there. The ease. The pure love. It left an ache somewhere within me, in a place I refused to visit.

Following the commotion, Emma and I walked outside through the sliding doors. There were few people here, and the cold air was welcome against my face and bare legs. A small bar stood against the far wall, decked out with white fairy lights and another congratulations banner for the band. We spotted a cushioned bench across from the bar, painted and varnished so it was silky smooth to the touch. Emma brushed her hair over her shoulder as she sat; it was dyed a darker blonde and much longer than the last time I had seen her. The bartender watched us for a moment and then turned back to his phone.

"I have to say, you look beautiful, Sam." She grazed her hand lightly across my face. "Look at those cheekbones, girl."

"Thanks. You look great too." Compliments made me uneasy, so I directed the focus to her dress, a notion I had taken from Rachel, who loved to direct topics this way. "Where's this from?"

"I've had it for years, thought it might like to see the light of day again. Although seems like we missed that."

The sky above was a deep purple; scattered balls of white moved through silently, spying on the world's conversation. It was a clear night after the hot afternoon Ellie and I had spent drinking on the decking. The heat had sapped the water from my body, and with the increasing amount of alcohol I was drinking, I was feeling the effects all the more.

"How's the big job in London?"

"Yeah. It's good, thanks. Been super busy with work lately."

"And the love life?"

"Pretty non-existent. I thought it would be easier to find someone in the capital, but I guess not."

"What about that woman from work?"

"Rachel? No, that ended."

"Shame. I liked her. She seemed very interesting."

"Interesting?"

"Yeah. You speak about people in pieces. I never get the full story, so it's fun to put it together."

"I don't do that."

She laughed. "*Rachel is fine, not seen her much 'cause of work,*" she mocked me with a slow and lazy tone. "*She's rich and a bit annoying, but fun in bed.*"

I nudged her with my elbow. "I don't sound like that."

"Yes, you do. But it's funny; I like it."

"Well, I could say the same for you. *More than that, even.*"

"What's that? I never say that."

I laughed. "You've got to be kidding. That's like your signature catchphrase."

"I've never said that in my life."

"You lie, Emma Carlton."

She smiled at me, shaking her head.

"What about *I'm at the bar tonight* and *I've just been playing some stuff...*" I tried to mimic her light and fluffy accent, but it sounded terrible. "Yet I never get to hear you play! It's been years, and I'm still imagining what your 'stuff' sounds like."

"You really want to hear it, don't you?"

"Well, yeah."

Her mouth flickered with amusement. "Maybe soon..." She necked the last of her drink, watching my face with delight.

"Really?"

She nodded. "Actually, there's something I wanted to tell you."

My eyes darted down to her torso, where her hand rested absent-mindedly.

"I'm not pregnant!" She swatted at me. "Honestly, woman. That's the first thing you think of."

"I would make a great auntie."

Her eyes cast down from mine and observed the garden, which was filling up with more people. "I know you would. But I doubt I would make a great mother with all the wine I've drunk tonight."

"What is it, then?"

"We're gonna need something to toast with. 'Cause it's pretty crazy."

"What? What?" I tugged on her arm. "What is it?"

She pulled me towards the bar and ordered two shots of tequila.

"Tequila? God."

"Don't you remember?" She giggled, handing over her card to the bartender.

"Of course. You *saved* me," I teased, taking the salt pot and sprinkling it below her thumb.

"It was my good deed for the day." She clinked our glasses together. "So," she began. "I am going on tour with Blue Rooms...as their guitarist."

"No way! That's amazing! How did that happen?" I put my glass back on the bar and hugged her. She spilled a bit of her shot down my front.

"I know, it's crazy, isn't it? First, drink. Then, we'll talk details." She handed my glass back to me. We knocked them together in a *cheers* and gulped the fierce liquid down our throats. Tequila was a lot harsher than I remembered.

"I'm too old for this now." I recoiled.

"Hey, speak for yourself. I'm older than you, and I've still got it."

"If you say so."

She laughed, ordered us two more, and told me to *shut up and drink*. So, I did.

★

"And then Petey suggested me to the boys, and they liked what they heard. That was that."

"She's being modest. Girl can *shred* on a guitar," Tom said. "Better than Ash."

"Don't be silly." Emma brushed her hair behind her ear and looked away.

Tom turned to me. "I'm telling you, she's so good. She should have her own band."

Tom and Ellie had spotted us in the garden outside after his interrogation had dwindled, and Emma, who had just finished telling me the story, had relayed a condensed version to Ellie.

"It's amazing news. Congrats, Emma." Ellie squeezed her arm. "How did you keep this quiet?" she asked Tom.

"Babe, I know! It was so hard to keep a secret. If I had seen you, I would've had to tell you."

"He's so bad at secrets," Ellie explained to us.

"It's true. Like when I told your mum that we had sex in her bed."

"*What*? Seriously, guys?" I said, my tone sounding alarmingly like my dad's.

"Yeah. Just kinda slipped out."

"No pun intended."

"Yes! Nice one." Tom high-fived Emma with a force that made her wince. "Man. Tour is gonna be so fun."

"At least now I know not to go telling you any of my secrets."

"I bet you have some dirty ones from your younger days."

"Excuse me?" she exclaimed. "My younger days?"

Tom continued, unaware, "Yeah, I bet you have some great tales from your day."

Ellie smacked him on his chest, and recognition flashed across his face.

"Not that you're old. Like older," he stuttered. "But, erm, you know, you're married."

Emma raised her eyebrows, and the frown on her face made me fear for Tom's safety.

"I just bet you have some good secrets. That's all. And you're still hot, by the way."

"It's true," Ellie added. She replied to my inquisitive look with a shrug. "What? She is."

Emma's face lifted. "Good. Now, where's my husband?" She peered over Tom's shoulder and into the party, where the DJ was blasting "Mr. Brightside" loudly. "I'll catch you kids later. I've got to take my night meds and wash my Zimmer frame."

She swayed her hips deliberately as she walked away, casting a smile over her shoulder as she went through the doors.

"You idiot." Ellie pushed Tom in his chest again, harder. "You don't speak about people that way."

"I'm sorry. It was a bit of a brain meltdown."

"Honestly." Ellie rolled her eyes. "You need to apologise to her."

"I will. I will."

The three of us bought another drink and drifted inside, avoiding the clusters of dancers and eagle-eyed men watching intently. I sipped at my drink slowly, regret filling my stomach at the thought of all the wine we devoured on the decking. The familiar fear of drunk-induced panic flooded my mind, and as we bumbled through the crowd, bile rose in my throat. Why had I agreed to those shots with Emma? Mumbling something resembling a "be right back" to Ellie, I dashed to the toilets. Rounding the corner, I found a small queue of women patiently waiting for their turn.

Frantically, I searched for an opening to get outside. My hand cupped my mouth involuntarily, a haphazard attempt to catch any of the alcohol that was threatening to rise. I pushed through some young dancers, whose top buttons had come undone. The smell of sweat mixed with cologne pinched my nostrils. Managing to stagger outside, I straightened my footing and continued to swallow, keeping the bile at bay. At the far end of the greenery, I took a seat on the fence, preparing to vomit into the plant pot nearby.

I noticed a damp patch on my dress, a dark splodge that I wiped at with my hand. The splodge faded out, creating a dark-blue mark on the turquoise ruffle. I drew closer to inspect it, and a sharp wind blew the gut-turning scent of tequila up my nose, out of my stomach, and into the poor plant pot by my feet.

That confirmed it: sophisticated was definitely not my thing.

I peered up sheepishly, catching the eyes of a few guests by the doors who were watching me with amusement. Sensing the worst was over, they drifted back inside, leaving me with the shame and stench of my vomit to mull over my night's decisions. I scooted away from the plant pot to breathe in the fresh air. My face was hot with the panic-induced retching, so I wandered to the barman for a glass of water, in hopes that he didn't see the horticulture abuse.

The party was approaching stage four: company was fighting over the dance floor space, sweaty bodies indifferent to unbuttoning or taking clothes off, revealing chest hair and patches of perspiration-dyed garments that nobody wanted to see. The music was in full swing, the DJ fulfilling the requests of popular songs to a cheering and loosened crowd. I spotted Ellie shrugging off one of the dancers attempting to pull her onto the dance floor, and her face shifted when she saw me standing outside. She wandered over, her expression unimpressed.

"Where did you go? Are you all right?"

"Yeah. I'm fine." I took a sip of my water.

"Woah. You stink." Ellie took a step back from me, looking closely. "Have you puked?"

"Shh! Keep your voice down!" I hissed, peering at the barman, who smiled and then looked away. "And yes. I puked."

"Jesus." She shook her head, the loose strands of her pinned hair wiggling against her face in protest. "Let's go fix you up."

After waiting in the estranged queue of shame, Ellie pushed us both into a cubicle and whipped out her makeup bag and compact mirror from her clutch. She gave me three extra-strong mints, touched up my foundation and mascara, and then topped me up with another mint, "just to be sure".

"How are you not more drunk?" I asked as she fiddled with my hair, pulling and straightening curls until she was satisfied.

"I am drunk. That's why Tom has been drinking for me all night." She burst out laughing. "I've been on Diet Coke for the last hour."

"I feel a lot better now."

"Me too. I think I'm ready to drink again."

Laughter enveloped us until my stomach hurt, causing someone to bang loudly on the door, expressing their urgent need to pee.

We sauntered out of the bathroom, confident and eager to see what the rest of the night held for us. Ellie pointed out where the boys were, and I headed to the bar to get in the next round. Something about it made my chest feel warm. A routine that had been forgotten since the five of us lived in Treaton Vale. It was a little nod to the past adolescent us who lived for that bar and the people surrounding us. I watched Tom greet Ellie with a big kiss, not any different from those years ago at Petey's, and the guys (plus Yvette) catch her up on what she had missed. I waited at the bar for my turn, moving into the gap when it emerged and edging closer to the front. Someone said my name. I turned but could only see eager partygoers trying to make their way through. A wave of groans rippled from the right, as well as my name once more. "*Sam!*" A space opened up, so I moved forward and ordered my drinks from the bartender.

"Hey, stranger." The voice was loud next to me, silky and definite. My gut. My hands. My knees. At once, subsiding at the sound.

"Hi, Tamara."

"How are you?" Her smile was genuine, showcasing her slightly crooked teeth. I stepped back, caught off guard, and caught a guy's foot behind me. I apologised and turned back to face her. I knew there was a possibility she could be here, but I didn't think I would be on my own when it happened.

"I'm good. How are you?" I cast my question downwards, cautious of my breath and hoping that the mints Ellie gave me were strong enough to mask any unpleasant smell.

Before she could answer, the barman returned with my drinks, and Tamara reached over to pay. She waved away my protest with a flick of her hand and handed over her card to him.

"I hoped you'd be coming," she said. "Here, I'll give you a hand." She clasped three glasses between her palms and parted a way through the crowd. I followed her, speechless, my mind betraying me with thoughts I had locked away in the back of my head for years. My heartbeat resuming an old and forgotten rhythm, *Tamara King, Tamara King, Tamara King.*

Chapter Nineteen

2021

Before continuing with the wedding evening celebrations, I excused myself to go to the bathroom. It was old-fashioned. Small, square pink tiles covered the walls, with dark wooden basins and cubicle doors that creaked open and shut. I could hear the conversations of the passers-by, eager, no doubt, to begin the booze-induced part of the evening. I looked at myself in the mirror, pulling at the skin by my eyes in an attempt to smooth it out. There was nothing to be done. Once the wrinkles had started to appear, it was a solemn reminder that not even Samantha Atlas, with her haphazard desire to wear makeup, could stop the turning of time. I wondered, if Mum were still alive, whether she would have encouraged me to moisturise. Or whether she would have a beauty routine of her own. I would never know.

Tamara's wedding gift stared at me from the side of the sink. I hated the uncertainty of the idea. Would people think it was meddlesome? *Why would Sam give a gift like that to Tamara? She obviously isn't over her.* It's true that even I had doubted these things in the past. How did you know for sure that you're over your first love? I guess the answer might be attending their wedding and seeing if you make it out the other side.

★

I had seen Tamara a handful of times since the events of the Blue Rooms party. One time, I was up visiting my dad. It'd been months since I had seen Jake, and I hoped he would be in too. Emma had told me he'd been in the bar a lot recently getting wasted, and he hadn't been responding to my texts. I walked the gravel pathway up to the door, spotting a redheaded woman with her back to the window.

In the living room, sitting around a takeaway pizza, were Jake, Tamara, and Dad. I lingered a little too long in the doorway, struggling to put the pieces together of the scene in front of me.

"Hey," Jake said, barely looking up from his plate of pizza.

"Hey," Tamara added casually.

Dad rose to greet me and pulled me into a big hug. I studied Tamara over his shoulder suspiciously. She didn't look at me.

I waited in the kitchen, boiling the kettle. Jake came in with his empty plate. Pizza sauce stained the right side of his mouth.

"What is Tamara doing here?" I hissed.

"What? We hang out sometimes." He grabbed a beer from the fridge and opened it on the side of the counter.

"What you doing that for? Use a bottle opener."

"Jeez. What's got into you?" He took a large gulp, letting out an audible sigh.

"Don't you think you should've mentioned that she would be here?" I brushed my hands over my orange jumper. I had bought it on the market for a fiver, and suddenly, it was super itchy. "It's weird."

"It's only weird for you. Tamara doesn't mind that you're here."

"Right. Nice to see you too, Jake."

I took my bag upstairs and rearranged the contents of my bedroom. It had slowly become the "junk" room since I moved out. I was tidying away a stack of magazines when there was a shy knock on the door. Tamara stood there, holding a plate of pizza in her hands.

"Peace offering?"

I sighed. "I'm not even mad at you. It's *him.*"

She didn't say anything but lingered in the doorway. It annoyed me.

"You can come in if you want. You don't have to just stand there."

Tamara clicked her tongue. "All right, then." She sat on the edge of the bed, laying the plate down beside her. "Why are you sulking?"

I scrunched up some old letters and took aim at the bin. I missed. "I'm not sulking. I just wasn't expecting this."

"Do you want me to go?"

"I...I don't know. I want Jake to be less of an arse."

"I'm not sure what we could do about that." She snorted. "Are you still mad at me? About what happened at the beach house?"

I sighed heavily, putting my head to my hands. "It was a moment of weakness on my part. That's all. I'm quite happy for you to do what you want."

"All right. Understood." Tamara fiddled with the pocket of her jeans. "I'd like it if we could be friends though?"

★

A young mother with her baby burst through into the ladies' toilets, making me jump. She looked at me apologetically as she ushered the toddler into a cubicle. I took the gift in my hand and headed out of the door. Were Tamara and I friends? I wasn't really sure. Would the gift make her uncomfortable? Again, I wasn't sure. Emma seemed to think it was a nice idea. *Very personal. Shows you care.* I needed more time to decide.

The corridor was empty, just the plants and the pictures and the faint thump of music coming from the hall. I walked the opposite way, back towards the dining hall and the gardens. I was surprised at how well I was navigating Tarnbourg Hall, as directions weren't usually my strong suit. I pushed through the big double doors, eyeing the willow tree and the steep hill behind it. I needed somewhere I could retrieve the gift if I changed my mind. I dipped down beneath the tree, following the curve of the hillside and stepping carefully in my heels. The grass was dry, and when I rounded the corner, I found a small rockery that looked the perfect place to hide something. I tucked the gift in between two rocks and made my way back to the hall, pleased with myself. A celebratory drink was in order.

Chapter Twenty

2014

"She really hates me."

"She doesn't."

"Of course she does." Tamara had a swig of her drink—rum and Coke, a concoction I hadn't seen her drink before.

"Well, can you blame her?" I said. "She's my best friend."

"I know. But those dagger eyes! It's enough to make me hyperventilate."

Ellie watched us dejectedly from the other side of the room. Tom, upon noticing, nudged her, and she tore her eyes away, taking big gulps from her glass.

"Every time I see her, it's the same," she scoffed. "Icy doesn't even come close."

"Well." I swallowed a mouthful of my drink, hoping the taste would settle my nerves and not bring up anything else. "I don't know what you expect."

"Hmm." Tamara watched me, and it made me uneasy. "You all right with that?"

"Yeah. Why?"

She tried to muffle her laughter with her hand. "I saw your incident with the plant pot."

"Oh my God!" My head fell into my palm. "No, you didn't!"

"I was about to come over and say hi, but then...you puked."

"Oh my God." Of course the first time that I saw Tamara in years would be when I was about to be sick in public.

"I didn't wanna make it worse. Wasn't sure if you'd be too pleased to see me."

"I can't believe you saw me throw up." I shook my head, trying to erase the memory. Talk about bad timing.

"Yeah. Was pretty impressive." She burst out laughing, a loud and melodic sound I hadn't realised how much I missed. "It's fine, Sam. You still look great."

I ignored her compliment and straightened up, ready to go back to the group, who were still watching us from across the room.

"Wait," Tamara said. "I do wanna talk to you."

"Go on, then."

"Not here. Not with all the eyes on us."

"I'm not leaving the boys' party just to hear a half-arsed apology from you, Tamara. That ship sailed a long time ago."

"A half-arsed apology?" She grabbed my arm and pulled me to face her. "That's what you think I'm about? Every day I regret what happened. And how I handled things. Every day I have to look at myself and face how I hurt you."

"Tamara," I hissed. "People are looking."

"So what? Let them. You need to hear what I'm gonna say."

"Do I though? This night is not about us. Or any of the bullshit you wanna call it."

"Bullshit? You think our relationship was bullshit?" Tamara's voice was loud and strained. Her eyes pierced into mine.

"Well...I don't know, really."

She shook her head, dissatisfied with my answer. "I can't believe you would say that!" she shouted above the noise.

"Can you blame me? *Really?* You were *cheating* on me!"

I could feel eyes on me, but anger was building in my gut.

"I wasn't *cheating*—"

"Tamara! I saw you with my own eyes. Don't insult me!" I shrugged her arm off mine and paced away, my heart pounding in my chest. She called after me, but I stormed across the room, avoiding the eyes of onlookers as I went.

"Sam. I'm sorry!"

"If that's all you have to say, Tamara, then it's fine. I don't wanna hear it."

She didn't follow me. I headed back to Ellie and the others and didn't look back. The nerve of her. I wanted to go back and unleash the rest of this pent-up anger that was eating me up.

I denied the offers to talk about it with the gang, insisting it was their night and I didn't want to steal any focus. Ten minutes later, the altercation with Tamara was forgotten, and the five of us headed to the dance floor with Yvette watching from the side. Petey joined us too, picking the boys up on his big shoulders and trying to pass them around above our heads. They managed to be carried between four people, familiar faces that I couldn't connect any names to, before they were drunkenly dropped and then cheered after rearing their heads from a crumpled mess on the floor.

The DJ continued his playlist of popular tunes, people hearing their favourites and pulling their friends closer to the booth to dance and sing along. After a few songs, Ash tugged on my arm, motioning for me to follow him. The room was humid from all the dancing bodies, so I was relieved when he led me out through the sliding doors and into the wispy night air. Instead of taking me to one of the benches or the wall beside the dreaded plant pot, he pulled me around the corner and down a path at the side of the building. The steady thump of the music continued inside, reverberating off the walls and echoing into the night.

"I thought you might want one?" Ash produced a packet of cigarettes from a crack in the wall.

"What about Yvette?"

"It's fine."

"Right," I said, accepting his offer. "That's why they're stashed in the wall."

He laughed, popping the tip in his mouth and bringing it to light. "I've got mints too." He tapped the wall, and a silver packet glistened.

"You're like Jesus. What else you got in there? A donkey and three wise men?"

"Nah. That's all." He took a deep drag. I thought he had quit smoking when he met Yvette.

"How long you two been together now?"

"Three years."

"Wow."

"I know." He exhaled. "Seems much longer." He caught the surprise on my face. "I know what the boys think about her. What you all do. And it's fine." His blue eyes regarded mine. "Really. I'm happy. She keeps me on my toes. Makes me wanna do better." He beamed, revealing his gap-toothed grin.

"You sure? You don't always seem it."

He shook his head. "We're not perfect. Far from it. I wanna make her happy, but...some things are best not said."

"Like smoking?"

"Exactly."

"I don't get it."

"I get what I want, and she gets what she wants. I want to smoke, and she wanted me to quit. Now we're both happy." He tapped ash onto the floor. "You do what you gotta do to make it work."

I thought about it for a moment, sucking on my cigarette.

"If you wanna talk to Tamara, don't think about the others," he said. "Whatever happens, they'll be there for you. If you work it out. Or just get closure." He shrugged as he took another drag. "You two had something. I don't know the ins and outs of what happened—but that was clear to see."

"Hmm." I digested this information; the night was certainly full of surprises. The atmosphere and the people here mirrored many nights back home, filling me with a youth-like desire for fun and the unspoken promise that things would be okay. I watched Ash put out his cigarette on the wall and toss it down the drain. All this time, we thought Yvette had him trained to her command, but he was still his own person. And he was happy. We had it all wrong.

Back inside, the party was winding down, stage five, in all its glory. People had started to leave, clearing space for the bar and the dance floor alike. The remaining guests rejoiced in this fact, taking advantage of the small queues at the bar to get the last squeeze of fun out of the night. I spotted Emma and Petey sitting in a corner, discussing something with intensity, their faces flushed. Their heads were close together in conversation, many empty glasses on the table between them. Emma caught my eye and looked away. I hoped they were all right.

Ellie and Tom were swaying to a slow song by the DJ booth (a trademark section of the winding down process). Blue and white balloons settled by their feet, and they nudged them gently as they rocked side to side, bouncing them back into the air. Many of the older guests had left already, aside from a few big-bellied men who lounged back in their chairs, red-faced and bloated with drink, their young companions nestled beside them in a day-dream. Kipper was still there too, chatting away with his bowtie undone around his open collar, glass still in hand. A small balding man listened to him in snippets, swaying to the music like a tree in the wind.

When I saw Tamara, she was already looking at me. Her face rested in thought, her brown eyes burning back into mine. My stomach gripped, and a wave of sadness crashed over me. All the memories that I had locked away in the back of my mind snapped off the bars to their cages and escaped, drowning me in their weight. The mass of it—of her—pressed on my chest, and as she rose and started to approach me, my breathing grew tight and wheezy.

She slowed as she drew closer, assessing my expression with the flicker of her eyes. "Can we please talk now?" she asked, her voice quiet and soft.

"I'll meet you outside."

Before following her through the doors, I said good night to the boys and congratulated them once more, squeezing them tight and ignoring the stench of alcohol and sweat. I couldn't find Emma or Petey; they must have already left.

Ellie watched me closely. "You sure you know what you're doing?"

I nodded, and she put the address for the beach house into my phone.

"Be careful."

"I will."

Tamara waited for me by the outside bar. The lights were switched off, and the whole space was empty and in darkness, apart from a young couple who were stargazing on the bench. In the absent light, I could still make her out from the way she leaned against the wood. One leg crossed in front of the other, arms folded across her chest, her hair hiding her profile as she stared at the ground. She straightened when she saw me exit through the doors, the moonlight casting light across her body.

"Wanna walk me home?" I asked her.

"Yeah, sure."

We took a few steps, turning down the side of the building where Ash had shown me his secret stash.

"Wait. Not to Treaton Vale, right?"

I laughed, a short singular sound resembling a snort. "No. Not to Treaton Vale."

The pathway led to the front of the building and the main road. Instinctively I headed the same way we came earlier in the car.

"Do you know where you're going?" she asked, peering at me from the side.

"Kinda. Don't you?" Our footsteps fell together in a quiet and comforting rhythm. The cold air was wonderful against my skin.

"No. I've never been to their beach house."

"Besides, I thought you liked getting lost?"

"Touché." Tamara cast into the dark. "You don't forget a thing, do you?"

Not when it comes to us, no.

I still remembered the first time we met, how the disappointment and hurt I had felt all melted away at her allure and her perfectly freckled face. I glanced at her from the side and caught those big brown eyes observing me right back. I wondered if she was thinking about the same thing, our first meeting. Or our first kiss.

We followed the road down towards the beach. I was pretty sure if we walked along it, we would get to Tom's beach house eventually. Large concrete steps led us down from the road, and I kicked my shoes off onto the beach and pushed my toes into the cold sand. The grains caressed my feet, easing some discomfort from being in heels all night, and I exhaled deeply. The salty air lifted me up, and with my shoes in hand, I started walking. Tamara unlaced her white trainers, pulled her socks off, and stuffed them inside. She jogged to catch up with me.

"I heard you moved to London," she said. It was more of a statement than a question.

"Yeah. Two years ago, now."

"Do you like it?"

"It's different."

"I can't imagine you there."

Tamara carried her trainers by the laces, throwing them over her shoulder so they dangled down her back.

"Why not?"

"I dunno." She shrugged. "I don't think you belong in the city."

"I miss home a lot."

"Yeah?"

"I used to love being in the Mayor's Gardens. Just doodling."

Tamara nodded, her shoes clunking against her back in sync with her footsteps.

"It was always quiet but not too quiet," I continued. "Know what I mean?"

"Yeah." She paused. "It wasn't the same place without you."

My heart leaped into my throat. I swallowed it away. "Thought you were back in Manchester anyway?"

"You been checking up on me?" She grinned playfully.

"Just heard from Tom."

"Ah, yeah." Her voice was laced with disappointment. "I got my own place now. Small but real homey. I wanna do it up and sell it on. I've seen people do that on TV, and they always make it look so good."

"Yeah? That sounds ideal."

"I'm good at hands-on stuff. Not really the arty part though. Like mine could use a bit of *painting*."

I nodded, not biting on her line. She cast another. "Bit of artwork to brighten it up maybe."

"There's a lot of great local artists."

I felt her gaze on me, a smile tugging at her mouth. Our arms brushed accidentally, and a shiver shot up my spine.

Her phone chimed in her pocket. She ignored it. The wind blew a soft chill through the air.

"Remember how much we used to hang out at the beach?" Tamara asked, her voice soft and innocent.

"Of course."

"And I still can't swim."

I laughed as the image of Tamara shrieking as I dragged her into the sea entered my mind.

"How's Puds?" I asked.

"He's good. Still the greediest Labrador in the county, but yeah."

The cold sand was damp underfoot, and in the moonlight, a calm settled upon us as we looked out across the black vastness of the ocean, pushed along by the wind as the two unspoken years flashed past us in conversation. We walked a little farther, passing closed ice cream parlours and arcades deserted in the darkness. The moon hung big and bright in the sky above us, the stars sprinkled upon the deep blue like fireflies lighting the way. We must have been nearing the beach house, but I didn't want the night to be over yet. I felt more myself than I had done in months under the eye of the night sky, walking barefoot in the sand. I didn't want to go back to London. I didn't want Tamara to leave. I just wanted to stay this way, protected by the darkness, pretending I was twenty-one again and just falling in love.

Chapter Twenty-One

2021

"Would you like a drink, miss?"

The voice made me jump. I thought I was alone. I had been studying the pictures the newlyweds had displayed in the corridor to the main hall. I had no desire to join in the celebratory rituals of the night, except to find something to quench my thirst and numb my head. Vodka maybe. Perhaps something stronger.

The congratulation banner had been pinned across the door slightly offset, reminding me of something that primary school children would use to decorate their class. Small tables stocking various sweets and pictures paraded to the doorway. I studied the pictures in front of me. Tamara's baby photos were so obviously her. She had the same dark eyes and fiery hair, just less of it and messier. I didn't look long at the pictures of April; she was just a stranger to me.

The voice came from the side of me, behind the bar, which I had thought was unmanned.

"Sorry. I didn't mean to make you jump," he said, placing red cloth table mats on the bar.

"I didn't realise you were open."

"I'm not yet. Just starting up." He flashed a cheeky, lopsided grin. "I'd be happy to serve you something. I think there's quite the queue in there, and I wouldn't want you to wait." Obviously a charmer. He must be used to hitting on the women here. I was embarrassed to have been singled out as a lonely wedding guest. How sad I must have looked, wandering around the corridor by myself.

"Sure. I'll have a double gin and tonic."

His smile grew wider, revealing a pointed incisor that nipped his lower lip. "Certainly, miss." He ducked behind the bar, finished polishing a glass, and filled it with ice. I walked over, eyeing the photo booth in the far right-hand corner.

"What is this supposed to be, then?" I gestured behind me, perching on a stool.

"This is an overflow room. The guests can come in here and take pictures, write things in the souvenir book." He sliced a lime into fine pieces. "It's just a bit quieter, miss."

"Right. How lovely." I eyed the seating area with distaste. The log fire and the red plaid draped over the tables reminded me of a hunting lodge. "And less of the 'miss'. It makes me feel about a thousand years old."

"Of course. I'm sorry. The last thing I would want to do is offend you." He poured the gin into the glass gracefully, finishing it off with a little flair.

I eyed his name badge. *Javier*. Something about him took me back to another time. A fancy restaurant. Expensive wine. Young and handsome, black slick hair combed over to one side, a cheeky smile and way with words. He would have been exactly Rachel's type.

I hadn't spoken to Rachel since I left London, but I heard that she was divorced now, which didn't surprise me. She had called me the eve of her wedding, tipsy and horny, and I wasn't having any of it.

★

"Don't you miss me?" she slurred into the speaker.

"Rachel. You're getting married tomorrow."

"Don't you think I know that?" she snapped. Her voice was heightened in an unfamiliar way. High pitched. Verging on desperation. It was strange to hear Rachel in this way when she scarcely lost control. Not in the time that I knew her, anyway. "It's my last night. And you, my love, are my last hurrah."

"Rachel." I glanced at my watch. "It's 1:13 a.m. You need to get some sleep."

"Samantha. Samantha. I'm going to call you Samantha."

I pulled the phone away from my ear as she continued to chant, and when she fell silent, I tried to say my goodbyes, growing impatient.

"Why aren't you coming tomorrow?" she asked. "I was disappointed when you said that you wouldn't be attending."

I sighed heavily, rubbing my eyes. "I didn't see the point."

"Aren't you happy for me? You said that you were."

"I am happy for you. I hope you would be happy for me too."

"Of course." She was quiet on the other end. A rustling sound. "Have you met someone?"

I paused. "Kinda. Yeah."

More quiet. Then, "I see. I'm sorry to have called."

"It's fine. I hope you're all right."

"I am. Don't worry about me."

"If you're not happy, Rachel. It's not too late, you know."

"I know, darling. It's just the wine talking. I'm sorry to have called. What will your girlfriend think? Late-night calls from old lovers."

"It's fine," I was going to say. "Get some sleep. Have a great wedding. Look after yourself."

Silence echoed through the receiver. She had already hung up the phone.

★

"Here you go." Javier slid the glass over to me, decorated nicely with lemon and lime.

"What do I owe you?"

"Nothing. The first one is free."

I shook my head, feeling too old to deal with a flirty youngster. "All right. Well, thank you, Javier. Have a good night now."

With a deep sigh and glass in hand, I jumped off the barstool and walked towards the hall. Surprisingly, for the first time that day, a lightness filled me. It could've been the champagne or the gin, but as I drew closer to the crowd and the booming music, I looked forward to the night ahead.

Chapter Twenty-Two

2014

Tamara sighed, her cool breath winding through the air in distortions. "Which way now?"

I pulled out my phone to check the address. It was only two streets away.

"I think it's just down here." I motioned the way down the beach. "Then up one of these paths into the garden. Ellie said it has a green gate."

"Okay. You know I have to wear contacts now?" Tamara said. "My vision is fucked."

"I think glasses would suit you."

"They're too faffy. I kept losing them all the time. Mum was going mad." She laughed, wind chimes ringing out into the night. "So, I don't know how much help I'll be."

"Is that your excuse?"

I felt her eyes on me. "Excuse for what?"

"For spending more time with me."

"Hmm. Maybe."

I turned to her, catching a new look on her face... What was that? Was Tamara *blushing*? It was difficult to tell in the lack of light.

"Sam, I do have something I want to say." Her voice was serious. Unusual for Tamara.

"Let's not ruin it."

"But we have to talk about it—"

"Do we though?" I stopped walking. "I don't want to drag up the past." The image of Tamara and Tyler flashed in front of my eyelids. I blinked it away, spotting a dark-green gate in the distance. "That might be it."

She lagged behind me as I strode out in front, adrenaline-fuelled anger nipping at my skin.

"You were always too good to be true," a soft voice said from the shadows. "I never deserved you."

I turned to face her. A pained expression gripped her face.

"You don't even realise how amazing you are. You're so delicate and thoughtful...but incredibly strong."

"Tamara, I really—"

"I was so used to being a fuck-up that I didn't want to hurt you. I didn't want to do anything to hurt you." Her voice wavered. "And I know that I did." The last word was encased in a sob. "I was so afraid of what could happen between us... I stopped myself... I tried to." She took a deep breath in to steady her breathing. "I wanted to earn you. To be someone you deserved. I just wanted to be that, but I knew I couldn't, and look what I did!" She gestured with her arm. Tears cascaded down her face and onto the sand. "The stuff with Tyler..."

I scowled at the mention of her name, and Tamara noticed.

"No, Sam, it was nothing. It was a distraction. I was trying to convince myself my feelings weren't real."

"Tamara—"

"It's no excuse. I know." She stepped towards me, dropping her trainers by her feet. "And I know how pathetic I was and how stupid. I am so, so sorry."

A gull cawed from the darkness, Tamara's sobs filling the rest of the silence. I took a seat on the sand beside her shoes, and she joined me. Her face was stained with black, covering her freckles with wet smudges.

"Here." I took my thumb and wiped under her eyes, smoothing the tears away. She pressed her cheek against my palm, cool and damp. Her eyes held mine. Deep brown and holding more sadness than I had ever seen.

Tamara was leaning into me, or was I her? Her plump pink lips edged closer to mine. I had forgotten the taste. Were they as soft as they looked? My brain ticked away the entangled thoughts until our lips touched. And *yes*. It all came back to me. The mint and the smoke. The soft and the cold.

I kissed her hard. Her cool fingers moved to my face, and she caressed my jawline carefully with her thumb. She pulled me on top of her, tumbling down in the sand, lacing her arms around my back. My stomach gripped with lust and the sudden reminder of all the things that inhabited this person I had loved.

My hands cupped her bum, squeezing it as I kissed her, making Tamara moan into my mouth. I jumped as her hand crept under my dress, feeling over my pants and the sensation she had caused. She smiled into my kiss, attempting to throw me onto my back and take control of the situation in there. Instead, she pushed a heap of sand onto both of us, stinging our faces and eyes as we jumped away from each other in pain.

"Jesus Christ!" I keeled over, rubbed the grains out of my eyes.

"Fuck!" Tamara yelled. "My fucking eyes!"

We lay crumpled in the sand, blinking and rubbing our eyelids until the pain subsided.

"I can't see," Tamara groaned. She sat with her head in between her knees, her fingers holding her eyelids open as she blinked rapidly. "It fucking stings."

I squinted at her, my eyes sore and red. "Lemme have a look."

She tilted her head to my voice, her eyes squeezed shut. I wiped my hand on my dress and then brushed off the grains that were stuck around her eyes. They fell onto Tamara's jeans with a pitter-patter.

"Better?"

She opened them slowly. "A little."

"Here. Come on." I grabbed her hands and pulled her onto her feet. "There might be some eye drops or something at the beach house."

I led her down to the green gate slowly, with her hand clasped in mine. She squeezed it tight when we went through the gate and began the slight incline up towards the decking. I spotted the two chairs Ellie and I had been drinking on earlier, lonely and eerie in the quiet night. The house appeared to be silent, and I wondered if Ellie and Tom were still back at the party. I produced a key from underneath a large plant pot by the door, reliving the not-too-distant memory of hurling into one a few hours earlier. Ellie and I had stashed the key there before we left "in case we split up". I swore that woman knew everything.

The door swung open, revealing the mess Ellie and I had left, empty bottles and wine-stained glasses over the white countertops. I escorted Tamara inside, her eyes still closed, and noticed the blinking lights in the corner of the wall. A burglar alarm? I didn't remember Ellie setting one. I glanced to the alarm box on the wall just as it burst into its loud and deafening song. I ran to the box, checking the notes in my phone for a code, but they were blank. *Fuck. Fuck. Fuck.*

My mind garbled numbers together, unable to think for the sound blaring in my ears. I jabbed my fingers quickly into the keypad, 170589. The alarm cut into silence. *Tom's birthday.*

"That scared the shit out of me," Tamara gasped. "Thought I was gonna have a heart attack."

"You okay?"

"Apart from being blind and narrowly avoiding cardiac arrest? Yeah, I'm good." She squinted at me, her face twisted in discomfort. She reminded me of a little mole.

I led her along the hallway into the bathroom and sat her on the edge of the bath.

"Don't lean back."

I searched the medicine cabinet above the sink, finding a small bottle of eye drops. I leaned her head back and tapped the bottle, the salted water running down her face and onto her clothes. She blinked, her eyes darting around the room.

"Lil more, please."

I complied. More drops and then more blinking.

She opened her eyes and looked at me, smiling. "There we go. I can see your lovely face."

"Your eyes are so red."

She laughed. "Could be worse." She stood and kissed me, pulling my body into hers. "So...grand tour? Or just of your bedroom?"

"My bedroom," I mumbled into her mouth. "You can see the rest of the house tomorrow."

★

The morning light filtered through the blinds, casting striped shadows along the walls. My head throbbed, my mouth painfully dry. What happened last night?

I rolled over and saw Tamara, and the night's events came catapulting back at me in quick succession: hands and mouths and the push and pull of our bodies. Her lips on my thighs. My fingers in her hair. Ragged breathing and sounds from her mouth that made my insides throb.

She was naked, the powder-blue covers tangled around her pale body. Her arm was stretched above her head, her bare leg straddling the duvet. I leaned over and kissed her shoulder, and she grumbled underneath me. She was never fond of mornings.

Her phone buzzed loudly on the nightstand. Tamara sighed loudly, rolling over to reject the call.

"Who's that?"

"Mother," she replied sleepily.

I looked down at her, her hair messy from sleep and the events of last night. "This is weird," I said.

"What d'ya mean?"

"Just...seeing you like this again."

"Good weird? Or bad weird?" Tamara slowly sat up in bed, propping herself up on her elbow.

"I'm not sure yet," I teased.

"Well. I was gonna offer to make you a cup of tea, but now you can bugger off." She tickled my ribs, and I collapsed on the bed, trying to push her off me.

"Stop! Stop!" I shrieked. She paused for a moment, revelling in the moment before continuing. I writhed around the bed in hysterics until she finally ended the tickle torture with a kiss.

We moved to the kitchen. Tamara perched herself at the breakfast bar, wearing her sand-dusted clothes from last night. I explored the hall, spotting Tom's and Ellie's shoes by the door. I wondered what time they got back last night.

I searched the cupboards for the teabags and cups as Tamara turned her phone over in her hands absent-mindedly. I heard movement in the hallway as the kettle hummed away, and Ellie popped her head around the corner.

"Is your head as fucked as mine?" she grumbled, her face falling when she saw Tamara perched on the stool. "What's she doing here?"

"Good morning to you too," Tamara said.

"Long story."

"I fucking knew it. As soon as I saw her...I just knew it." Ellie shook her head, pulling out a glass and filling it with water. "Whatever, man."

"You want a cup of tea?"

Ellie glared at Tamara, who looked at me pleadingly. "Okay. I'll have an extra sugar though, please." She sat at the opposite side of the breakfast bar, her back to Tamara.

"What time did you get in?" I asked her.

"About five."

"What happened?"

She rubbed her head, sipping her water delicately. "We went to some rich guy's house. He had a pool and everything." She popped some paracetamol out of the packet. "I think there was a duck? I don't remember much more." She offered the packet to me and then Tamara. We both took two each.

I poured the tea and passed them their cups. The silence was unnerving.

"Anyway. I'm gonna drink this in bed." Ellie gave me a look. "Tom was so drunk. I should check he's still breathing." She shuffled out of the room, clutching her water in one hand and tea in the other.

"Yeah. She *defo* hates me," Tamara said.

We took our drinks outside and sat on the decking. The morning sun was peeking out from behind the clouds, hinting at another warm day. The salty sea air was refreshing. My knees were pulled up to my chest, my tea cupped in my hands.

"Last night was crazy." Tamara blew into her cup before taking a sip. "I didn't expect any of this."

"Me neither." I glanced at her, a tingle rising in my belly.

Tamara's phone buzzed again, lighting up on the table between us. Instinctively, I looked at the name. Tamara leaped at the screen and swiped it off.

"Who's Kelly?" I asked.

She waited before responding. I suddenly felt sick.

"Urgh." She gulped her tea, but it was too hot to drink.

"Who is she?"

"Just this girl?"

"*Just this girl?* Are you fucking kidding me?"

Her eyes widened at my heightened voice. "Calm down, Sam. It's nothing."

"Yeah." I slammed my cup down, and it spilled onto the table. "You seem to say that a lot."

I stormed into my room and shut the door, my hands shaking. I caught my reflection in the mirror and cursed myself.

You stupid woman. You stupid fucking woman.

Then I cursed Tamara King for making me look a fool once more, vowing to never let it happen again.

★

"I swear on Puds's life. I'm not gonna make that same mistake again."

"Don't bring your dog into this. I'm not as naïve as I was four years ago, Tamara." I stormed out of the house, dragging her behind me.

"I just want you to come for a drive with me. That's all I'm asking for. For old times' sake?"

"For old times' sake? Isn't that just what last night was?"

She turned away from me.

"When I told you to go and not come back, I didn't mean *go and get your car, let's go on a road trip*!" I spat. "How stupid do you think I am?"

"I don't think you're stupid. I've told you the truth! She's a girl I've been seeing, and it's nothing serious." She pulled on my arm, and I yanked it away from her.

"Please. That's probably what you told Tyler about me."

Tamara rolled her eyes. "Sam, we've been through this."

"And yet, here we are again."

We both stood on the driveway, not saying anything. Tamara pulled out a packet of cigarettes and offered me one. I accepted. We stood there for a while, inhaling and exhaling, letting the seagull noise above fill in the silence.

"Look. I should've been honest about Kelly from the start. I know that. But this—" She moved her hand to mine and held it. "This is more than any of that. This is real, and you know it, Sam."

Her fingertips made soft circles on my wrist. She pulled us closer together, her hair falling across her face. I stood still. The only sound was the two of us breathing, soft and slow, and the steady hum of the occasional car in the distance. Her hands found my waist. I craned my neck in response, and she raised her head to meet my eyes. That same old smirk.

I tugged on her hair. She studied me for a moment, her dark eyes holding mine before she kissed me hard. I kissed her back, welcoming the taste of fresh mint and old cigarettes. Her fingers were in my hair, moving rhythmically as she kissed me. They wandered down to my face, her smooth fingers tracing the outline of my jaw. I stopped suddenly and stepped away, wiping my mouth. I lingered for a moment, conscious of the pulse in my ears and the heart in my throat.

"Don't fucking do that again."

She nodded, her smile fading. "I guess I'll see you around, then." She watched for a moment and then spun on her heels.

I stood and watched her walk to her car.

And I stood and watched as she got inside and pulled away.

Then I stood.

Alone.

Thinking about Tamara King.

Chapter Twenty-Three

2021

Tom's parents had secured a table for us in the hall and waved me over from their seats. Men and women dotted themselves along the bar, collecting orders of beverages for their groups. Jake waited patiently at the end of the bar for his turn, unaware of the bar opening next door. The room was warm. Debbie was flushed with a light coat of sweat as she fretted over the children. Phil went to help Jake with the orders.

The hall had filled fast; old couples sparred off for the limited seating at the back of the room. Women draped their handbags and shawls over chairs before they sat, gossiping with anybody nearby who would listen to coo over the decorations. The red theme had continued from the wedding, down the hall and into this room too. Red ribbon decorated the centrepieces and the backs of the chairs, chequered white-and-red tablecloth covered the tables. It was a lot of red.

People waltzed around the room, greeting new guests who were arriving through the doors for the evening do and making toasts to one another. As the gathering dispersed, I spotted two tables by the doors. One exhibiting a huge white wedding cake topped with vanilla swirls and crushed almonds. The other, a display of wedding gifts, small and large and wrapped in a multitude of different colours and patterns. I thought of my gift that Jake had fetched from the car, resting in the rockery until I decided what to do with it.

Catherine would be joining the evening part of the wedding soon—that was something I needed to deal with first.

Jake and Phil approached with our drinks, ice cubes rattling together. A whooping cheer erupted around us as Tamara and April burst through the doors, hand in hand. The DJ called into the microphone that it was time for the first dance, and people made way for the newlyweds to get to the wooden dance floor.

"Jake," I hushed into his ear. "I need to talk to you."

"What, now? They're gonna have their first dance." He clapped his hands together loudly. "Woo!"

"Jake." I tugged at his sleeve.

"Yeah, okay. After this." His focus never strayed from the two women waiting on the dance floor. Every eye in the room watched them—apart from mine. I was busy watching the door, hoping to see my date walk in or, in another scenario, to see Catherine waltz in and kick her ass. I had never been much of a fighter, but the thought of her breaking Jake's heart made me want to drag her to the floor by her pretty black hair.

A slow song belted out from the speakers (thankfully, not a song that I knew, so it wouldn't be ruined forever), and the guests clapped and cheered as the two swayed together to the music.

Two thirds of the way through the song, Tamara and April started to pull other people onto the floor with them, encouraging them to dance. I took this opportunity to drag Jake out into the hall to finally get him alone.

"Jeez. What is wrong with you?" He shook me off his arm. "I thought you'd played the *crazy ex* part of the wedding already."

"I haven't been a *crazy* ex. You moron. I'm being serious here. I have a problem."

"What is it?" He peered at me, his blue eyes a reflection of mine.

"You might wanna sit down."

His face shifted. "What is it? Is it Dad? Is he okay?"

"Yeah, Dad's fine." I took Jake's arm again and led him to a large leather sofa, nodding at Javier as I did.

"Hey," Jake said, distracted. "I didn't know there was a bar in here."

"Yeah. It's not open yet though. I don't think."

"I waited fifteen minutes for our drinks before."

"Jake. Just listen to me, for Christ's sake."

He tore his eyes away from Javier, who was pretending not to listen.

"I don't know how to tell you this. So, I'm just gonna say it." I couldn't look at him. My gaze flittered around the room and settled on the stupid photo booth. "If it was me, I would want you to tell me, so I'm just going to have to."

"Okay. Tell me, Sam. You're scaring the shit out of me."

I took a deep breath in and blurted out the words as I exhaled. "I saw Catherine with another guy."

Jake's face fell the exact way I imagined it would. Like the time his hamster Furball had died or when he found out I was moving to London. I watched him carefully as he absorbed the news, his brow raising and dropping with deep thought. I wasn't sure if he was going to get angry or if he would stay level-headed. He wasn't doing anything at all.

"Who was it?" he asked.

"Some caterer guy. He slapped her arse, and they were laughing and giggling. I'm here for you. Whatever you need." I sighed. "She's a stupid bitch."

He let out a laugh.

I looked at him, bewildered. "What?"

"You never liked her, did you?"

"I don't know what you mean."

"It's okay, Sam. Really." He smiled at me, no trace of anger in his features.

"You know what I'm saying, right?"

"Yeah. I'm not an idiot."

"Then what's wrong with you?" My voice was a lot shriller than I had intended. Jake sighed. His thick brows knotted before he spoke.

"Catherine and I are not together." He pulled a hand over his head, ruffling his hair. "We're getting divorced."

"*What*? Since when? Why haven't you said anything?"

"To be honest..." he started. "I'm embarrassed. I never imagined getting divorced, *never mind* before I was thirty. I know how people talk." He shook his head.

"But I'm your sister. I'm not gonna judge you."

"I know. I just thought it'd be easier this way. I can deal with it on my own and not have to deal with all the sympathy. Like the look you're giving me right now."

I straightened my head, not realising I had tilted it towards him. "I just care about you, Jake."

"I know. And I'm fine, really." He smiled.

"Really?"

"Really really."

We sat for a moment as the DJ bellowed on the microphone, telling everyone to get on the dance floor.

"How long?" I asked.

"Couple of months. But I've known a lot longer. Sure she has too."

"And you're really okay? What about Lottie?"

"She doesn't know yet, but we'll figure it out. Stop worrying, worry wuss." He flashed a grin at me. "Come on. Let's go dance." He stood and held out a big hand towards me so he could pull me up in one swift motion.

I noticed a guest book on a table by the door, a giant cardboard sign above asking for people to write comments and well-wishes for the newlyweds. As Jake tugged me back down the hallway, I tried to sneak a peek, but I couldn't read the handwriting. Back inside the main room, the music drummed out the thoughts in my head about what I would write—if I should write anything. Would they even expect me to?

"I love this one!" Jake called behind him as he beelined for the dance floor, dragging me with him into the crowd of people orchestrating the cha-cha slide.

Chapter Twenty-Four

2015

The digits on the clock refused to move. I had been staring at the computer screen for what felt like the longest minutes of my life. To my left, Beth chatted away to somebody on the phone. A high-pitched whinny sounded from the front desk. Tina was attempting to flirt with the new co-director again. I closed my tabs on screen and switched off the computer. I'd pulled on my jacket before the machine had time to process my requests. Tina looked up as I approached, waving goodbye to the co-director with a painted hand.

"Have a nice weekend, Sam," she squawked. "Hope the drive isn't too busy."

"Thanks, Tina. You too."

I took the lift to the top-floor car park and searched for my car. Stella had conked out last year on the drive back to London after the Blue Rooms party. After overhearing Tina say on Tuesday morning (which was near impossible with her foghorn mouth) that she was getting rid of her small and worn little blue car, I couldn't resist.

I had managed without a car in London for a good few months. There was no real need for one there; in London, a car was a privilege, not a necessity. But my plans to travel home for the weekend were tainted by the thought of having to get two trains, so I bargained the price down, and she sold it to me for a cheap sum. The paintwork had a couple of scrapes on the bonnet and the back. Clearly, Tina, too, had trouble with the multistorey car park and the steel pillars lining the spaces. This didn't bother me; it actually made me less worried about keeping the car pristine. Plus, if anybody asked me about any bumps, I could just blame it on Tina's driving.

The car sighed heavily as I sat in the driver's seat and started the engine. I was itching to be in Treaton Vale, and the whole day had dragged. I pulled out of the space, re-adjusted the rear-view mirror, and descended the spiral exit to the ground floor. Work was boring, and the days were long. I had experienced more eye contact with the clock the last few weeks than I had with any other person. This didn't bother me much; the gossip and the politics bored me, and I was misunderstood by the other women in the office.

I followed the road signs for the north, relief enveloping me at the thought of heading out of the city. Fashion had never interested me much, and yet there I was in the same job revolving around the stuff. The concepts were a little too "out there" for my taste, and as this was a common topic in the office, especially surrounding any new lines, I was painfully out of place. I hadn't heard from Rachel since we had dinner, only snippets of information fed from Tina and the other women, usually followed by laughter and hushed whispering in my direction.

The long and busy road opened up into three lanes, and I let my mind wander as I reduced the space between work and my hometown.

Two hours later, I turned off the exit for Treaton Vale, my newly cut brown bob fluttering around my face. The familiar landmarks of the town welcomed me as I drove through the city, past the train station and the Mayor's Gardens. Nostalgia rolled over me as a flash of memories jumped into my mind's eye, countless summers and evenings I had spent there with the people closest to me. The temperature dipped as clouds grouped overhead, and the sudden drop sent a shiver through my body. I turned past Diamond as I fiddled with the window, winding it up in a painfully slow motion. A few shops had changed names since I had last been home. It made me feel like a tourist in my own town.

I pulled onto the kerb outside my house and spotted Dad waiting by the window. He shot to the door when he saw me arrive and bounded through the doorway in his brown slippers.

"Pumpkin!" He hugged me tightly as soon as I stepped out of the car. "How are you? The car drive okay?" He stepped back, taking me in. "New hair? I like it!"

"Yeah? You don't think it makes me look really young?"

"What's wrong with looking young? I would have my hair cut that way if I could pull it off."

"If you had any."

"Hey." He felt over his thinning hair, more grey now than brown. "I'm coming into my Clooney years."

"Sure. It suits you."

"Here. Lemme get that." He took my bag from my hand and closed the boot. It bounced back up in defiance. "Huh." He tried again, slamming the boot shut with a loud bang. "She been checked over properly?" he asked. "I'll top her up with oil and coolant before you go." He peered in through the windows to inspect the interior. "Do you have a name for her yet?"

"One question at a time, please. And after I've had a cup of tea."

★

I settled on the sofa, cup between my hands, and I waited for Dad to join me. As he clattered about the kitchen, I took the opportunity to have a quick look at the house. He had appeared to be keeping it tidy, aside from the stack of teabags by the kettle and the opened letters piled on the table. I made a mental note to inspect it later and make sure he was taking care of himself. He came and sat in the cosy reclinable chair (purchased after I moved out) perfectly angled towards the TV. He beamed at me as he pushed back in the seat, the chair moving horizontally with a squeak.

"It's good to see you, Pumpkin."

"I know. I miss you too, Dad."

He nodded, accepting this response eagerly as he blew into his cup. "I've found some things I want to show you."

He drew my attention to a box by the mantelpiece overflowing with paper and pictures. I spotted one on the top of the pile. Mum and Jake, their bodies splattered with paint. She was holding him on her hip, laughing as Jake pulled a face at the camera. He must have only been four or five.

Mum always encouraged us to be creative. In the springtime, around when the blossom trees in the garden would get their first buds, Jake and I were allowed to re-decorate our bedrooms. It was my favourite season. Jake loved the concept too for the first few years. Then when the excitement wore off, I ended up doing his room for him.

One year, I had slaved over a school project, building a huge Ferris wheel out of lollipop sticks, toilet roll, and glue. I came back from school one day to find it had collapsed into a gloopy mess. (Jake swears to this day that it wasn't him, but he isn't a very good liar.) Mum stayed up all night with me making a new one and continued working on it long after I had been put to bed. In the morning, she claimed that fairies came and fixed it for me.

"There's so many of Jake pulling faces." Dad heaved himself out of the chair and handed me a stack of photos to flick through. "Look."

"He still does that face now." I laughed at a picture of us together, both covered head to toe in chocolate cake. "Have you heard from him recently?"

"I saw him last weekend. He brought that girl around again."

"What's her name again? L? L..."

"Catherine," Dad jumped in. "She's...a fiery one."

Hmm. Jake sure had an interesting taste in women. "You don't like her?"

"She will keep him on his toes," he said diplomatically.

"Hmm." I found one of Mum and Dad posing for the camera at Gardeners, Dad carrying her in his arms like she was a damsel in distress.

"That was one of the last photos we had." He peered at the photo more closely. When he spoke again, his voice was weakened. "I still miss her every day."

"I do too." I glanced at him just in time to see his face laced with sadness before he plastered on his smile to cover it up.

He put his hand on mine and squeezed it, just like the day when he told me the news all those years ago.

Mum has been in a car accident. I need you to stay with Grandma and Grandad while I go and wait for her to come out of theatre. Don't cry, Pumpkin. It'll be okay. I promise.

I'd seen the worry in his eyes that day. The wave of uncertainness in his voice. The details were still so clear to me, something I could never unsee. The swollen puffiness of his eyes when he returned later that evening. The emptiness to his face that I couldn't quite comprehend. The news I would never forget. *Mum didn't make it.*

It was a Wednesday, of that I was sure. Wednesday nights were pizza night, and we would each make our own toppings and combinations for the pizza oven. Dad had won it as a raffle prize at work the previous year. Jake and I loved making our creations, and so the tradition ensued. The proofed dough was waiting on the kitchen counter. Mum was on her way home from work, a ten-minute journey she had done a thousand times. Except for that particular time, on that Wednesday evening, a man travelling too fast in a black BMW was also making a similar journey. And as he rounded a corner, his car drifted onto the wrong side of the road, colliding into Mum's little Polo and crashing abruptly into all our lives.

"She would be so proud of you, you know," Dad said, bringing me swiftly back to the present.

I sighed, unsure of what to say. My mind had replayed the memories so many times I wasn't sure what was real or what was a figment of my imagination. Guilt panged my stomach.

"She would. The way that you are so true to your authentic self. She would be so proud." He hugged me suddenly, knocking the air out of my lungs. "And I am too." He sniffed into my ear. "So proud of you both. I'm so sorry that she can't see you two all grown up."

"At least we have you."

He sniffed loudly. "And if I ever let you kids down at all, with the cooking and—"

"Dad. Stop it. You are more than enough."

"You're gonna make me bawl like a baby. Look at me." He dabbed the back of his hand beneath his eyes, smudging the tears across his cheeks. "I don't know why I'm so emotional today. You'd think it was my time of the month."

He placed the picture back into the box and reached for the tea that he had placed on the hearth.

"Dad."

"Uh-huh."

"Do you think you'll ever drive again?"

His eyes snapped up to mine. "I, um, I don't think so, no."

"I think you should."

"What? Why?"

"I think it's time. Mum would want you to."

He sat on this thought for a moment and then took a long sip of his tea. "We'll see, honey."

That meant no.

"Dad, you're getting too old to be taking the bus."

"I'm not too old!" He waggled his eyebrows. "I've still got the best of my prime on the horizon. I was just thinking the other day I should pack in nursing and pursue a career in modelling."

I snorted, and he grinned, pleased to have made me laugh.

"I still think it's a good idea."

"We'll see, honey. We'll see."

★

With the promise that I would be home for tea, I set off walking to Emma's house. I took the route through the Mayor's Gardens, feeling brave and emotionally evolved. The Gardens had been tainted since that day five years ago in April I saw Tamara with Tyler. Hurt had been planted in the bedding with the Alstroemerias, and pain had rained onto the rose bushes, casting a mist of sadness I had tried for many years to avoid. After seeing Tamara last year, despite our differences and misunderstandings, a part of that had healed.

We had stayed in contact since that night at the beach house. After she explained to me that she and Kelly were on very casual terms, whether I believed her or not, a calm indifference had possessed me. I was angry that she hadn't told me about the girl, but then, also, it didn't really *matter* to me. It dawned on me that Tamara probably wasn't my soulmate, if such a thing existed. We agreed to stay in touch, which surprisingly we had—a few messages and updates as life would allow. The invisible tie that rooted in our hearts in our first meeting that autumn had been cut, allowing us to roam freer, in search of whatever it was we were searching for. I felt lighter than I had in years. I bounced through the gardens, taking in every flower and every person who was enjoying the serenity—and I was warm. I was full.

I crossed under the arches, leaving the Gardens, and down over the road that led to Emma's flat. Her white Mini was parked outside, sparkling clean and immaculate. I swung open the gate, still paint-chipped, and side-stepped her potted plants that were no longer plants but just pots. I gave three sharp knocks on the door. She answered quickly, her hair pinned up messily in a bun, dyed pink and blue.

"Oh my God, your hair!" I screamed excitedly as she pulled me into a hug. Her perfume filled my nose, and I hugged her tighter.

"What about *your* hair? Miss Bob." She bounced one of my tufts.

"It's nothing compared to yours! It looks so great!"

Emma turned, modelling it. "You really like?"

"Uh-huh!"

She beamed, escorting me inside. I placed my boots by the door and hung my jacket on the hanger before I noticed all the boxes on the floor.

"What're you... Are you moving?" I asked uncertainly.

"Yeah. I'm moving back here." She scratched the back of her neck. "Permanently."

"How come? Is everything okay?" I fussed, studying her face for any cracks in her poise.

"Yeah. It's great." She paused. "Do you want a drink?"

"Sure." I manoeuvred around the boxes to get to the kitchen. "What's Petey doing?"

"A twenty-year-old. A couple of them, actually." She spoke the words so casually it took me a moment to understand the content.

"*What?*" I exclaimed, anger erupting in my gut. "Emma, I'm so sorry... Why didn't you say? You should've told me." My voice was loud. "I'll go get that son of a bitch—"

"It's all right. I'm good." She smiled at me warmly. "I was suspecting for years, and I was right. I should've known. Hot chocolate?"

"Erm. Sure." Emma turned her back to me so she could mix the powder into the mugs and boil the kettle. My eyes narrowed, my heart hammering hard in my chest. "How are you so...okay with this?"

"I've known for years, Sam. I've just been too scared to find out the truth."

"But. You guys are married."

"Not for much longer."

"You're getting divorced?"

"Uh-huh."

She poured the boiled water into the two Christmas mugs and stirred them gently before handing one to me.

“Really. You don’t have to look at me like that. This is good for me.” She sat on the white leather sofa, and I joined her.

“I don’t understand.”

She blew into her mug and then looked me in the eye, her green irises glowing. “I finally get my independence back. I can do what I want and be with somebody who actually gives me some attention instead of wasting every minute of every damn day in that bar!” She shook her head. “All the sacrifices I made for him. Then I get my big break, and *he* can’t handle it. Starts sleeping with some singer-songwriter he wants to play at the bar. Like are you *fucking* kidding me?”

“Hey,” I said gently. She looked at me, her eyes welling with tears. “You deserve better.”

She nodded, tears spilling down her cheeks. “I know. I know I do. I just feel like such a fool.”

“What did you say to me when Tamara cheated?”

She sniffed. “That she was the stupid one. It wasn’t your fault.”

“Exactly. Don’t cry. Here.” I leaned back into the sofa, putting my arm around her. She rested her head on me, her chest heaving with big sobs. It had been a long time since I had held someone so close. I missed it. I held her tightly, breathing in the smell of her coconut shampoo until her cries subsided. Emma sat up, pulling me with her.

“This is a good thing.”

“Totally. You can do anything you want.”

“I want to open a business.”

“Really? Yeah, what kind?”

"A café. With music and art. Somewhere people can go to…gather inspiration." She smiled at me.

"That sounds great."

"We should do it together." Her eyes lit up. "We could combine my music and your art and—you said you wanted to move back here, right? Move in here with me? I've got the room. It would be great!"

"Wow. I…erm. It sounds so great, but—"

"I scared you, didn't I?"

I laughed. "A little, yeah." She joined in.

"Sorry. I got a bit carried away. So much opportunity now I don't know what to do with myself." All sadness melted away from her face. "Seriously, though, the offer still stands."

I looked around the room. Could I see myself living here? It would be great to live so close to the Mayor's Gardens…and to Dad. What about my job? And Ellie?

"You'd have your privacy, I promise," Emma continued. "And I'll stop crying soon, and then we'll have a much more fun time."

"Tell me more about this café."

"Well. I know all the ins and outs about business 'cause I've run the bar for the last five years for that lazy bastard. So, you don't have to worry about that." Her mouth ran away with the words. "You can design the whole space, and we could have different themes and have different exhibitions for artists and sell their pieces, so it's like a gallery, but it's also a café and a safe space!" She spoke so fast it was hard to keep up with her.

"What about the band?"

She paused, her lips pursed in thought. "I love the band. You know that." She sipped her drink, her eyes flickering from me to the mug. "But the whole tour life isn't for me. It was a fantastic experience—don't get me wrong—and I'm super grateful...but I'm a home girl at heart." She beamed at me, her green eyes a little red from the tears.

A silence settled between us as the idea consumed me. Emma bounced her leg in anticipation.

"What do you think?" she asked.

"I can't lie. It sounds amazing."

"Yes!" She grabbed me and kissed me on the cheek. "It will be amazing! I can feel it."

"I need to talk to Ellie though."

"Of course." She squeezed me. "Sam, it's gonna be a dream!"

My stomach tingled at the thought. Excitement flittered up and down my nerve endings, making me twitchy like Emma was. "You know. I think you're right."

My phone vibrated in my pocket. I pulled it out. I had three missed calls from Ellie. It jumped to life again in my hands, and I answered it.

"Sam? Oh my God, you answered! *Oh my God*!"

"Ellie? What's up? Are you okay?"

Emma's eyes widened at the concern in my voice; her twitching leg ceased and rested still.

"Oh my God. Sam. Fuck. Fuck. Oh my God."

"What is it? Do you need me to come home? What's wrong?" I stood and moved towards the fireplace, nerves and worry itching at me.

“I don’t know. Fuck. I just don’t know.”

“Ellie. Talk to me. What is it?”

“Fuck. Fuck. Fuck. Fuck. Fuck.”

“Ellie. What’s happened?”

She was quiet at the other end. And then spoke in a very small voice, “I’m pregnant.”

Chapter Twenty-Five

2021

"And that's why it's so important to keep your bits clean," she announced. "My Gerald's was immaculate. Every day as clean as a whistle."

"Uh-huh." Jake swallowed, his teeth gritted together. He looked away from Mrs Hairy Mole, who had wandered over to our table fifteen minutes ago for more delightful wedding conversation.

"I had to show him of course. The man was clueless." She looked around the group before continuing. Ellie shot me a look. Her mouth twitched up, threatening to burst into laughter. "The foreskin goes much farther back than you think. It's important to really get in the nooks and crannies. Don't be afraid, son."

Jake looked horrified as the woman placed her wrinkled hand on his shoulder. He took a step back, and she shrugged it off.

"Some men get so sensitive when we talk about their bits, not like they haven't been speaking of ours for years."

"I need a drink," Jake said.

Mrs Hairy Mole watched him as he left the group, shaking her head in disappointment. "It clearly must've been a shock to him. Bet he's going to give himself a good clean in one of the cubicles."

"Mama, there you are. I wondered where you'd gone." A woman appeared from behind dressed in a smart black pantsuit. Her forehead creased when she noticed the look on our faces. "Mama. What are you talking about?" She had a slight accent, but I couldn't identify it.

"Your father. And the importance of maintaining the private parts."

"Mama! You cannot talk about this to strangers!" The woman looked to be in her mid-thirties and had purple-rimmed glasses that sat too far down the bridge of her nose. "I've told you about this. It's inappropriate!" She tugged on her mother's arm, who was offended by the gesture.

"Celeste! I am not an ignoramus. Your father would agree with me if he were here. God rest his soul."

Celeste shook her head in disbelief, her hand still clutching her mother's. "Mama. You are scaring these poor people." She glanced to Ellie and then to me. I looked down into my glass. "Come on," she urged.

Mrs Hairy Mole held her hands up in a sigh. Each finger was decorated with rings that bulged over her plump digits. "It appears I am an embarrassment to my daughter. Please excuse me."

They both left our table, arguing until they disappeared through the double doors and out of sight.

Ellie sat down and rested her head against the table. "Jesus Christ," she muttered into the cloth. "That woman...is something else."

I sat next to her, watching the door after they left and hoping to see someone else walk in. I was feeling homesick. It was probably a mixture of emotions. That, and the topic of our last conversation.

"I think she's scarred Jake for life."

"Well. Can't say we didn't warn him earlier," Ellie said. With a sigh, she lifted her head from the table. "She's coming back. She's coming back!" She scrambled to her feet and ran onto the crowded dance floor, leaving me alone and unguarded.

I held my eyes on the DJ booth, hoping she would walk on past to the next table of unsuspecting guests. Instead, she moved into my eyeline, forcing my attention onto her pale complexion.

"I would like to apologise for my mama. She does not have any boundaries when it comes to inappropriate topics." Celeste towered above me, frown lines etched deep beside the corners of her mouth.

"It's okay. Don't worry about it."

"Do you mind?" She gestured to the empty seat beside me and, when I nodded, sat down. "She drives me crazy. I told Tamara it was a bad idea to invite her. But what can I say?" She shrugged. "The woman loves her. Thinks she's *hilarious*. But for me, no. It is worse than babysitting." Celeste moved her straight black hair behind her ears. I noticed how tiny they were, with little pointed tips and a small diamond stud in each lobe.

"How do you know Tamara?" I asked.

"We work together."

I nodded, pretending I knew anything about what she was talking about. "What is it that you do?"

She peered at me from behind her purple rims as though I had asked a peculiar question. “I help her scout out the properties for development. Do all the legal documents and such.” She glanced behind her, uninterested in the conversation or worried about the return of her mother. “And you? How do you know her?”

“I knew her a long time ago.” I hesitated, unnerved by her beady eyes. “I’m her ex-girlfriend.”

“Ah, really?” The surprise caught in her voice. Her little eyes perked up behind her glasses as she scouted me. “I would have never thought.”

“That’s funny. Your mother said the same thing.”

“Mama...she does not understand these things. But she loves to talk. And she loves Tamara.” Her eyes moved over the room before flicking back to me. “Interesting that you are here. I’m not sure I would attend my ex-boyfriend’s wedding.” She shrugged. “Though, of course, he is a pig.”

I smiled politely in agreement, unsure of what to say. Pretending to have some knowledge of Celeste and her dating history, like we were old friends of sorts.

“Well. It was a long time ago. A lot has changed since then.”

“I see. Interesting. It is a nice thing, I’m sure.”

A loud cackle erupted from behind us, and Celeste jumped to her feet, muttering something in another language.

“This night will never end. I told her to stop drinking, but there she is again. Excuse me.” She scurried towards a group of guests where her mother had gathered. Mrs

Hairy Mole spotted her, and they both sauntered towards the doors in another heated argument.

My phone vibrated on my seat, and I pulled up the latest message.

I'm setting off now, be there soon. Love you x

I smiled into the screen, typed a quick reply, and put my phone back on the seat. I turned towards the back wall, eager for the doors to swing open and to see her walk in, my heart full and my body craving her greedily. Instead, Celeste and her mother were quarrelling over an empty wine glass, pulling and pushing each other beside the doors.

Chapter Twenty-Six

2016

I waved goodbye to Mr Gablehouse and locked the door shut behind him, pulling the cream blinds shut. Since we opened last week, he had been in every day for a black coffee and one of Emma's homemade scones. I picked up my tray, collected the last of the dirty cups and plates, and placed them in the dishwasher behind the counter. After I wiped the cream countertops clean, I leaned back, admiring the artwork on the back wall. Last Saturday, with Emma's assistance, I had painted a big colourful mural to brighten up the white walls. Taking inspiration from the Gardens, I painted perennials, poppies, and sunflowers snaking up to the ceiling. Dotted throughout the flowers was a variety of animals: squirrels, birds, a small fox, and a dog hiding behind the rosebush.

I heard footsteps down the stairs. Emma appeared, a white apron tied around her waist. "Stroking your own ego?"

"Shut up."

"I don't blame you," she said, following my gaze. "It's brilliant."

"When are the Smyth pieces coming in?" I asked, judging the blank walls beside the staircase.

"On Friday, I think."

"Good. You all set for tomorrow?"

"I believe so." She switched off the lights upstairs. "Nervous though. You turned the coffee machine off?"

"Yeah. Don't be nervous—you're brilliant. Can you grab my jacket?"

"Sure. Catch." She tossed my black suede raincoat from the hanger, and it landed on the counter with a thud.

"You throw like such a girl."

"If you mean that in a negative way, then you're just insulting yourself." Emma zipped her cream coat up to the top and pulled the faux fur hood over her head.

"Fine. You throw like my grandma."

"Shut up. I'll do the alarm. You grab the keys."

I waited outside the door as she set the alarm, the quiet road dimly lit by the streetlights. The September chill was upon us, chasing away the last of the summer's warmth. We'd had a hot summer, the warmest in years. Emma and I hadn't been able to take advantage of it much because we were so busy with preparing The Hideout for opening. It still hadn't sunk in.

The steady beeps sounded from the box, and Emma dashed outside, catching a heel on the step. "Woah! I'm so paranoid that I won't make it in time."

"You have a whole minute to get out," I said, turning the key in the lock. "You could probably grab another cuppa on your way out the door."

"I fancy something a bit stronger tonight. It's been a long day."

"A busy one." I pulled the shutter down, double-checked the locks, and then linked my arm through Emma's. The night was clear, and white stars shone out in the distant sky. A chill grew up my spine, and Emma rubbed my arm in an effort to warm me.

"You wanna swap coats?"

"Nah, it's not far. Plus, I don't think I can pull off the fur look."

"You're probably right."

We waited at the red light to cross the street, even though no cars were coming.

"It feels later than it is, doesn't it?" Emma whispered into the air. "Like midnight and we're breaking curfew."

"Feeling reckless?"

"Might bring out the tequila bottle."

"Don't you dare."

"Why not?"

"Emma Carlton, if I didn't know any better, I would think you were trying to get me drunk."

The green man lit up, and we cut across the road. A cat joined us and then scuttered over a wall into a garden.

"You are a very amusing drunk. Pukey."

I shook my head, and Emma laughed, the sound echoing out into the air. "I'm never gonna live that down, am I?"

"Probably not." Her green eyes met mine, and she smiled, her face full of mischievousness.

“You have an unfair advantage though.”

“How so?”

“You worked in a bar for years, so you can handle your liquor way better than me.”

“True. True. But I don’t know many people who handle it worse than you.” Emma misplaced a heel on the pavement, and I caught her as she stumbled.

“Least I can walk properly,” I muttered. “Next time I’ll let you fall.”

“You wouldn’t,” she teased, prodding me in the ribs.

“Maybe.”

We turned the corner, pushed through the freshly painted gate, and went inside. I hung my jacket on the hanger, glancing at the framed drawing I had given Emma for her birthday a few years ago. I remembered posting it from my old flat in London, a sketch I had done one evening on the tube home from work. An elderly woman wearing black dungarees and a straw hat nursed a guitar and sang softly as we moved from station to station. She had initially reminded me of Emma, a much older version, with less style and more wrinkles, though I hadn’t told her this until I moved in last year. We had named her Susan, and she had become something of a good luck charm.

“You want one?” Emma asked, holding up a bottle of gin in one hand, an empty glass in the other.

“Yeah, go on, then.”

I lit the fire and lay back on the sofa, feeling the ache in my feet ascend through my body. Emma joined me after inspecting the fire, pulling a grey wool blanket over the two of us. My feet rested across her lap, and she handed me my glass, the ice cubes clinking together.

"You're getting the hang of the fire. Finally." She rested her warm hands on my feet.

"It's tricky. It was never explained to me properly, I think that's what it is."

"A poor workman blames his tools," she teased.

"I'm not blaming my tools—I'm blaming you." I nudged her with my toe, and she flicked it away. The blue and pink of her hair was fading, blending together into a fused lilac colour. She brushed the stray hairs out of her face, and She watched her lips move as she spoke.

"You're hard to teach. You get so easily distracted."

I gulped my drink. The gin was strong and overpowering. I peered at her, drinking her own mix, and wondered if she had done that on purpose. Her hands caressed my feet slowly.

"You can hardly blame me for that," I said.

"Why?"

"You're very distracting."

A pause. "You think?" Her hands briefly stopped on my feet. My heartbeat pulsed as her eyes locked with mine. Suddenly, I was hot. Warmth spread up my neck and to my face. I wished it away.

"You're blushing," Emma commented, a soft smile playing on her lips. I was drawn to them, her perfect pink bow-lips, and my mind wandered to places it shouldn't. Emma's body underneath her clothes, her large round breasts that I had caught a glimpse of when she was in the shower. It was an innocent accident, easily done by roommates who shared a bathroom, but the door was left unlocked, and Emma didn't seem surprised when I had walked in.

Emma's hand moved to my calf, her fingers rubbing in small circular motions. Her green eyes studied my face, which was reddening at a fast rate. My eyes flickered to hers. Serious and sultry in a way I hadn't seen before. Her hand moved to my inner thigh, and I gasped, both of us laughing the potential awkwardness away.

"Is this okay?" she asked, inching her hand farther up my leg.

"Yeah." My heart hammered in my chest, watching her fingers make circles on the inside of my jeans. My stomach tightened as she inched closer, her eyes pinned to my lips. I licked them self-consciously.

"I've been thinking about you a lot," she said softly. "In different ways."

"Like what?" I asked, my breathing shallow.

"Like us. Together." She finished her drink and set it on the glass coffee table. Her other hand never left my thigh. Her fingers drummed near my crotch, sending pulses through me.

"Like together-together?"

"Uh-huh." She watched me closely, her fingers pressing harder against me.

"You think that's a good idea?" My voice was low as I inched closer to her, her lips parting slightly.

"I think so."

"Yeah?" My voice was more of a whisper. My stomach ached as I thought about her naked and underneath me. I leaned into her, feeling her sweet gin-tainted breath on my face. I moved closer, just the sound of the two of us breathing, loud and rasped. I swallowed loudly, and we both laughed, a short exhale of breath that was quickly forgotten. I pulled her to me, our lips finally touching and melting into a kiss. She pushed me down on the sofa, kissing me hard. Her lips were pillowy and soft as she moved from my lips to my neck and back to my mouth. I tugged her T-shirt off over her head, teasing her first with the flick of my tongue. Emma kissed me harder, her breasts pressing against me.

"This is crazy," I groaned into her mouth. "Is this a good idea?"

"Do you want me to stop?" Emma pulled back, leaving my lips empty.

"God, no." I kissed her again, feeling the tension build in my trousers. As if reading my mind, Emma popped open the buttons to my jeans and slid down my zipper.

"I want you," she breathed onto my neck.

I unclipped her bra and threw it across the room. I caressed her pink nipples in my mouth. I flipped her onto her back and slipped off her trousers, taking in her skimpy black underwear. Had she been planning this all along? Her eyes pinned mine, filled with desire and longing. Something I hadn't seen in Emma before. This was crazy. But a brilliant kind of crazy.

I kissed her hard and moved my hands slowly, taking my time, teasing up her legs and across her pants. She whimpered softly as I tucked my hands inside, moving slow and feeling her grind against my movement. I pinned one of her legs on my shoulder—she was surprisingly flexible—and moved my fingers deep inside her. Her back arched, and she released a deep moan, making my insides throb.

"You're so wet," I whispered into her ear, feeling her push herself into me more.

Her eyes locked onto mine, big and full and begging me to satisfy her urge. She ground against me, her eyes burning into mine, my stomach tightening at the sensation on my fingers. Emma and Me. Fucking.

I kissed her again. My insides doing flips. Her soft mouth encouraging me with every movement. My mouth explored all of her. Her shoulders, her breasts, her stomach. I could feel her tightening around me, a feeling I could have never imagined being so sexy. Her legs jiggled with the tension, begging for the big release. I obeyed, applying my complete concentration to the woman underneath me, watching her mouth shape into an *O* and pushing harder, her eyes rolling into her head in pleasure. A noise escaped her mouth, a soft squeal that was equal parts sexy and cute, her legs shuddering around me as I kissed her, feeling her body roll in ecstasy.

"Fuck," Emma said, quiet and breathless.

"I can't believe it."

She turned to me and kissed me, her tongue teasing mine. "I can't believe it either. After all this time."

"What do you mean?" I cupped her right breast, rolling her nipple between my fingers.

"Us. Me and you. Just something of daydreams and now this."

"You daydream about me?"

Her face turned away, embarrassed at what she had said.

"You do?" I planted a kiss on her delicate neck. "How long for?" I traced the spatter of small brown moles with my lips.

"That's a secret."

"You can tell me."

"No, there are other things that require my attention first." I jumped as she rose quickly to her knees and directed my arms above my head as she pulled off my jeans. "And I've thought about doing these things to you for a long time." My breath caught in my lungs, my heart racing along with the pulse in my pants. Emma watched me closely as she ran a painted nail up the inside of my thigh and made circles on the front of my underwear. "Do you want to know what they are?" she asked softly, the fire covering her in a beautiful orange glow.

I nodded, my legs twitching in anticipation. My lips craving hers once more.

"Okay, then. No more questions." She smiled. "For now." A sexy and sultry gesture that made me ache. In one movement she rolled down my underwear and replaced it with her hot mouth. I pushed into her tongue, her hands exploring my body. My mind spotting white and my legs tingling all over. Her fingers teased me, leading into me, gentle at first and then faster, bringing me closer and closer to the white mountains. Her eyes followed mine with an intensity that grabbed my gut. The way she watched me. The desire and focus, so sexy and poised, the moment so whole in a way that confused me and also made complete sense. My emotions joined together in a peak, forcing a moan from my throat as my body filled with light. The white mountains carried my body, the momentous heaves of my breath filling the fog.

The room was different. The whole world had propelled forward on its axis now that Emma's body lay naked on mine. Our hearts beat hard and triumphantly as they fell together in rhythm, and we watched the fire crackle and then fade out into the dark.

★

I woke to a gentle pressure on my lower back. Soft and slow circles, clockwise and then anticlockwise. My eyes opened to the blinding white walls as the morning sun-light streaked through the partially open blinds. I wasn't in my room. Or my bed.

I rolled over. Emma smiled, and my stomach tight-ened, the events of the night before flashing back to me. She reached over to her bedside table and passed me a steaming cup of tea in a Christmas mug. Her dainty pink lace top and shorts combo matched her pale complexion perfectly. I immediately pictured her body underneath it and accepted the mug enthusiastically as something to distract myself with.

"You're extremely cute when you sleep," Emma said. "You talk as well."

"Do I?" I propped myself back against the purple headboard, trying to gather my morning scatterbrain.

"Yeah. Something about pasta and your dad?"

I sipped at my tea. It was still too hot. "He was prob-ably burning the dinner or something."

"So." She paused. "How're you feeling this morning?" She was a little reserved, worried almost.

"I'm good." I smiled, trying to reassure her. "Last night was amazing."

"It was, wasn't it? I still don't fully believe it. When I saw you next to me this morning, I thought I must still be asleep."

"I didn't know where I was at first."

She laughed, and it made me want to kiss her. She was so cute. Even first thing in the morning. Even with no makeup and bed hair. She was beautiful.

"What?" she asked, seeing me staring.

"Nothing," I said, blowing into the steamy mug. "What time is it?"

"Six forty-five. We have to get ready soon. As much as I would love to sack it all off and stay in bed with you all day...we have a business to run." She leaned in to kiss me on the cheek, and I turned, catching her lips. This seemed to surprise her, but she kissed me back, tasting of mint.

"Have you brushed your teeth already?" I asked.

She giggled. "I didn't want to have bad morning breath. Like yours."

"Do I?"

"No, I'm only kidding." She laughed. "Ah, you're so sweet. Look how worried you are." She squeezed my arm and turned back to her mug. "I think this is ready to drink now."

★

We got ready for work in our separate rooms, which was normal for us, but after last night, it felt wrong. It was a small ache in my gut like I missed her, which was absurd, as she was only a few walls away. I spent longer picking out my outfit, even though I knew it would be mostly covered by the apron anyway, and settled on a light-blue shirt and my work jeans. I waited for her by the door, peering out of the window into the musky morning. She appeared a minute later, also wearing a similar light-blue shirt.

"One night together and now we're like twins. The lesbian stereotype is real," I said.

"Shut up."

Before I could say anything more, she kissed me, pressing me up against the big wooden door. Her hands gripped my waist firmly, the smell of her perfume inhabiting my senses. She pulled away and grabbed her coat off the hanger in a swift movement.

"Ready, hot stuff?"

We walked to work the same route we did every day, but we were different. I felt it in every step, the clunk of my boots and Emma's small heels, the synchronicity of our movements, the rising and falling of our breath into the damp air. Every touch of her body on mine sent ripples of messages to my brain, flaring up my senses and my nervous system. Alarm bells rang in my head, but I didn't want to listen. My heart flinched as my brain prodded at old wounds, trying to initiate the guard system, trying to shut the trespasser out.

Emma was lighter. She bounced with each step, her lilac hair down and blowing gently in the wind. I felt safe with her. I pushed away the negative thoughts and listened to her voice.

"Are you surprised?" she asked. "That I like you?"

My breath caught in my throat. "Erm, I had a few inklings... The shower. Trying to get me drunk."

She laughed. "God, yeah...the shower. In my defence, I had no idea what you were thinking. I wasn't sure if it was all in my head. 'Cause you've always been a bit of a flirt."

I pulled my hood up over my head, the cold dewy air dampening my hair. "Really?"

"Yeah. I was like, does she mean to say those things, or is she just used to it? So, I thought I'd send you a little hint."

"You call that a little hint? You might as well have draped a giant banner across the flat saying *come and look at me naked.*"

"Well. You did. And it worked so...go me."

I shook my head. "You should've just said."

"I was so scared. 'Cause with living together and the business, it could've just gone tits up."

"What changed your mind, then?"

"Yesterday. When you said I was distracting...and you blushed. You only blush when you're thinking with your lady bits."

"Fuck off, that's so not true!" I nudged her arm as we walked. "And please, please, don't call them *lady bits.*"

"All right, I won't. But it's true."

The Hideout looked eerie in the morning fog. We rolled up the shutters and unlocked the door. I disabled the alarm, and Emma took off her coat. She shivered as she shrugged out of her sleeves.

"It's cold in here, isn't it? I'll put the heating on."

I snuggled into my coat against the counter, thinking of the day to come. We were open for business until the afternoon. Then we were having our first music night, and Emma was going to perform, along with a few guest appearances. I sighed, feeling tired, and dragged myself behind the counter to switch on the drink machines. They buzzed to life, eager to start the day with a happy hum. I pulled out two big white mugs with small red foxes on them. The crockery set we picked out had an assortment of wildlife on them, from birds to squirrels and dogs and foxes. They matched the theme well.

"Coffee or tea this morning?" I called to Emma. She was turning on the fairy lights upstairs, bringing the room to life with each flick of the switch.

"Coffee today, please." She descended the spiral staircase, one hand holding the oak banister. I thought of her hands on me yesterday, making soft slow circles. I concentrated on the cups, adding an extra lump of sugar in my tea to wake me up. Emma flipped the sign over in the window and pulled on an apron. She tied it neatly behind her back in a knot. She glided over and inspected the cups, a smile spreading across her face.

"Here. It's all tangled." She unravelled my makeshift knot, the ends of my apron hanging loosely by my side. Her hands grabbed my waist as she pulled it tight, her breath tickling my neck. In a quick movement, she wrapped it neatly in a bow and folded her arms around my front, her neck resting on my shoulder.

"Thank you." I handed her the mug of fresh coffee, the steam pillowing upwards like a train. "Think it'll be busy today?"

Emma shrugged her delicate shoulders. "I'm not sure. We might be tonight. There were a lot of invites. Just depends who turns up, I guess."

"Dad is coming. Jake too. Think he's bringing his girlfriend."

She nodded. "A few of them from the bar are coming. Is Tamara?"

"No. She's still in Manchester."

A small smile crept onto her face. "Good."

I was thankful too. That could have been a whole lot of awkward. "Are you nervous about tonight?"

She thought about it, finally answering, "No."

"How come?"

"I think I was more nervous about all this with you." She reached out and touched my waist. "I don't feel nervous about tonight anymore."

"Good. You needn't be."

She glanced at my lips, and I thought she was going to kiss me. I was disappointed when she didn't.

"You know last night?" I asked sheepishly.

"Yeah?" Emma rested back against the wooden counter.

"Was I your first? You know...with a woman?"

She raised her eyebrows, blonde and pixie-like. Her features softened. "No. You weren't. I had a girlfriend when I was at university, back in Leeds."

"How come you never spoke about it?"

"I don't know. It's just the past. It's not really relevant anymore." She glanced out of the window at a passer-by. "Petey never liked talking about exes, and I don't know. It's private."

"But I'm your best friend—I'm your, you know, thingy."

She smiled. "You are my *thingy*, yeah. I hope so."

I cringed at myself, embarrassed for feeling so jealous. "So, you've always liked women too?"

Emma took a deep breath in like she was weighing up how to answer the question. “To be honest, I don’t like labels. I just fall for people. I’m happy to be with anyone I have a great connection with regardless of any gender.”

“I can’t believe you never mentioned this.”

“Well.” She took a swig of her coffee. “You never asked.”

The bell jingled as two elderly women poked their heads in through the door. They were sharing a black-and-white polka dot umbrella that spattered raindrops on the floor as they bustled through and wiped their boots on the welcome mat.

“Good morning, ladies,” Emma chimed, jumping up from the counter. “What can I get you?”

★

I rinsed the dishcloth in the sink, squeezed it dry, and threw it in the wash pile. The day had passed quickly, and before I knew it, we were closing to get ready for the evening do. We had a steady flow of customers, mainly elderly couples or mums with their babies. It was enough to keep us busy, stealing glances and touches with Emma whenever I could. She had left early to go get ready and prepare Harrison the guitar for his Hideout debut. I breathed a sigh of relief once I finished the cleaning, moving the Hoover into the cupboard and stuffing it in, refusing to wind up the wire. Emma tidied it away perfectly usually. It just seemed like a waste of time to me, undoing it all again the next day and having to suffer the same repetitive motion.

A loud knock on the door made me jump. The handle moved up and down, but I had already locked myself inside.

"We're closed!" I called from the cupboard, picking up the mop that I had knocked over with my elbow.

The door rattled again, and I went to investigate, finding a figure leaning on the glass and peering through the window.

"Let me in. I have a child." The figure took down their hood. "It's freezing!" Ellie said, her voice muffled through the glass.

I unlocked the door, and she scurried inside, pushing Jasper in the pram. He was in a blue all-in-one shell suit, his pink face slumped against a teddy as he slept.

"You're early," I said, giving her a quick hug. "How are you?"

"I'm good. Just wanted to get out of the house. Going a bit stir-crazy."

"How's he doing?" I nodded to Jasper, who grunted mid-dream.

"Good. He's good. It's me that's knackered!" Ellie collapsed in a faux-fur chair, rolling the pram beside her. "I haven't slept in three months. I haven't drunk in twelve. I miss wine, Sam. *Big time.*"

"When can you drink again?"

"Whenever I stop breastfeeding. Would be so much easier if Tom could do it for me."

"Where is he?"

"He's coming up in a bit."

I nodded. "You want a drink?"

"Double vodka Coke, please." She snorted, relaxing further into her chair. "Just an orange juice, if you don't mind."

I pulled one out of the fridge, poured it into a glass, and returned to her a moment later.

"The place looks so great." Ellie's eyes darted around the room. "I'm proud of you."

"I'm proud of you too. Look at us all grown up."

"I know. It's gross, isn't it?" She shook her head. "I can't believe I have a kid. Like I am responsible for another life. That's terrifying."

Instinctively, we turned to look at Jasper, still sleeping soundly. His dark hair stuck up in tufts across his head, and his red cheeks were plumper than the last time I had seen him. He had been born two weeks premature in June, weighing just shy of five pounds, and was so tiny. He had grown into his features over the last couple of months, inheriting Tom's strong face shape and Ellie's dark-brown eyes.

The door jingled behind us, and I cursed myself for forgetting to lock the door. Luckily, it was Emma, her face freshly painted in foundation and a silver eyeshadow. Her eyes met mine as she entered, my heartbeat rising slightly. She shrugged out of her coat to reveal a burgundy skater skirt and a black crop top. Her navel exposed her belly button piercing. My eyes wandered there for a second too long, flashbacks of the night before disrupting my vision. The way Emma had giggled when I had seen it for the first time. The added sexiness the jewellery had given the experience, with the way it moved against her naked body and mine.

"Hey, *Mummy*," Emma teased. "How are you coping?"

"Hey. I'm good. Tired but good." The two of them hugged, and my eyes were drawn to Emma's piercing again. Ellie watched me over Emma's shoulder, and I looked away.

"Excited for tonight?" Ellie asked, her gaze darting between us.

"Yeah! It's a dream come true. People should be arriving soon. You want anything?"

Ellie lifted her glass in one hand. "All good, thanks. Can we have a sneak peek?"

"I just need to set the equipment up, won't take long."

Emma excused herself to the back of the room, where we had set up a chair and stand for the evening performers. She unpacked the amps and wires and started to assemble them.

"What is going on with you two?" Ellie hissed, her eyes lighting up with mischief.

"Nothing." I hesitated. "Why?"

"Oh my God. Something is going on. I can feel it."

Emma looked over as she untangled a wheel of red wires.

"Shut up. I don't know what you're talking about."

Her mouth hung open. "*Samantha*, I know when you're hiding something."

"Don't *Samantha* me."

Ellie rolled her eyes. "You really not gonna tell me?"

"Not right now," I hissed. "Woman, be cool!"

Ellie leaned back in her chair, satisfied with my answer. The room lit up as Emma switched on more white fairy lights. She plucked at her guitar strings perfectly, the sound echoing around the room.

"You hear that okay?" she called, her pick between her teeth.

★

Tom was the next to arrive with both his parents. Then Kipper and his guest, a young, impeccably dressed woman wearing shades, even though the weather outside was dreadful. Familiar acquaintances appeared from Blue Rooms' days at Petey's, followed by customers who had frequented the café this week in a whole array of ages from teens to elderly. Ellie's parents arrived with Dad, dressed in an old checked shirt I had bought him many moons ago for a birthday or a Christmas—I couldn't remember which.

Everyone muddled together cupping steaming mugs or glasses of juice, conversation humming throughout the room until Emma announced over the microphone for people to take a seat. I perched myself on the back counter, what I thought was the best seat in the house, as I could see perfectly clearly without being watched by others. Emma sat casually on the chair, Harrison hanging over her shoulder. She readjusted the guitar strap once more before she commanded the room.

"Hello, everyone! Thank you for coming. Can I just say, first of all, how great it is to see so many familiar faces, new and old, and I hope you feel very welcome here." Her eyes wandered around the guests, each of them watching her intently. "This whole experience has been a dream come true for me. Especially getting to work with so many talented local people. Treaton Vale is the place I call home because of all of you. You are the reason that this town is so special." The guests murmured in agreement, eyes darting about the room. "We have a brilliant line-up tonight... The Rodaye twins, the youngest cover group in Yorkshire and the best." She winked at the young girls sitting near the front. "Then the songwriting talents of Mr James Camwell, one of my favourite artists, who has been in the business, well, probably as long as I have, if not longer."

"You wish, you cheeky sod!" James called out from the right.

Emma laughed, shaking her head. "The wonderful Marlene Simpson is here." The crowd turned to the woman wearing shades at the back of the room, who waved a hand in greeting. Kipper nodded enthusiastically beside her, bringing his hands together in applause. "But first, I would like to play you a few songs." A cheer erupted from the front, and Emma smiled. "Thank you. I've had a rollercoaster journey with music, but it has always been a constant throughout my life." Emma's eyes lifted above the guests to rest on me, and a smile tugged at her lips. "I'd like to dedicate this one to Sam Atlas, who is not only my business partner, my bestest friend, but the most special person in my life, and I am so grateful that this crazy world has bound us together...because I would not know what to do without her."

The room erupted into cheers, led by Emma's applause, and everyone turned to face me. I shied away, waving the attention and noise away with my hand. Emma studied me the whole time, the biggest grin stretched across her face. The room settled into a comfortable silence, and Emma began to play.

The song started slow and soft, and I racked my brain to try to place it. I knew most of Emma's songs, had seen her perform on stage with Blue Rooms and listened to her practice in our living room hundreds of times. But this moment was so intimate, as if it was only me and her in the room. Emma's fingers plucked the strings as she swayed her head gently side to side, feeling the rhythm of the music. She smiled at the crowd, her eyes flickering to me, just as she opened her mouth to sing.

I spoon you into my tea each morning
A love that is hidden away
Now I feel the tide is turning
And we both want a taste

The redness flushed my cheeks, and I was sure that everyone looking at me. I tore my eyes away from Emma for a minute, but all the attention was on her.

Something is different
Can we follow the clues
I've been waiting my whole life for you

My stomach tightened; a strange tingling sensation captured my hands. Had she written this about me? Her eyes held mine. In the white glow from the fairy lights, she was angelic. The song picked up pace heading into the chorus, the strum of the guitar and Emma's hand becoming a blur across the strings. Her voice sounded out throughout the room, lifting high above all our heads, sending my hairs rippling over my body as they stood to attention. She closed her eyes as she belted the chorus.

Feels like I've been living blind
Till the Gods put us side by side
Listening out for a change of the tide
Watching you out of the corner of my eye

She brought the song to a close, the acoustics of the guitar bouncing through the room. Everyone watched her, captivated by her performance. The crowd stayed quiet until the last note hung in the air, slowly drifting out into silence. Then applause, hands meeting hands with great force, cheers and whoops and whistling. All of this sent my head into a spin, with my eyes on Emma and hers on mine. The smile on her face, and those bold eyes looking at me, was enough to bring me to my knees in front of the entire café. Luckily, the counter supported my weight, leaving just me and her, watching each other from across the room, as the crowd bellowed and boomed in applause around us.

Chapter Twenty-Seven

2021

I finished my drink, keeping a mindful eye on the dance floor as Tom, Jake, Lottie, and Jasper played keepy-uppy with a red balloon. It started just the four of them, and then, one by one, people joined in until the game took up most of the floor. The kids shrieked as they dived on the ground, giving everything they had to keep the balloon in the air. Jake was the same, covering his navy suit in dust from the floor.

"They're nuts, aren't they?" Ellie said, reapplying her pink lipstick.

"Yep." I checked my phone again. No new messages. I took another sip of my drink.

After the balloon game had died down, guests danced and sang along to the music. Tamara and April were making their way around the room, thanking people for coming and exchanging pleasantries. I wondered if April knew everything that had happened between Tamara and me. I hoped she didn't; it would be a breach of privacy between us. My memories of our relationship had a special place in my heart, and it would be a trespassing of sorts to go to those places and share those secrets with somebody else.

"How're you holding up?" Ellie asked, peering at me from behind her straw.

"Yeah, you know... I'm actually good." I watched as April accepted a gift from a couple, Tamara kissing them both on the cheek in thanks.

"Good?" Ellie smiled. "That's what I like to hear."

Tom flung Jasper onto his shoulders, both of them doing silly moves to the music. Lottie squeaked with joy, her laughter lifting above the sound, and she joined in, trying to copy their doing the robot.

"When do you think you'll get married?" I asked Ellie.

"Who knows? We practically already are, but yeah, it would be nice to have everyone together." She shrugged. "Something similar to this, maybe."

"You have to. You're the perfect couple."

"We're not," she scoffed. "We're really not. But we love each other. And if we've made it this far, I don't see anything coming between us." She nodded towards Jasper. "Look at the size of him now. I can't believe he came out of me!"

Jasper was dashing from one side of the dance floor to the other, trying to avoid the red and green lights from the DJ booth as they moved across in swift orchestrated movements. Middle-aged women waved their partners over from the safety of their tables to encourage them to join in the dancing.

"What about you?" Ellie asked, nudging me. "When we going to get me a bridesmaid dress?"

I laughed. "Not yet. But who knows?" I took a sip of my drink, forgetting the glass was empty.

"I can see it."

"Yeah?"

"Yeah." Her eyes flickered behind me. "Hey, Sam. Are you thirsty?"

"Huh?"

"Slush Puppy is here."

I whipped my head around to the door, where I spotted Emma scanning the room for familiar faces. She spotted me, her face stretching into a big smile, and my stomach tightened. Her half-blue, half-pink hair was pinned sexily above her head, the two colours complementing her grey ankle-length dress. It clung to her hips as she swayed over to us, her neckline sparkling as the chandelier's light reflected in her jewellery. I recognised the necklace as one I had bought her for our first anniversary.

"Hey!" Emma called as she came closer. She kissed me on the lips. Instantly, I was reminded of how much I had missed her. I pulled her back for another one. Her mouth was cold from being outside, but I didn't care. "You both look stunning," she said, looking us up and down.

"You don't look too bad yourself," Ellie replied.

"How's the wedding? Have I missed much?" she asked.

"Yeah. You've missed...everything." I laughed.

"God. I know. I'm sorry I was so long. Are you all right? Sorry I wasn't here for you."

"I'm good. I'm great, actually, now you're here." I kissed her again, tasting her strawberry-flavoured gloss.

"Get a room, you guys," Ellie murmured, sucking hard on her straw. "I need another drink."

"I'll get them. Vodka Coke?" She turned to Ellie.

"I'm impressed."

"And for you?"

"I'll come with. I missed you."

She giggled. Her green eyes, neatly painted with smoky eyeshadow, shimmered.

"You both make me sick."

"Shut up."

Ellie winked at me and then turned her attention to Tom and Jasper, who were starting a conga line.

Emma took my hand in hers, squeezing slightly, and led us away from the table and towards the bar.

"Are you all right?"

"Yes, I'm good! Stop worrying." I kissed her on the cheek.

"Have you spoken to Tamara?"

I thought of our shared cigarette outside. "A little bit."

"Did you smoke?"

I hesitated. "A little bit."

Emma laughed. "It's okay. I'll let you have that today."

"Thanks. It's been a weird day."

"I bet." We took our place in the queue, waving as the conga line went past us. I caught a glimpse of Tamara on the other side of the room.

"Oh, yeah!" I squeezed Emma's arm. "How did your meeting go?"

"Well..." We edged forward in the line, moving closer to the front. "I think it's time for some more *tequila*!" she said.

"Why? What happened? Did you get it?"

"We need something to toast with first."

"And your choice is still tequila? Babe, seriously."

She waggled her finger at me. "It's the only way. We're adults. We have to keep the tradition going." A sternness laced into her voice. I liked it.

"Baby!" I protested as she ordered ten shots of tequila from the bartender. "You're gonna be the death of me, I swear."

She laughed, a little belly roll from deep in her gut. "Don't be so dramatic. They're not all for you, Pukey. Here." She handed me a small tray with the glasses neatly lined up, the deadly liquid burning my nose as I sneaked a whiff. A small pot of salt and ten slices of lime rested in a glass bowl beside them. I carried them back to the table carefully, Emma guiding the way.

"No. No. No. No. No. No," Ellie uttered as we approached with the contents of the tray. "Shots? Guys? Really?"

"Time to get *fruity!*" I winked at her, and she shook her head in embarrassment.

"I knew that would come back and bite me in the ass. Tom! Jake! Get over here!"

Tom dashed over, detaching himself from a group of older women who had flocked around him.

"Baby, they're so not my type," he teased. "Don't worry."

"Whatever you say, Romeo. Here, surprise." Ellie handed him a shot glass, and his face fell.

"Shots? No, guys! What about the kids?"

"Your parents are here, so drink up. You'll be fine."

Jake strolled over from a nearby table. "Shots? Nice! I didn't think you guys had it in ya!" He reached for the salt pot. When he tried to sprinkle it over his hand, he spilled it on the floor.

Emma and I handed out the rest of the glasses, making sure everyone had a sufficient amount of salt and access to a lime wedge.

"So. Can we raise our glasses," she began, speaking in a slow and wonderstruck tone. "Because as of today, I am now in partnership with *the* Robert Kipper himself as a solo artist on his new film! Three of my songs! Three!"

We whooped and whistled, clinking our glasses together and drinking, flinching and then gipping in unison, all except for Jake.

"That's amazing, baby. You deserve it!" I kissed her, still feeling the burn of tequila inside my mouth.

"Three of my own songs. I can't believe it."

We swarmed around her, offering our congratulations and praises, trying to ignore the burns in our oesophagi.

"What are those ones for?" Jake asked, pointing at the next five shots staring back at us.

"To celebrate the wedding! Can't all be about me, can it?" Emma handed out the next glasses, and the group accepted them begrudgingly, all except for Jake.

"I don't know if I can handle another," I groaned.

"When did you get so old?" Jake said, nudging me with his elbow. "Don't be such a worry wuss."

"Shut up, you."

"To the happy couple!" Emma said.

"To the happy couple!" we chorused.

A few guests surrounding us also lifted a glass in a toast, laughing at us as we flinched once more against the sting of the alcohol.

"Trust you lot to be causing a scene," Tamara said, approaching the table, April's arm linked with her. "I told you they'd be the ones to watch." April smiled beside her. "Hey, Emma, glad you could make it."

"I'm sorry I'm so late! I had a meeting I couldn't miss. Congratulations to you both," Emma said, leaning forward and hugging the two of them. "You look stunning." Emma had a way of defusing what could be a very awkward situation and making it a normal event: *just a couple of exes with their new partners, no big deal.*

"Thank you. It's really nice to meet you," April said. She had a quiet and high-pitched voice that didn't seem to suit her.

Tamara glanced around the group, her eyes flickering from face to face and then lingering on mine. "Something to celebrate?"

"No, no," Emma said, shaking her head. 'It's your big day."

Tamara waved the statement away with the flick of her hand. "Come on, what is it?"

"Emma's got a contract with Kipper for his new film. She's got three of her songs on the soundtrack," Ellie commented.

An excited squeal came from Emma's mouth, and she squeezed Ellie's arm. "God, it sounds so insane when I hear it!"

"That's amazing. Congrats, Em," Tamara said, beaming at her. April's smile never faded from her face. I bet her cheeks were sore.

"Time to really get the celebrations started!" Jake declared, appearing from behind Tamara and April with another tray of shots. I didn't see him leave in the first place.

"Jake! You've got to be kidding me," I wailed.

He shook his head. "It would be rude not to. There's one for everyone. Here. Time for a great night!"

"He's in high spirits," Emma whispered to me. "Is he okay?"

"I think so, yeah. I have a lot to fill you in on."

"Three, two, one!" Jake led the countdown, his glass high in the air. "Cheers!"

"Cheers!"

Three shots in one night. I was gonna pay for that later. The image of the vomit-covered plant pot flashed into my mind, and I cringed at the memory.

A cool hand rested on my arm. "Do you have a minute?" Tamara said. "I'd like to talk to you."

I glanced at Emma, who had been ambushed by Lottie. She fussed over her while Lottie giggled, jumping up and down. "Yeah, sure. One second."

I glided over to Emma, who was balancing Lottie on her hip. They both smiled as I approached. "Aunty Sam, Emma is a princess too! See!" She pointed to the ribbon I stole for her this morning, now intertwined around Emma's bun.

"I'm a princess," Emma declared. "And you must obey my every command."

Lottie nodded, listening intently as Emma placed her back on the floor.

"You see your daddy?" Emma continued. "Tell him he dances like an old man."

Lottie galloped away, humming as she went.

Emma laughed. "I love winding him up." Her voice turned serious when she saw my face. "What's up?"

"Nothing. I'm just so proud of you and want you to know that."

"Thanks, baby. I couldn't do it without you."

I wrapped my arms around her, pulling her close to me and breathing her in. The sweet tang of her perfume and her cocoa body butter comforted me. She squeezed me tight, planting a kiss on my neck.

"Tamara wants to have a chat with me," I said, studying her face. "Are you all right with that?"

"Yeah, of course. You don't have to ask my permission," Emma said, a smile pulling at her lip. "Cute, though, for asking."

"I love you."

"I love you too. Don't look so worried."

"I'm not."

"Come find me when you're back 'cause I wanna dance with you."

"Sure."

I turned to find Tamara waiting by the door, leaning back on one leg, her arms crossed across her chest.

"You ready?" she said, not waiting for my response and pivoting. She strutted outside into the cool dark night, expecting me to follow her.

Chapter Twenty-Eight

2019

I eyed the small furry creature suspiciously from the driver's seat. How could I be scared of something so small? Two large eyes peered through the plastic bars, watching me with as much wariness as I was watching him. A small meow sounded from the cat's tiny throat, revealing an array of razor-sharp white teeth. A black paw clawed the door of the pet carrier, and I suddenly felt sorry for him.

"You'll be okay," I said, offering a finger of condolence through the gap in the bars. A wet sandpaper tongue scraped across the tip of my finger, and I pulled it away, confused by the sensation. Another meow filled the car, this time much louder.

"You'll be fine. Stop making so much racket." I turned the volume up slightly on the stereo. An upbeat pop song filtered through the speakers. "Katy Perry? You like her, do you, boy?"

The cat's mouth stretched wide in a yawn, showcasing again the ferocity of its incisors. I imagined the damage those teeth could do and cast the thought aside. I had to get used to the idea of having a cat—for Emma's sake.

"A cat?" Ellie had said the week before at The Hideout. "Why on earth are you getting a cat? You don't even like them."

"It's for Emma's birthday," I said, clearing away Ellie's empty mug. "And you can't say anything."

"I won't. I won't. But a cat? *Really*?"

"Why not? We can't get a dog because we're here all the time. And she had cats when she was younger, so I thought it would be nice."

"You *so* could have a dog!" she protested. "He could come to work with you. He'd love it. The smell of the scones...and the coffee. What more could a dog want?"

I paused for a second as I considered it. The wet cloth hung limp in my hand.

I thought of Emma sitting in her cream chair, legs swung over the arm, cradling Harrison the guitar as she played. The soft and sweet tone of her voice as she plucked the strings, singing "Killing Me Softly" to herself. Sometimes I would linger first in the hallway and listen to her sing. She would play for me when I asked, but something about these moments was pure and intimate, as though it wasn't meant for others to hear. The fire crackled and popped against the pluck of the strings, Emma's voice carrying the melody throughout the room as I tiptoed down the laminate flooring towards the living room. Her eyes would raise to meet mine, innocent and adorable as if she had just been someplace else and my presence had brought her swiftly to the present. *Hey, baby*, she would say. *I didn't see you there.*

I had always wanted a dog...but no, this was for Emma.

"You're too soft," Ellie had said. "Don't say I didn't tell you so when it scratches your eyes out in your sleep."

The Katy Perry song ended and went straight into adverts. A loud man gabbled nonsense from the speakers about some kind of life insurance, and I turned it over, trying to find a station with music. By the time I had flicked through a few, the cat started meowing again, making escape attempts with his little paws.

It was an hour's drive from Stockport, and the road back to Treaton Vale was long and wound up through the hillside. I had spotted the post about the litter of kittens online a few days before and contacted the seller, *puscatz4life,* immediately. Cats were more expensive than I had initially thought. I figured that a lot of the time people became cat mothers by accident. Contrary to the canine world, the cat would choose the owner, wandering into the garden, scratching and meowing at the door, and edging into their lives, one paw at a time. One day, you were feeding it the stray scraps from the Sunday roast, and the next, it was prodding you in the face at three in the morning, demanding belly rubs. I had considered getting a cat from a shelter, but I had no idea what to look for. Plus, the idea terrified me, and knowing my luck, I would pick the feline with natural scissor hands and a track record for using them on human skin.

The lady selling the kittens was nice enough. She lived in an end-terrace that mirrored many similar ones around Treaton Vale. I had driven past the property twice. The house number had fallen off, and nobody had bothered to replace it, instead propping it lazily on the window ledge, blocked from view by the large Range Rover on the driveway. She welcomed me in—*Lisa, just call me Lisa—*

offered me half a dozen beverages, all of which I politely declined, and then ushered me in to see the kittens. I didn't have time to take in much of the décor before being swept into the small dining room containing a makeshift cage made out of fireguards and some old leftover scraps of carpet. I recognised the pattern from the living room, and it surprised me that Lisa not only kept the horrific pattern that covered the living room into the hallway but assumedly chose it herself. The burgundy-and-green swirls were unpleasant to the eye, as was much of the inside. Rugs and sofas were scratched and clawed at, revealing the bare wood of the structure and the workmanship underneath. The sight of the furniture, chewed and diced, made me second-guess my birthday present for Emma. Our modern and clean apartment might not take kindly to the new guest, who could interpret everything in there as its own personal playground and litter tray. The image of a cat staring me dead in the eye as it squatted and pissed on Emma's guitar flashed across my eyelids. I blinked it away. I could not see any kittens inside the pen and was about to ask Lisa when something rubbed against the inside of my leg.

"That's Potter," Lisa said, her shrill voice piercing my ears. "I've called him that 'cause he has a little patch on his head like a scar, see?" She collected him from my feet and pointed out the white mark. "Of course, you don't have to call him that. I just give them all nicknames to try and keep them apart." She plonked the little black ball of fluff onto my chest and darted about the room, pointing out the other kittens that, like Potter, were scattered about, making the makeshift pen irrelevant. "This one is Percy, that one is Spot, this little devil is Bowie—look at his little lightning bolt across his back there..." Lisa's chipper voice buzzed around my ears as she pranced about the room, but I was focused on Potter, who lay casually across my chest. His big green eyes looked up at mine with curiosity and intrigue, reminding me somewhat of Emma's.

The road began to decline as we came over the moor, my finger still idly resting on the door of the cage. The clouds above opened up, and fog descended over the hillside, bringing with it showers of scattered rain. The kitten pressed his face against the bars, meowing at the rapid speed of the windscreen wipers as they moved from side to side. I stroked his furry face with my finger, keeping my eyes on the road ahead. He nuzzled into me, his small bony skull nudging me as he purred. We passed the sign for Glossop, rounding the bend past the steep cliff edge, and I thought of Jake. I considered stopping by for a quick cup of tea but immediately decided against it. The day was already going to be a tough one for the little cat, never mind introducing him to a troublesome one-year-old. I hoped that Jake was coping well enough and made a mental note to call him soon.

Jake had taken the news that he was about to enter fatherhood quite well. Aside from the first night, where I had received a call from Dad about Jake being so drunk that he had thrown up in the kitchen sink and all over the carpet. "Catherine can't see him like this," Dad said. "You've got to come and help me, Sam." I was asleep before I got the call, and Emma and I headed over in our pyjamas to put Jake to bed.

In the morning, I pulled him aside. He had no obvious signs of a hangover, apart from a soft blue bruise that ran under his chin where he must have fallen. "I'm fine," he said. "Stop mothering me."

I asked him about it on the day Lottie was born. We were in the hospital waiting room, giving the mother and baby some quiet time to sleep. The room was a bright illuminated white, with a handful of basic wooden chairs lined up in three rows. A small TV hung in the corner, and a game show flashed across the screen with the sound muted. “Remember the day you found out about the baby?” I asked.

“Oh, yeah.” He sipped at his plastic cup, pulling a face at the taste of the coffee.

“What happened to you?”

“I lost a bet with the boys.”

“A bet?”

“The first of us to get somebody pregnant had to drink a dirty pint.” He looked at me, a serious hold on his face. “Pretty sure it had piss in it.”

I braked suddenly, almost missing the turning for Treaton Vale. A van behind me beeped, and I held a hand up in apology as he zoomed past me. The cat meowed once more, a loud and squeaky sound, perhaps in shock from whiplash. I offered a finger of forgiveness through the cage door and was met with a sharp sting as he clamped his jaws firmly around it.

Emma’s car was already outside our flat when I pulled up. The living room light was on. She must have finished work early. I imagined her sitting by the fireplace, singing a song to herself. I gathered the pet carrier, peering at the little black fluff ball inside. He had seemed to quite enjoy the car ride and now appeared to be more nervous. His small paws clawed the door repeatedly as we walked down the pathway. I closed the gate quietly behind me, hoping to sneak in and surprise Emma. I tried the door, but it was locked. Dammit.

I fiddled with the key in the lock, having to place the carrier on the floor, as I couldn't quite balance it and didn't want to risk the poor kitty having two knocks in one night. Emma sat by the fire, reading a birthday card that must have come in the post.

"Hey, how was the dentist? Do you want a cup of—" She paused mid-sentence, eyeing the carrier in my hand. "What is that?"

"I want you to meet the newest member of the Atlas-Carlton household." I held the carrier up so she could see inside. Emma squealed and ran to me. The empty envelope on her lap fell to the floor.

"Are you serious?"

"Happy birthday, babe."

"Oh my God! Thank you so much. Put him? Him? Down on the rug and let him explore a bit."

I did as I was asked, settling the carrier down on the cream rug and opening the gate. In a few seconds, the kitten sauntered out, eyeing Emma inquisitively and then his surroundings, turning to me last. Emma held out a closed fist and he sniffed it eagerly. After deciding she was safe, he rubbed his head against her hand, purring quietly.

"He is perfect!" she said. "What's his name?"

I sat on the floor, resting my back against the sofa. "Currently, Potter. 'Cause he has that mark on his head, see?"

"Oh, yeah."

"You can call him anything you like though."

Emma smiled mischievously. "Anything?"

I nodded.

"Okay. Meet Mr Squigglefluff the Third. But we can call him Squiggle."

I raised a brow. "Squiggle?"

"Yeah." Her eyes met mine, and she burst out laughing. "You should see your face. I love cats, but I'm not that mental...yet." She stroked his back, and he arched against the touch, stretching his legs. "I like Flic. What do you think?"

"Flic," I said, rolling the name over in my mouth. "Flic. Yeah. Flic is cool."

★

Sundays were usually a day of rest in the Carlton-Atlas household. It was the one day that the café was closed, and we took advantage of that by spending most of the morning in bed, sipping tea and watching TV in our pyjamas. Since Flic joined the family, these quiet Sundays were replaced by hectic playtime segments, resting only when Flic would sleep, curled up on a pillow beside the fire.

Emma's hand moved slowly through Flic's fur. His eyes flickered left and right in a deep slumber, his small pink nose twitching and jerking his whiskers. She watched him with a peaceful smile.

"Look at you," I said. "You're almost smothering him."

"He's so cute. I can't help it."

I held up my pink slipper, turning it to reveal a big hole in the sole. "Cute, sure. Lunatic, certainly."

She came over to inspect it. "How many is that?"

"This is the fourth one." I threw it towards the door, and it clattered against the coat hanger. Flic sprung to his feet, his hair standing on end. "Sorry Flic! Go back to sleep."

Flic stretched out his legs, took three steps, and then curled up again, nudging his head into his chest.

"You're a bad cat mum," she teased, tidying away dry cups on the draining board. "The baby needs his sleep."

I put my arms around her waist, squeezing tight. "I bet you're knackered after staying up with him last night."

"He was fine when he was in the bedroom."

"He seems more than fine to be destroying the contents of my wardrobe."

"I think he was doing you a favour destroying those awful slippers."

A scratting sound came from the door, followed by a short meow. I glanced to the fireplace, but Flic was gone.

"God, what has he got now?" I asked.

Flic lay on his back, a piece of card in his mouth. He swatted at it with his paw.

"Give it here, Flic," Emma said. "Good boy." She tugged on the card and, despite Flic's efforts, managed to pull it free. Smoothing out the paper, her expression fell.

"What is it?" I asked.

Without saying anything, she handed me the card. Three bite marks had left holes in the paper, but it was still clear to read.

> *Tamara King and April Peterson joyfully invite you to attend their wedding celebration, August 23rd, 2021*

I glanced over the rest of the invitation and handed it back to Emma.

"Are you okay?" she asked, folding the card over in her hand.

"Yeah, I'm fine. Why wouldn't I be?"

"Well." She paused. "I felt a little weird when I found out Petey was getting remarried. You are bound to feel a little strange."

I took the note from her palm and stuck it onto the corkboard beside the dentist reminder and the shopping list. Emma put her arm around my waist, and I leaned into her.

"We don't have to go if you don't want to."

"No," I said. "I think we should."

Flic rustled in the bin next to the fireplace and dragged out a sheet of newspaper.

"It's up to you, babe. You don't have to decide yet." Emma kissed my cheek and then picked up the kettle. She refilled it from the tap before flicking it on. "Cup of tea?"

I turned and kissed her before she finished asking the question. "Yeah," I said, kissing her again and watching her smile. "Cup of tea sounds great."

Chapter Twenty-Nine

2021

I followed Tamara outside, past the wall where we had shared our pre-wedding cigarette, across the terrace where she had got married just a few hours ago, and onto a bench that overlooked the gardens. She held her suit jacket over one arm, revealing a crisp white shirt underneath that was tucked into her trousers. The night breeze nipped at my legs as I walked, and I hoped that we would be shaded from the wind beneath the arms of the willow tree. Tamara sat on one side and motioned for me to sit next to her. The image of the two of us sitting on a bench back at Oktoberfest all those years ago flashed into my mind and made me smile. So much had happened in our lives since then, good and bad, and yet here we were mirroring that past life again, a decade in the future.

"Are you all right?" I asked. Tamara's face was in shadow, the profile of her nose and chin barely visible in the darkness. "Should we be here? It's a bit...weird."

"Weird?"

"Yeah. Don't you think?"

She shrugged. "I guess. I don't know."

"I can't believe that you're married."

She laughed, a singular sound into the darkness. "I know. I don't quite believe it either."

A silence settled in the air. "April seems nice."

"She is. She's amazing." Tamara smiled into her lap, her jacket resting across her knees. I folded my legs over one another in an attempt to coax away my goosebumps. I didn't know if she noticed or not.

"You look good together."

"Yeah? Thanks, Sam."

Birds rustled in the treetops above. Neither one of us spoke. The cold made me shudder. "Tamara," I began. "What am I doing here?"

"I just wanted to talk to you. I've never been good at the stuff, but...here goes." She shook her head, her auburn hair falling across her face. She brushed it behind her ears and turned to face me. "You are the reason that I'm here today. I don't think I would've ever been here if it wasn't for you."

"What're you talking about?"

She held her hand up to silence me. "Please, Sam. Just let me."

I nodded and she continued.

"You were the first person I ever loved who truly loved me back. And I know I fucked it all up, that much is obvious, but you meant so much to me and I just hope you know that. I didn't care much about myself back then or give much thought to the things that I did, because I didn't think people cared or that I mattered. But you changed that for me. You showed me that I didn't have to be scared—that I shouldn't be—because hiding from your feelings just fucks you up anyway." She sighed and looked out across the gardens, though it was just a vast blue nothingness in the night. "Losing you and hurting you was the worst thing I've done this far. What I have with April is amazing, and this wouldn't have happened if it wasn't for us. I learned a lot, and...I'm sorry."

I placed my hand on hers. "I don't regret a thing with you, Tamara." The wind rustled between the leaves, the sound comforting like rain pattering against a windowpane. "I'm glad you're happy."

She flashed a quick smile before her face fell serious once more. "Are *you* happy?" Her eyes, jet black in the lack of light, pierced mine. She pursed her mouth, waiting for my response.

"I am, yeah." I smiled. "Emma is everything to me."

"I'm glad." She paused. "It was a surprise. I would've never thought it, but it does make sense when I see you both together."

"Yeah. She's great."

Silence settled between us. I removed my hand from hers and placed it on my cold knee.

"I do wonder though," she said quietly. "If we would've stayed together. If we'd be here today instead."

My mind wandered to the main hall, where Emma was, and I thought of her dancing with Jake, Tom, and Ellie, my favourite people in all the world.

"If it was meant to be, then it would have been," I said. "Everything worked out the way it was supposed to."

"Yeah, I think you're right."

"Wait here a second," I said, standing to leave.

"Where are you going?"

"Just. Wait there, I'll be right back." I parted the willow branches like curtains and disappeared from Tamara's sight.

I heard her sigh as I rounded the back of the tree and down into the dip behind it. I squinted my eyes in the darkness, placing my feet carefully and guiding my way down the hill. The silver package reflected in the moonlight like a piece of treasure that had washed up on the shore. I picked up the present, feeling a wave of stupidity crash over me for hiding the damn thing in the first place. I swallowed away my nerves and headed back up towards Tamara. The sky above was a deep blue, the countryside's lack of light allowing every star to be seen. My foot caught in a ditch, and I tripped, yelping like a dog that'd had its tail trodden on. I managed to catch myself before I hit the ground, steadying myself with my hands.

"Are you all right?" Tamara called from the darkness.

"Yeah, I'm fine." I followed her voice and the movement of the branches as they drifted in the soft breeze. I parted the leaf curtains again and sat next to Tamara, who watched me with amusement.

"Here," I said, handing her the silver package. "It's a wedding gift for you."

"Ah, that's sweet. You really didn't have to get us anything."

"Well." I scratched my neck, feeling a prick of heat. "It's more of a gift for you. I wasn't going to give it to you, but I changed my mind."

"Hmm." Tamara raised a dark brow, turning the package over in her hands. "It feels like a book."

She teased under the edge of the paper, lifting it up and tearing across the top. Fiddling with the end, she finally pulled it off with a tug, revealing the black-and-red cover of a record.

Her face lit up. "'Don't Stretch The Moon'. Merlot and the Bakers." She swallowed. "Sam." Her voice was small. She turned over the record in her hands. "I don't know what to say."

"You don't have to say anything. Apart from thank you 'cause it never hurts to have manners."

She snorted. "Yeah." Her eyes darted over the artwork as she turned the record over and then back again. She was silent for a minute.

"Do you like it?" I asked. "I haven't upset you, have I?"

"No, of course not. And I love it. I wish we could listen to it now. I haven't heard it in a long time." She looked at me for the first time since she opened the present. "Thank you. It means a lot." Her eyes narrowed. "Where did you hide this?"

I laughed. "Erm, in the garden, just down there." I waved my hand in the general direction, and she shook her head.

"Of course you did. Why did you hide it?"

"I don't know. I guess I was...scared."

Tamara contemplated this, her mouth pouting. "What of?"

"I'm not sure. Making a fool of myself? Or just weirding you out."

Tamara's face shifted. "I don't know why you would think this would weird me out."

"I don't know. It was your wedding."

"Hmm."

Here it was again. The famous Tamara King shut-down. The record rested across her lap as she looked out into the darkness. The silence between us was unnerving, and I longed for the busy happenings inside the crowded hall.

"We should probably head back inside," I said. "I bet people are looking for you."

"Yeah. I guess we should." She stood, straightening her back, the record tucked under her arm casually. "Thanks again, Sam. For the present. For all of it."

"You're welcome." I smiled. "Congratulations again." I started towards the large doors, lit dimly overhead, and paused when she didn't follow me. "Are you coming?"

Tamara hung back by the pathway as if something had struck her mid-step. "Yeah. I just need a minute." I noticed her eyes, full and sad, her wet cheek reflecting in the light. She turned her back to me, but I had already seen. "You go ahead," she said. "I'll be in in a minute."

The inside of the hall hummed with laughter and music. I hesitated inside, waiting by the door, pondering whether to check on Tamara. In the end, I figured she probably wanted space. I hated seeing her cry though; it was an uncommon thing. It made me feel uncomfortable, like it was still my responsibility to stop that hurt from happening. But looking after her wasn't my job anymore. I didn't think it ever was in the first place.

Sweaty bodies and recirculated hot breath made the air in the room humid. Guests danced red-faced to the music, swirling their drinks around as they moved across the dance floor, slapping each other on the back. I spotted our table, my ripped wrap hung carelessly on a chair. Emma's bag and Ellie's coat, plus an extraordinary amount of empty glasses collected in the middle. My eyes panned to the dance floor, finding Lottie on Emma's shoulders and Jasper on Tom's, waving their arms to a Lady Gaga song. Their smiles grew wider when they saw me walking over. Emma passed Lottie over to Jake, who clambered on top of his wide shoulders hastily.

Emma pulled me into an embrace, asked me if I was okay, and offered me a sip of her drink. I declined. We had been drinking almost the entire day, and the mix of the shots had left a weary ache in my stomach. Not wanting to risk any puking repetitions, I decided to stick to lemonade. Emma's eyes glazed over with the flow of alcohol. Her smile was relaxed and wide, showing her lovely teeth. I watched her as she moved side to side, pulling me towards her and moving my arms for me like I was incapable of doing it myself. She laughed loudly, shaking her head and swatting me with her pink hand.

"Dance with me!" she pleaded, swaying her head to the beat and waiting for me to join her. "I miss dancing with you."

In the early stages of our friendship, back when she was the bartender at Petey's and I was a naïve undergraduate, we would dance almost every weekend. Never for long, because she was on shift, but I remembered it well. She was a good dancer, with a great sense of rhythm, probably aided from her musical talents. Sometimes she would dance so close to me I could feel the heat of her body and the smell of her perfume. I never thought much of it at the time. But since we got together, my memories replayed everything in a different light.

The DJ transitioned into a slow song met by oohs and aahs from the dance floor. A few people left, beelining for the bar or a well-deserved sit down at their respective tables. I heard Ellie laugh, and Tom spun her into his chest. Jasper and Lottie galloped off someplace else, bored by the sudden change in tempo. Debbie and Phil strode over to a space on the dance floor, Phil trailing behind her like a scolded puppy.

Emma placed both hands around my waist. She was taller than me by a good few inches, even more so assisted by the black stilettos she was wearing. I looped my arms around her neck, and we moved across the floor, mingling among the other couples. I was never much of a dancer, so I let Emma lead the way, enjoying the peace that was descending over me as our limbs swayed together in rhythm. It was the first part of the night where I could truly relax. The night was drawing to an end, that was obvious, and the stress of the wedding had taken its toll. I rested my head into Emma's collarbone, the cool and sharp edges familiar to my touch. I could draw them with my eyes closed: the curve and structure of each bone, the exact co-ordinate of every mole that enriched her pale skin. She held me closer to her, inhaling deeply, and I wondered what she was thinking about. I pulled back a little, curious of her facial expression. She peered down at me, amused.

"What is it?" she asked, squeezing her grip on my waist playfully.

"What're you thinking?" I said quietly, feeling childish.

Her mouth pursed before stretching into a grin. "I was thinking." She spun me around a nearby couple, my dress fanning against the movement. "How great this would be if it were our wedding."

"Really?"

"Oh, yeah. You in a gorgeous white gown, professing your love for me, forever. What's not to want about that?"

"You're crazy."

"What for?"

My fingers stroked the back of her neck. "For wanting me. You could be touring the world and have whoever you want."

"Sam," she said with a strong firmness, like whenever I forgot to put the bins out or left things untidy. "Being with you is all I could ever want. It's more than that, even." Guests cooed at a nearby commotion. I glanced towards the noise. Tom was lifting Ellie up above his head, to the thrill of the dance floor. "The idea that you still doubt my feelings for you is the crazy part. You're crazy."

I shook my head. "What did I do to deserve you?"

She kissed me. "Must've done something right in a past life. 'Cause you've made some questionable decisions in this one."

I pinched her neck, and she laughed, spinning me into nearby space. I spotted Tamara and April on the far side of the dance floor. Tamara caught my eye and winked. I smiled at her, and she returned her famous Tamara smile, full of warmth and heart, and then turned her full attention back to her bride, who was looking back at her adoringly.

I nuzzled myself closer into Emma, breathing her perfume in deep. She pulled me close to her as the music descended into quiet silence and polite applause while the DJ selected another track. I longed to pause the moment, knowing there were only a few songs left to dance to. I wished I had spent more time with Emma but then relished the thought that I would have as much time with her as the world would allow. A man with a gruff voice announced the last song through the microphone, scratching his head absent-mindedly as he did so. The lights above flickered on, blinding the eyes of everyone on the dance floor. People rushed down to enjoy the last song, herding the guests together like cattle, but we didn't care. We laughed as the beat kicked in and everyone sang "Love Is in the Air" as loud as they could, like they truly believed every word. And I believed it too.

More than that, even.

Acknowledgements

If somebody came up to fifteen-year-old Emily and told her that one day she would be able to publish the stories she craves to read, she would think they were a few crumbs short of a biscuit.

The truth is, I was desperate to read an LGBTQ+ story that wasn't just about coming out or didn't involve one of the characters dying in an unbelievably tragic way just before the end. I wanted to read a story that reflected real-life relationships, a story where first loves aren't always endgame.

I learned so much from these characters, and they have a special place in my heart. A part of me is sad that their stories are over. However, without the help of some incredible people, these characters that I love so dearly would have only ever lived inside my head. I am forever grateful to each of them for helping bring them onto the page.

A special thanks to Conor O'Callaghan for giving me the "lightbulb" moment that would change the way I write forever. Big hugs to all my beta readers, who continue to amaze me with their comments and support. A massive thank you to Beth Kent, the greatest friend and cheerleader anyone could ask for. My family and friends, whose excitement and encouragement always keeps me going. To Elizabeth and everyone at NineStar Press, thank you for making this dream a reality. Finally, none of this would have been possible without the love and support from my amazing other half, Laura. You always make me laugh when I need it the most and believe in me even when I don't. Thank you for being my Emma.

About Emily Wright

Emily is a dog-loving, book-sniffing, ukulele-playing author who lives in Sheffield in the UK. When she isn't attached to her computer writing, she loves the outdoors, especially the crash of the ocean, the smell of pine, and starry night skies that make her feel absolutely obsolete. When not drinking tea and eating an unthinkable amount of Bourbons, she spends the rest of her time chasing her two naughty Cocker Spaniels around the house to stop them from eating anything and everything.

Email

emilywrightwriter@outlook.com

Twitter

@emziewriter

Website

www.emilywrightwriter.co.uk

Also from NineStar Press

You Know I'd Never by Kara Lowndes

How do you get over the love of your life when you can't even admit you loved her?

Janey has been in the closet her entire life—even when she fell for her first girlfriend, Elise, back in high school. After Elise left their small hometown of Clitheroe to pursue her dreams of becoming a musician, Janey knew that the only thing she'd have to remember her by was the song that Elise had written about Janey.

But that love song soon turned into the biggest hit of the decade, and Elise and her band return to Clitheroe a few years later to pay tribute to their hometown. Janey, still stuck where she was five years ago when Elise left, knows that she can't let her ex slip through her fingers again.

But she's still in the closet, and has no intention or idea of coming out to her homophobic family. How can she make amends with the woman she loved when she can't even be honest with herself or the people closest to her?

NINESTAR PRESS

Connect with NineStar Press

www.ninestarpress.com

www.facebook.com/ninestarpress

www.facebook.com/groups/NineStarNiche

www.twitter.com/ninestarpress

www.instagram.com/ninestarpress

Printed in Great Britain
by Amazon

67838505R00182